found

(book #8 in the vampire journals)

morgan rice

Cover model: Jennifer Onvie. Cover photography: Adam Luke Studios, New York. Cover makeup artist: Ruthie Weems. If you would like to contact any of these artists, please contact Morgan Rice.

ISBN: 978-0-9849753-2-7

Also by Morgan Rice

ARENA ONE
(BOOK #1 OF THE SURVIVAL TRILOGY)

turned
(book #1 in the Vampire Journals)

loved
(Book #2 in the Vampire Journals)

betrayed
(Book #3 in the Vampire Journals)

destined
(Book #4 in the Vampire Journals)

desired
(Book #5 in the Vampire Journals)

betrothed
(Book #6 in the Vampire Journals)

vowed
(Book #7 in the Vampire Journals)

FACT:

Although the exact date of Jesus' death remains unknown, he is widely believed to have died on April 3, 33 A.D.

FACT:

The synagogue in Capernaum (Israel), one of the oldest in the world, is one of the few places that remain where Jesus taught. It is also where he healed a man "who had the spirit of an unclean devil."

FACT:

The current Church of the Holy Sepulchre in Jerusalem, one of the most sacred churches in the world, was built on the spot of Jesus' crucifixion, and on the supposed spot of his resurrection. But before this church was built, for the first 300 years after his crucifixion, paradoxically, this spot was occupied by a Pagan Temple.

FACT:

After the Last Supper, Jesus was betrayed by Judas in the ancient garden of Gethsemane.

FACT:

Both Judaism and Christianity hold that there will be an apocalypse, an end of days, during which a Messiah will come, and during which those who have died will be resurrected. Judaism holds that when the Messiah comes, the first to be resurrected will be those buried on the Mount of Olives.

"I will kiss thy lips;
Haply some poison yet doth hang on them,
To make die with a restorative.
O happy dagger!"
--William Shakespeare, *Romeo and Juliet*

CHAPTER ONE

Nazareth, Israel
(April, 33 A.D.)

Caitlin's mind raced with fast, troubled dreams. She saw her best friend, Polly, fall off a cliff, reaching out and trying to grab hold of her, but just missing her hand. She saw her brother Sam, run from her, through an endless field; she chased after him, but no matter how fast she ran, she couldn't catch him. She saw Kyle and Rynd slaughter her coven members before her eyes, chopping them into pieces, the blood spraying over her. This blood morphed into a blood-red sunset, which hung over her wedding ceremony to Caleb. Except in this wedding, they were the only two people there, the last ones left in the world, standing at the edge of a cliff against a blood-red sky.

And then she saw her daughter, Scarlet, sitting in a small wooden boat, alone on a vast sea, drifting in turbulent waters. Scarlet held up the four keys that Caitlin needed to find her father. But as she watched, Scarlet reached up and dropped them into the water.

"Scarlet!" Caitlin tried to scream.

But no sound came, and as she watched, Scarlet drifted further and further away from her, into the ocean, into the huge storm clouds gathering on the horizon.

"SCARLET!"

Caitlin Paine woke screaming. She sat up, breathing hard, and looked all around her, trying to get her bearings. It was dark in here, the only light source from a small opening, about twenty yards away. It looked like she was in a tunnel. Or maybe a cave.

Caitlin felt something hard beneath her and looked down to realize she was lying on a dirt floor, on small rocks. It was hot in here, dusty. Wherever she was, this was not Scottish weather. It felt hot, dry—as if she were in a desert.

Caitlin sat there, rubbing her head, squinting into the darkness, trying to remember, to distinguish between dreams and reality. Her dreams were so vivid, and her reality so surreal, it was becoming increasingly hard to tell the difference.

As she slowly caught her breath, shaking off the horrific visions, she began to realize that she was back. Alive somewhere. In some new place and time. She felt the layers of dirt on her skin, in her hair, her eyes, and felt like she needed to bathe. It was so hot in here, it was hard to breathe.

Caitlin felt a familiar bulge in her pocket, and rolled over and saw with relief that her journal had made it. She immediately checked her other pocket and felt the four keys, then reached up and felt her necklace. It had all made it. She was flooded with relief.

Then she remembered. Caitlin immediately spun around, looking to see if Caleb and Scarlet had made it back with her.

She made out a shape lying in the darkness, unmoving, and at first she wondered if it was an animal. But as her eyes adjusted, she realized it took the shape of a human form. She got up slowly, her body aching, stiff from lying on the rocks, and began to approach.

She walked across the cave, knelt down, and gently pushed the shoulder of the large form. She already sensed who it was: she didn't need for him to turn over to know. She could feel it from across the cave. It was, she knew with relief, her one and only love. Her husband. Caleb.

As he rolled over onto his back, she prayed he'd made it back in good health. That he remembered her.

Please, she thought. *Please. Just one last time. Let Caleb survive the trip.*

As Caleb turned over, she was relieved to see that his features were intact. She did not see any signs of injury. As she looked closely, she was even more relieved to see him breathing, the slow rhythms of his chest rising and falling—and then, to see his eyelids twitch.

She let out a huge sigh of relief as his eyes fluttered open.

"Caitlin?" he asked.

Caitlin burst into tears. Her heart soared, as she leaned over and hugged him. They'd made it back together. He was alive. That was all she needed. She wouldn't ask for anything more from the world.

He embraced her back, and she held him for a long time, feeling his rippling muscles. She was flooded with relief. She loved him more than she could possibly say. They had come back so many times and places together, had seen so much together, the highs and lows, had suffered so much and had celebrated, too. She thought of all the times they almost lost each other, the time he didn't remember her, his being poisoned... The obstacles in their relationship seemed to never end.

And now, finally, they had made it. They were together again, for the final trip back. *Did that mean they would be together forever?* she wondered. She hoped so, with every fiber of her being. No more trips back. This time, they were together for good.

Caleb looked older as he looked back at her. She stared into his glowing, brown eyes and could feel the love pouring through him. She knew he was thinking the same thing she was.

As she looked into his eyes, all the memories came flooding back. She thought of their last trip, of Scotland. It all came rushing back like a horrible dream. At first, it was so beautiful. The castle, seeing all her friends. The wedding. *My God, the wedding.* It was the most beautiful thing she could have ever hoped for. She looked down and checked her finger, and saw the ring. It was still there. The ring had made it back. This token of their love had survived. She could hardly believe it. She was really married. And to him. She took it as a sign: if the ring could make it back in time, through all this, if the ring could survive, then so could their love.

The sight of the ring on her finger really sank in. Caitlin paused and felt what it felt like to be a married woman. It felt different. More solid, more permanent. She had always loved Caleb, and she had sensed that he loved her, too. She had always felt that their union was forever. But now that it was official, she felt different. She felt that they were both truly one.

Caitlin then thought back and remembered what happened after the wedding: their having to leave Scarlet, and Sam, and Polly. Finding Scarlet in the ocean, seeing Aiden, hearing the awful news. Polly, her best friend, dead. Sam, her only brother, gone to her forever, turned to the dark side. Her fellow coven members slaughtered. It was almost too much for her to bear. She couldn't imagine the horror, or a life without Sam in it—or Polly.

With a jolt, her thoughts turned to Scarlet. Suddenly panic-stricken, she pulled back from Caleb, searching the cave, wondering if she made it back, too.

Caleb must have been thinking the same thing at the same time, because his eyes opened wide.

"Where's Scarlet?" he asked, reading her mind, as always.

Caitlin turned and ran to every corner of the cave, searching the dark crevices, looking for any outline, any shape, any sign of Scarlet. But there was none. She searched frantically, crisscrossing the cave with Caleb, canvassing every inch of it.

But Scarlet was not here. She was simply not here.

Caitlin's heart sank. How could it be? How was it possible that she and Caleb made the trip back, but that Scarlet did not? Could destiny be that cruel?

Caitlin turned and ran for the sunlight, for the exit of the cave. She had to go outside, to see what was out there, to see if there was any sign of Scarlet. Caleb ran beside her, and the two of them ran to the lip of the cave, out into the sun, and stood at its entrance.

Caitlin stopped short, and just in time: a small platform jutted out from the cave, then fell off, straight down a steep mountain face. Caleb stopped short beside her. There they were, standing on a narrow ledge, looking down. Somehow, Caitlin realized, they'd landed back inside a mountain cave, hundreds of feet high. There was no way up or down. And if they took one more step, they would plummet hundreds of feet below.

Spread out below them was an enormous valley, stretching to the horizon as far as the eye could see. It was a rural, desert landscape, dotted with rocky outcroppings and the occasional palm tree. In the distance were rolling hills, and directly beneath them was a village, comprised of stone houses and dirt streets. It was even hotter here in the sun, unbearably bright and hot. Caitlin was beginning to realize that they were in a very different place and climate than Scotland. And judging from how rudimentary that village looked, they were in a very different time, too.

Interspersed between all the dirt and sand and rock were signs of agriculture, occasional patches of green. Some of these were covered with vineyards, growing in neat rows down the steep slopes, and among these were trees Caitlin could not recognize: small, ancient-looking trees with twisted branches and silver leaves that shimmered in the sun.

"Olive trees," Caleb said, reading her mind again.

Olive trees? Caitlin wondered. *Where on earth are we?*

She looked over at Caleb, sensing he might recognize the place and time. She saw his eyes open wide, and knew that he did—and that he was surprised. He stared out at the vista as if it were a long-lost friend.

"Where are we?" she asked, almost afraid to know.

Caleb surveyed the valley before them, then finally, he turned and looked at her.

Softly, he said: "Nazareth."

He paused, taking it all in.

"Judging from that village, we're in the first century," he said, turning and looking at her in awe, his eyes alight with excitement. "In fact, it looks like we might even be in the time of Christ."

CHAPTER TWO

Scarlet felt a tongue licking her face and opened her eyes to blinding sunlight. The tongue would not stop, and before she even looked over, she knew it was Ruth. She opened her eyes just enough to see that it was her: Ruth was leaning over, whining, and grew even more excited as Scarlet opened her eyes.

Scarlet felt a stab of pain as she tried to open her eyes further; struck by the blinding sunlight, her eyes teared up, more sensitive than ever. She had a bad headache, and peeled open her eyes just enough to she was lying on a cobblestone street somewhere. People rushed by, walking past her, and she could tell she was in the midst of a busy city. People hurried to and fro, bustling in every direction, and she could hear the din of a crowd in midday. As Ruth whined and whined, she sat there, trying to remember, trying to figure out where she was. But she had no idea.

Before Scarlet could get her mind around what had happened, she suddenly felt a foot prodding her in the ribs.

"Move on!" came a deep voice. "You can't sleep here."

Scarlet looked over and saw a Roman sandal near her face. She looked up, and saw a Roman soldier standing over her, dressed in a short tunic, a belt around his waist, from which hung a short sword. He wore a small brass helmet with feathers on it.

He leaned over and nudged her again with his foot. It hurt Scarlet's stomach.

"Did you hear what I said? Move on, or I'm locking you up."

Scarlet wanted to listen, but as she opened her eyes further, the sun hurt them so much, and she was so disoriented. She tried to get to her feet, but felt as if she were moving in slow motion.

The soldier leaned back to kick her hard in the ribs. Scarlet saw it coming, and braced herself, unable to react quickly enough.

Scarlet heard a snarl, and looked over to see Ruth, hair standing up on her back, lunge at the soldier. Ruth caught his ankle in mid-air, digging her sharp fangs into it with all she had.

The soldier screamed, and his screams filled the air as blood poured from his ankle. Ruth would not let go, shaking it with all she had, and the soldier's expression, so haughty a moment before, now turned to one of fear.

He reached down, into his scabbard, and extracted his sword. He lifted it high and prepared to bring it down on Ruth's back.

That was when Scarlet felt it. It was like a force taking over her body, as if another power, another entity, were inside her. Without realizing what she was doing, she suddenly burst into action. She couldn't control it, and she didn't understand what was happening.

Scarlet jumped to her feet, heart pounding with adrenaline, and managed to grab the soldier's wrist in midair, just as he was bringing down his sword. She felt power coursing through her, a power she had never known, as she held his arm. Even with all his strength, he could not budge.

She squeezed his wrist, and managed to squeeze it hard enough that, as he looked down at her in shock, he finally dropped his sword. It landed on the cobblestone with a clang.

"It's OK, Ruth," Scarlet said softly, and Ruth gradually let go of her grip on his ankle.

Scarlet stood there, holding the soldier's wrist, keeping him locked in her deadly embrace.

"Please, let me go," he pleaded.

Scarlet felt the power coursing through her, felt that, if she wanted, she could really hurt him. But she didn't want to. She just wanted to be left alone.

Slowly, Scarlet released her grip and let him go.

The soldier, fear in his eyes, looking as if he'd just encountered a demon, turned and ran away, not even bothering to retrieve his sword.

"Come on Ruth," Scarlet said, sensing he might come back with more soldiers, and not wanting to stick around.

A moment later, the two of them ran into the thick crowd. They hurried through the narrow, twisting alleyways, until Scarlet found a nook in the shade. She knew the soldiers wouldn't find them here, and she wanted a minute to regroup, to figure out where they were. Ruth panted beside her, as Scarlet caught her breath in the heat.

Scarlet was scared and amazed by her own powers. She knew something was different, but she didn't fully understand what was happening to her; she also didn't understand where everyone else was. It was so hot here, and she was in a crowded city she didn't recognize. It looked nothing like the London she grew up in. She looked out and watched all the people busting by, wearing robes, togas, sandals, carrying large baskets of figs and dates on their heads and shoulders, some of them wearing turbans. She saw ancient, stone buildings, narrow twisting alleyways, cobblestone streets, and wondered where on earth she could be.

This definitely was not Scotland. Everything here looked so primitive, she felt as if she had gone back thousands of years.

Scarlet looked everywhere, hoping for a glimpse of her mom and dad. She scrutinized every face that passed, hoping, willing, that one of them would stop and turn to her.

But they were nowhere. And with every passing face, she felt more and more alone.

Scarlet was beginning to feel a sense of panic. She didn't understand how she could have come back alone. How could they have left her like that? Where could they be? Did they make it back, too? Didn't they care enough to come and find her?

The longer Scarlet stood there, watching, waiting, the more the realization sank in. She was alone. Completely on her own, in a strange time and place. Even if they were back here, she had no idea where to look for them.

Scarlet looked down at her wrist, at the ancient bracelet with the dangling cross that had been given to her right before they left Scotland. As they'd stood there in the courtyard of that castle, one of those old men in the white robes had reached out and slipped it on her wrist. She thought it was very pretty, but she didn't know what it was, or what it meant. She had a feeling that it might be some sort of clue, but had no idea what.

She felt Ruth rubbing up against her leg, and she knelt down, kissed her head, and hugged her. Ruth whined in her ear, licking her. At least she had Ruth. Ruth was like a sister to her, and Scarlet was so grateful she had made it back with her, and so grateful she had protected her from that soldier. There was no one she loved more.

As Scarlet thought back to that soldier, to their encounter, she realized her powers must run deeper than she thought. She couldn't understand how she, as a small girl, had overpowered him. She felt that somehow she was changing, or had already changed, into something she had never been. She remembered, back in Scotland, her mom explaining it to her. But she still didn't quite understand it.

She wished it would all just go away. She just wanted to be normal, wanted things to be normal, back to the way they were. She just wanted her mommy and daddy; she wanted to close her eyes and be back in Scotland, in that castle, with Sam, and Polly, and Aiden. She wanted to be back at their wedding ceremony; she wanted everything to be right in the world.

But when she opened her eyes, she was still here, all alone with Ruth in this strange city, this strange time. She didn't know a soul. No one seemed friendly. And she had no idea where to go.

Finally, Scarlet couldn't take it anymore. She had to move on. She couldn't hide here, waiting forever. Wherever her mommy and daddy were, she figured, it was out there somewhere. She felt a hunger pang, and heard Ruth whining, and knew she was hungry, too. She had to be brave, she told herself. She had to go out there and try to find them—and try to find food for them both.

Scarlet stepped out into the bustling alleyway, on the lookout for soldiers; she spotted groups of them in the distance, patrolling the streets, but they didn't seem like they were looking out for her specifically.

Scarlet and Ruth squeezed their way into the masses of humanity, jostled as they headed down the twisting alleyways. It was so crowded here, people bustling in every direction. She passed vendors with wooden carts, selling fruits and vegetables, loaves of bread, bottles of olive oil and wine. They were adjacent to each other, crammed in the thick alleys, screaming out for customers. People haggled with them left and right.

As if it were not crowded enough, also filling the streets were animals—camels and donkeys and sheep and all sorts of livestock—being led by their owners. Amidst these ran wild chickens, roosters and dogs. They smelled terribly, and made the noisy marketplace even noisier, with their constant braying and bleating and barking.

Scarlet could feel Ruth's hunger mounting at the sight of these animals, and kneeled down and grabbed her by the neck, holding her back.

"No Ruth!" Scarlet said firmly.

Ruth reluctantly obeyed. Scarlet felt bad, but she didn't want Ruth to kill these animals and cause a huge commotion in this crowd.

"I'll find you food, Ruth," Scarlet said. "I promise."

Ruth whined back, and Scarlet felt a hunger pang, too.

Scarlet hurried past the animals, leading Ruth down more alleys, twisting and turning past vendors and down more alleyways. It seemed like this maze would never end, and Scarlet could hardly even see the sky.

Finally, Scarlet found a vendor with a huge piece of roasting meat. She could smell it from afar, the smell infiltrating her every pore; she looked down and saw Ruth looking up at it, licking her lips. She stopped before it, gawking.

"Buy a piece?" the vendor, a large man with a smock covered in blood, asked.

Scarlet wanted a piece more than anything. But as she reached into her pockets, she found no money whatsoever. She reached down and felt her bracelet, and more than anything, she wanted to take it off and sell it to this man, to get a meal.

But she forced herself not to. She sensed it was important, and so she used all her force of will to stop herself.

Instead, she slowly, sadly shook her head in response. She grabbed Ruth and led her away from the man. She could hear Ruth whining and protesting, but they had no choice.

They pressed on, and finally, the maze opened up into a bright and sunny, wide-open plaza. Scarlet was taken aback by the open sky. Coming out of all those alleyways, it felt like the most wide-open thing she'd ever seen, with thousands of people milling around inside it. In its center sat a stone fountain, and framing the plaza was an immense stone wall, rising hundreds of feet into the air. Each stone was so thick, it was ten times her size. Against this wall stood hundreds of people, wailing, praying. Scarlet had no idea why, or where she was, but she sensed that she was in the center of the city, and that this was a very holy place.

"Hey you!" came a nasty voice.

Scarlet felt the hairs rise on the back of her neck, and slowly turned.

There sat a group of five boys, sitting on a crop of stone, staring down at her. They were filthy from head to toe, dressed in rags. They were teenagers, maybe 15, and she could see the meanness on their faces. She could sense that they were hoping for trouble, and that they'd just spotted their next victim; she wondered if it was obvious how alone she was.

Among them was a wild dog, huge, rabid-looking, and twice the size of Ruth.

"What you doing out here all alone?" the lead boy asked in a mocking way, to the laughter of the other four. He was muscular and stupid-looking, with broad lips and a scar on his forehead.

As she looked at them, Scarlet felt a new sense overcome her, one she had never experienced before: it was a heightened sense of intuition. She didn't know what was happening, but suddenly, she was able to read their thoughts clearly, to feel their feelings, to know their intentions. She felt immediately, clear as day, that they were up to no good. She knew that they wanted to harm her.

Ruth snarled beside her. Scarlet could sense a major confrontation coming—which was exactly what she wanted to avoid.

She leaned down and began to lead Ruth away.

"Come on Ruth," Scarlet said, as she began to turn and walk away.

"Hey, girl, I'm talking to you!" yelled the boy.

As she walked away, Scarlet turned over her shoulder and saw the five of them jump down off the stone and begin walking after her.

Scarlet burst into a run, back into the alleyways, wanting to put as much distance between herself and these boys as she could. She thought of her confrontation with the Roman soldier, and for a moment wondered if she should stop and try to defend herself.

But she didn't want to fight. She didn't want to hurt anyone. Or take any chances. She just wanted to find her mommy and daddy.

Scarlet turned down an alley empty of people. She looked back, and within moments, could see the group of boys chasing after her. They weren't far behind, and they were gaining speed fast. Too fast. Their dog ran among them, and Scarlet could see that in moments, they'd catch up. She had to make a good turn to lose them.

Scarlet turned another corner, hoping she'd find a way out. But as she did, her heart stopped.

It was a dead-end.

Scarlet turned slowly, Ruth by her side, and faced the boys. They were now maybe ten feet away. They slowed as they approached, taking their time, savoring the moment. They stood there laughing, cruel smiles on the faces.

"Looks like your luck has run out, little girl," the lead boy said.

Scarlet was thinking the same thing.

CHAPTER THREE

Sam woke to a splitting headache. He reached up with both hands and held his head, trying to make the pain go away. But it wouldn't. It felt like the entire world was coming down on his skull.

Sam tried to open his eyes, to figure out where he was, and as he did, the pain was unbearable. Blinding sunlight bounced off of desert rock, forcing him to shield his eyes and lower his head. He felt himself lying on a rocky, desert floor, felt the dry heat, felt the dust rising up into his face. He curled up in a fetal position and held his head tighter, trying to make the pain go away.

Memories came flooding back.

First, there was Polly.

He remembered Caitlin's wedding night. The night he proposed to Polly. Her saying yes. The joy on her face.

He remembered the next day. His going on his hunt. His anticipation of their night to come.

He remembered finding her. On the beach. Dying. Her telling him about their baby.

Waves of grief came rushing back. It was more than he could handle. It was like a terrible nightmare re-running in his head, one he could not switch off. He felt that all he had left to live for was stripped away from him, all in one grand moment. Polly. The baby. Life as he knew it.

He wished he'd died at that moment.

Then he remembered his vengeance. His rage. Killing Kyle.

And the moment that everything changed. He remembered Kyle's spirit infusing him. He remembered the indescribable feeling of rage, of another person's spirit and soul and energy invading his, possessing him completely. It was the moment Sam stopped being who he was. It was the moment he became someone else.

Sam opened his eyes completely, and he sensed, he knew, they were glowing bright red. He knew they were no longer his. He knew they were now Kyle's.

He felt Kyle's hatred, felt Kyle's power, racing through him, through every ounce of his body, from his toes, through his legs, up his arms, all the way to his head. He felt Kyle's need for destruction pulsing through every ounce of him, like a living thing, like something stuck in his body that he could not get out. He felt as if he were no longer in control of himself. A part of him missed the old Sam, missed who he was.

But another part of him knew he would never be that person again.

Sam heard a hissing, rattling noise, and opened his eyes. His face lay flat on the rocks of the desert floor, and as he looked up, he saw a rattlesnake, just inches away, hissing at him. The rattlesnake's eyes looked right into Sam's, as if it were communing with a friend, sensing a similar energy. He could sense that the snake's rage matched his—and that it was about to strike.

But Sam was not afraid. On the contrary—he found himself filled with a rage not only equal to the snake's, but greater. And reflexes to match.

In the split second in which the snake geared up to strike, Sam beat him to it: he reached out with his own hand, grabbed the stake by the throat in mid-air area, and stopped it from biting him just an inch away from his face. Sam held the snake's eyes to his, staring at it so close that he could smell its breath, its long fangs only an inch away, dying to enter Sam's throat.

But Sam overpowered it. He squeezed harder and harder, and slowly drained the life from it. It went limp in his hand, crushed to death.

He leaned back and hurled it across the desert floor.

Sam jumped to his feet and took in his surroundings. All around him were dirt and rocks—an endless stretch of desert. He turned, and noticed two things: first, was a group of small children, dressed in rags, looking up at him curiously. As he spun towards them they scattered, hurrying back, as if watching a wild animal rise from the grave. Sam felt Kyle's rage rush through him, and felt like killing them all.

But the second thing he noticed made him change his focus. A city wall. An immense, stone wall, soaring hundreds of feet into the air, and stretching forever. That was when Sam realized: he had awakened on the outskirts of an ancient city. Before him sat a huge, arched gate, in and out of which streamed dozens of people, dressed in primitive clothing. They looked like they were in Roman times, wearing simple robes or tunics. Livestock hurried in and out, too, and Sam could already sense the heat and noise of the crowds beyond its walls.

Sam took a few steps towards the gate, and as he did, the kids scattered, as if running from a monster. He wondered how scary he looked. But he didn't really care. He felt the need to enter this city, to figure out why he had landed here. But unlike the old Sam, he didn't feel the need to explore it: rather, he felt the need to destroy it. To smash this city to bits.

A part of him tried to shake it off, to bring back the old Sam. He forced himself to think of something that might bring him back. He forced himself to think of his sister, Caitlin. But it was hazy; he couldn't really summon her face anymore, as much as he tried. He tried to summon his feelings for her, their shared mission, their father. He knew deep down that he still cared for her, that he still wanted to help her.

But that small part of him was soon overwhelmed by the new, vicious part. He could barely recognize himself anymore. And the new Sam forced him to stop his thoughts and to move on, right into the city.

Sam marched through the city gates, elbowing people out of the way as he went. An old woman, balancing a basket on her head, got too close, and he bumped her shoulder hard, sending her flying, knocking off her basket, fruit spilling everywhere.

"Hey!" yelled a man. "Look what you did! Apologize to her!"

The man marched up to Sam and stupidly, reached out and grabbed his coat. The man should have realized that it was a coat he couldn't recognize, black, and leather, and skin-tight. The man should have realized that Sam's garment was from another century—and that Sam was the last man he wanted to mess with.

Sam looked down at the man's hand as if it were an insect, then reached out, grabbed his wrist, and with the force of a hundred men, he turned it back. The man's eyes open wide in fear and pain, as Sam kept turning. The man finally turned sideways, and dropped to his knees. Sam kept turning, though, until he heard a sickening crack, and the man shrieked out, his arm broken.

Sam leaned back and finished the man off by kicking him hard in the face, knocking him, unconscious, to the ground.

A small group of passersby watched, and they gave Sam plenty of space as he continued walking. No one seemed eager to get anywhere near him.

Sam kept walking, heading into the throng, and was soon enveloped by a new crowd. He blended into the never-ending stream of humanity that filled the city. He wasn't sure which way to go, but he felt new desires overwhelming him. He felt the desire to feed coursing through. He wanted blood. He wanted a fresh kill.

Sam let his senses take over, and felt himself being led down a particular alleyway. As he turned down it, the alley became narrow, darker, higher, shut off from the rest of the city. It was clearly a seedy part of the city, and as he went, the crowd grow more sketchy.

Beggars, drunks and prostitutes filled the streets, and Sam brushed elbows with several roguish, fat men, unshaven, missing teeth, who stumbled by. He made sure he leaned over and bumped shoulders hard with them, sending them flying in every direction. Wisely for them, none stopped to challenge him, other than shouting an indignant: "Hey!"

Sam kept going and soon found himself in a small square. Standing there, in the middle, backs to him, was a circle of about a dozen men, cheering. Sam walked up and pushed his way through to see what they were cheering about.

In the midst of the circle were two roosters, tearing each other apart, covered in blood. Sam looked over and saw the men placing bets, trading ancient coins. Cockfighting. The oldest sport in the world. So many centuries had passed, yet nothing had really changed.

Sam had enough. He was getting antsy, and he felt the need to stir up some havoc. He marched into the center of the ring, right up to the two birds. As he did, the crowd burst into an indignant cry.

Sam ignored them. Instead he reached out, grabbed one of the roosters by its throat, lifted it high and spun it over his head. There was a cracking noise, as he felt it go limp in his hand, its neck broken.

Sam felt his fangs protract, and sunk his teeth into the rooster's body. He gorged with blood, and it poured out and ran over his face, down his cheeks. Finally, he threw down the bird, unsatisfied. The other rooster scurried away as fast as it could.

The crowd stared at Sam, clearly shocked. But these were rough, crude types, not ones to walk away easily. They scowled back, prepared for a fight.

"You ruined our sport!" one of them snapped.

"You will pay!" another yelled.

Several burly men pulled out short daggers and lunged at Sam, slashing right for him.

Sam hardly flinched. He saw it all happening as if in slow motion. His reflexes a million times faster, he simply reached out, grabbed the man's wrist in mid-air and twisted it back in the same motion, breaking his arm. Then he leaned back and kicked the man in the chest, sending him flying back to the circle.

As another man approached, Sam lunged forward, towards the man, beating him to it. He got in close, and before the man could react, sank his fangs into the man's throat. Sam drank deeply, blood squirting everywhere, as the man shrieked in pain. Within moments he drained his life, and the man slumped to the floor, unconscious.

The others stared, terrified. Finally, they must have realized they were in the presence of a monster.

Sam took a step towards them, and they all turned and sprinted away. They disappeared like flies, and in just a moment, Sam was the only one left in the square.

He had beaten them all. But it wasn't enough for Sam. There was no end to the blood and death and destruction he craved. He wanted to kill every man in this city. Even then, it would not be enough. His lack of satisfaction frustrated him to no end.

He leaned back, face to the sky, and roared. It was the shriek of an animal finally let loose. His cry of anguish soared up, into the air, reverberated off the stone walls of Jerusalem, louder than the bells, louder than the cries for prayer. For just a brief moment, it shook the walls, dominated the entire city—and from end to another, its inhabitants stopped and listened and learned to fear.

In that moment, they knew, a monster was among them.

CHAPTER FOUR

Caitlin and Caleb hiked down the steep mountain face, heading towards the village of Nazareth. It was rocky, and they slid more than walked down the steep face, stirring up dust. As they went the terrain began to change, the rock giving way to clumps of weeds, the occasional palm tree, then to real grass. They finally found themselves in an olive grove, walking amidst rows of olive trees, as they continued further down, towards the town.

Caitlin looked closely at the branches and saw thousands of small olives, shimmering in the sun, and marveled at how beautiful they were. The closer they got to the town the more fertile the trees were. Caitlin looked down and from this vantage point had a bird's eye view of the valley and the town.

A small village nestled amidst enormous valleys, Nazareth could hardly be called a city. There looked to be only a few hundred inhabitants, only a few dozen small buildings, one story high and built of stone. Several of them appeared to be built of a white limestone, and in the distance, Caitlin could see villagers hammering away at the enormous limestone quarries surrounding the city. She could hear the soft ping of their hammers echoing, even from here, and could see the light limestone dust lingering in the air.

Nazareth was encased by a low, winding stone wall, maybe ten feet high, which looked ancient even now. At its center was a wide, open arched gate. No one stood guard at the gate, and Caitlin suspected they had no reason to; after all, this was a small town in the middle of nowhere.

Caitlin found herself wondering why they had awakened in this time and place. Why Nazareth? She thought back and tried to remember what she knew of Nazareth. She vaguely remembered once learning something about it, but she just couldn't remember. And why the first century? It was such a dramatic leap from Medieval Scotland, and she found herself missing Europe. This new landscape, with its palm trees and desert heat, was so foreign to her. More than anything, Caitlin wondered if Scarlet were behind those walls. She hoped—she prayed—that she was. She needed to find her. She couldn't rest until she did.

Caitlin walked through the town gate with Caleb and entered with a great sense of anticipation. She could feel her heart pounding at the thought of finding Scarlet—and of figuring out why they had been sent to this place to begin with. Could her Dad be inside, waiting?

As they entered the town, she was struck by the vibrancy of it. The streets were filled with children running, screaming, playing. Dogs ran wild, as did chickens. Sheep and oxen shared the streets, ambling about, and outside every home there was a donkey or camel tied to a post. Villagers walked casually about, wearing primitive tunics and robes, carrying baskets of goods on their shoulders. Caitlin felt as if she'd entered a time machine.

As they walked down the narrow streets, past small houses, past old women washing laundry by hand, people stopped and stared. Caitlin realized they must have looked so out of place walking down these streets. She looked down and noticed her modern clothing—her tight, leather battle outfit—and wondered what these people must have thought of her. They must have thought she was an alien that had dropped down from the sky. She didn't blame them.

In front of each house was somebody preparing food, selling goods, or working on their craft. They passed several families of carpenters, the man seated outside the home, sawing, hammering, building things from bed frames, to dressers, to wooden axles for plows. Before one house a man was building a huge cross, several feet thick, and ten feet long. Caitlin realized it was a cross meant for someone to be crucified on. She shivered and looked away.

As they turned down another street, the entire block was filled with blacksmiths. Everywhere flew anvils and hammers, and the ping of metal rang throughout the street, each blacksmith seeming to echo the other. There were also clay pits with large flames roasting slabs of red-hot metal, on which they were forging horseshoes, swords, and all sorts of metal work. Caitlin noticed the faces of children, black with soot, sitting by their father's sides, watching them work. She felt badly that the children worked at such a young age.

Caitlin looked everywhere for a sign of Scarlet, of her Dad, of any clue of why they were here—but she found none.

They turned down yet another street, and this one was filled with masons. Here, men chipped away at huge blocks of limestone, crafting statues, pottery, and huge, flat presses. At first, Caitlin didn't realize what they were for.

Caleb reached over and pointed.

"They're wine presses," he said, reading her mind as always. "And olive presses. They use them to crush the grapes and olives, to extract the wine and oil. See those cranks?"

Caitlin looked closely and admired the craftsmanship, the long slabs of limestone, the intricate metal work of the gears. She was startled to see what sophisticated machinery they had, even for this time and place. She was also startled to realize what an ancient craft winemaking was. Here she was, thousands of years in the past, and people were still making bottles of wine, bottles of olive oil, just like they were in the 21st century. And as she looked at the glass bottles, slowly being filled with wine and oil, she realized they looked just like the olive and wine bottles she'd used.

A group of children ran past her, chasing each other, laughing, and as they did, clouds of dust rose up and covered Caitlin's feet. She looked down and realized the roads were not paved in this village—it was probably, she figured, too small to be able to afford paved roads. And yet she knew that Nazareth had been famous for something, and it was bothering her that she could not remember what. Once again, she was kicking herself for not paying more attention in history class.

"It is the town where Jesus lived," Caleb said, reading her mind.

Caitlin felt herself redden once again, as he plucked the thoughts so easily from her mind. She withheld nothing from Caleb, but still, she didn't want him to read her thoughts when it came to how much she loved him. She might be embarrassed.

"He *lives* here?" she asked.

Caleb nodded.

"If we've arrived in his time," Caleb said. "Clearly, we are in the first century. I can see by their dress, by the architecture. I was here once before. It's a hard time and place to forget."

Caitlin's eyes opened wide at the thought.

"Do you really think he could be here now? Jesus? Walking around? In this time and place? In this town?"

Caitlin could hardly comprehend it. She tried to imagine herself turning the corner and running into Jesus in the street, casually. The thought seemed inconceivable.

Caleb furrowed his brow.

"I don't know," he said. "I'm not sensing he's here now. Maybe we missed him."

Caitlin was flabbergasted at the thought. She looked around her with a new sense of awe.

Could he be here? she wondered.

She was speechless, and felt an even greater sense of importance to their mission.

"He might be here, in this time period," Caleb said. "But not necessarily in Nazareth. He traveled a lot. Bethlehem. Nazareth. Capernaum—and Jerusalem, of course. I don't even know for sure if we are in his exact time or not. But if we are, he could be anywhere. Israel is a big place. If he were here, in this town, we would sense it."

"What do you mean?" Caitlin asked, curious. "What would it feel like?"

"I can't explain it. But you would know. It's his energy. It's unlike anything you've ever experienced before."

Suddenly, a thought occurred to Caitlin.

"Have you actually *met* him?" she asked.

Caleb slowly shook his head.

"No, not up close. Once, I was in the same city, at the same time. And the energy was overwhelming. Unlike anything I've felt before."

Once again, Caitlin was amazed by all the things Caleb had seen, all the times and places he had experienced.

"There's only one way to find out," Caleb said. "We need to know what year it is. But the problem is, of course, that no one started counting the years, like we do, until long after Jesus died. After all, our calendar year is based on the year of his birth. And when he lived, no one counted the year based on Jesus' birth—most people didn't even know who he was! So if we ask people what year it is, they'll think we're crazy."

Caleb looked around, carefully, as if searching for clues, and Caitlin did, too.

"I do sense that he's in this time," Caleb said slowly. "Just not in this place."

Caitlin examined the village with a new respect.

"But this village," she said, "it seems so small, so humble. It's not like a great, biblical city, like I would imagine. It just looks like any other desert town."

"You're right," Caleb answered, "but this is where he lived. It wasn't some grand place. It was here, among these people."

They continued walking and finally turned a corner and came to a small square in the center of town. It was a simple little square, around which were small buildings and in the center of which sat a well. Caitlin looked around and spotted a few elderly men sitting in the shade, holding canes, staring at the empty, dusty town square.

They made their way over to the well. Caleb reached out and turned the rusty crank, and slowly the weathered rope pulled up a pail of water.

Caitlin reached out, cupped the cold water with her hands, and splashed her face. It felt so refreshing in the heat. She splashed her face again, then splashed her long hair, running her hands through it. It was dusty and greasy, and the cold water felt like heaven. She'd give anything for a shower. She then leaned over, cupped some more, and drank. Her throat was parched, and it hit the spot. Caleb did the same.

They both finally leaned back, against the well, and surveyed the square. There didn't seem to be any special buildings, any special markers or clues of where they should go.

"So where now?" she finally asked.

Caleb looked around, squinting into the sun, holding his hands to his eyes. He seemed as at a loss as she.

"I don't know," he said flatly. "I'm stumped."

"In other times and places," he continued, "it seemed like churches and monasteries always held our clues. But in this time period, there is no church. There is no Christianity. There are no Christians. It was only after Jesus died that people began to create a religion after him. In this time period, there is only religion. Jesus' religion: Judaism. After all, Jesus was Jewish."

Caitlin tried to process it all. It was all so complex. If Jesus was Jewish, she figured, that meant he must have prayed in a synagogue. Suddenly, she had a thought.

"So then, maybe the best place to look is the place where Jesus prayed. Maybe we should be looking for a synagogue."

"I think you're right," Caleb said. "After all, the only other religious practice of that time, if you can even call it that, was paganism—the worshipping of idols. And I'm sure Jesus wouldn't worship in a pagan temple."

Caitlin looked around the town again, squinting, searching for any building that resembled a synagogue. But she found none. They were all just simple abodes.

"I don't see anything," she said. "All the buildings look the same to me. They're all just small houses."

"I don't either," Caleb said.

There was a long silence, as Caitlin tried to process it all. Her mind raced with possibilities.

"Do you think that my Dad and the shield are somehow connected to all this?" Caitlin asked. "Do you think that going to the places where Jesus was will lead us to my Dad?"

Caleb narrowed his eyes, as he seemed to think for a long time.

"I don't know," he said finally. "But clearly, your Dad is guarding a very great secret. A secret not just for the vampire race, but for all humanity. A shield, or a weapon, that will change the nature of the entire human race, for all time. It must be very powerful. And it seems to me, that if anyone was meant to help lead us to your father, it would be someone very powerful. Like Jesus. It would make sense to me. Maybe, to find one, we have to find the other. After all, it is your cross that unlocked so many keys to get us here. And nearly all of our clues we found in churches and monasteries."

Caitlin tried to take it all in. Was it possible that her Dad knew Jesus? Was he one of his disciples? The idea was staggering, and her sense of mystery around him deepened.

She sat there on the well, looking around the sleepy village, stumped. She had no idea where to even begin to look. Nothing at all stood out to her. And even more, she was feeling increasingly desperate to find Scarlet. Yes, she wanted to find her Dad more than ever; she felt the four keys practically burning in her pocket. But she saw no obvious way to use them—and it was hard to even focus on him with thoughts of Scarlet in her mind. The idea that she was all alone out there tore her apart. Who knew if she was even safe?

But then again, she had no idea where to look for Scarlet either. She felt an increasing sense of hopelessness.

Suddenly, a shepherd appeared through the gate, walking slowly into the town square, followed by his flock of sheep. He wore a long white robe and hood covering his head from the sun and headed towards them, holding a staff. At first, Caitlin thought that he was walking right to them. But then she realized: the well. He was merely coming to get something to drink, and they were in the way.

As he walked in, the sheep swarmed all around him, filling the square, all heading for the well. They must have known it was watering time. Within moments, Caitlin and Caleb found themselves in the midst of the flock, the delicate animals nudging them out of the way so they could get to the water. Their impatient bleating filled the air, as they waited for their shepherd to tend to them.

Caitlin and Caleb moved aside as the shepherd approached the well, turning the rusty crank, and slowly raising the pail. As he went to lift it, he pulled back his hood.

Caitlin was surprised to see that he was young. He had a large shock of blond hair, a blonde beard, and bright blue eyes. He smiled, and she could see the sun lines in his face, crinkling around his eyes, and could feel the warmth and kindness radiating off of him.

He took the overflowing pail of water, and, despite the sweat all over his forehead, despite the fact that he appeared thirsty, he turned and poured the first bucket of water into the trough at the base of the well. The sheep crowded in, bleating, muscling each other out of the way as they drank.

Caitlin was overcome by the strangest feeling that perhaps this man knew something, that perhaps he was put in their path for a reason. If Jesus lived in this time, she figured, maybe this man would have heard of him?

Caitlin felt a pang of nervousness, as she cleared her throat.

"Excuse me?" she asked.

The man turned and looked at her, and she felt the intensity in his eyes.

"We are looking for someone. I'm wondering if you might know if he lives here."

The man narrowed his eyes, and as he did, Caitlin felt as if he were seeing right through her. It was uncanny.

"He lives," the man replied, as if reading her mind. "But he is in this place no longer."

Caitlin could hardly believe it. It was true.

"Where has he gone?" Caleb asked. Caitlin heard the intensity in his voice, and could sense how desperately he wanted to know.

The man shifted his gaze to Caleb.

"Why, to the Galilee," the man responded, as if it were obvious. "To the sea."

Caleb narrowed his eyes.

"Capernaum?" Caleb asked tentatively.

The man nodded back.

Caleb's eyes opened wide in recognition.

"There are many followers on the trail," the man said cryptically. "Seek and ye shall find."

The shepherd suddenly lowered his head, turned, and began to walk away, the sheep following. Soon, he was heading across the square.

Caitlin could not let him go. Not yet. She *had* to know more. And she sensed that he was holding something back.

"Wait!" she cried out.

The shepherd stopped and turned, staring at her.

"Do you know my father?" she asked.

To Caitlin's surprise, the man slowly nodded back.

"Where is he?" Caitlin asked.

"That is for you to find out," he said. "You are the one who carries the keys."

"Who is he?" Caitlin asked, desperate to know.

Slowly, the man shook his head.

"I am merely a shepherd on the way."

"But I don't even know where to look!" Caitlin responded, desperate. "Please. I *have* to find him."

The shepherd slowly broke into a smile.

"Always, the best place to look is right where you are," he said.

And with that, he covered his head, and turned and crossed the square. He passed through the arched gate, and a moment later, he was gone, his sheep following.

Always the best place to look is where you are.

His words rang through Caitlin's mind. Somehow, she sensed it was more than just an allegory. The more she dwelled on it, the more she felt that it was literal. As if he were telling her there was a clue right here, where she was.

Caitlin suddenly turned and searched the well, the place they had been sitting. Now, she sensed something.

Always the best place to look is where you are.

She knelt down and ran her hands along the ancient, smooth stone wall. She felt all along it, feeling more and more certain that something was there, that she had been led to a clue.

"What are you doing?" Caleb asked.

Caitlin searched frantically, scanning all the cracks of all the stones, feeling she was onto something.

Finally, halfway around the well, she stopped. She found one crack that was slightly larger than the others. Just large enough to get her finger in. The stone surrounding it was just slightly too smooth, and the crack was just slightly too big.

Caitlin reached in and pried it open. Soon, the stone began to wiggle, then to move. The stone came loose, out of the base of the well. Behind it, she was amazed to see, was a small hiding place.

Caleb came close, huddling over her shoulder, as she reached down into the darkness. She felt something cold and metal in her hand, and pulled it out slowly.

She raised her hand into the light, and slowly opened her palm.

She could not believe what was in it.

CHAPTER FIVE

As Scarlet stood there with Ruth, at the end of the dead end, her back to the wall, she watched in fear as the group of bullies set their dog loose on her. Moments later, the huge, wild dog was charging, snarling, aiming right for her throat. It was all happening so fast, Scarlet hardly knew what to do.

Before she could react, Ruth suddenly snarled and charged for the dog. She leapt into the air and met the dog halfway, sinking her fangs into its throat. Ruth landed on top of her, pinning her to the ground. The dog must have been twice Ruth's size, yet Ruth pinned her effortlessly, not letting her get up. She clamped her fangs down with all she had, and soon, the dog stopped struggling, dead.

"You little bitch!" screamed the lead boy, furious.

He burst out of the pack and charged right for Ruth. He raised a stick, sharpened at one end into a spear point, and brought it down right for Ruth's exposed back.

Scarlet's reflexes kicked in, and she burst into action. Without even thinking she sprinted for the boy, reached up and caught his stick in mid-air, right before it hit Ruth. She then pulled him towards her, leaned back and kicked him hard in the ribs.

He keeled over, and she kicked him again, this time in the face with a roundhouse kick. He spun around and landed face-first on the stone.

Ruth turned and charged the group of boys. She leapt high in the air, and sank her fangs into one boy's throat, pinning him to the ground. That left only three of them.

Scarlet stood there, facing them, and suddenly, a new feeling overtook her. No longer did she feel afraid; no longer did she want to run from these boys; no longer did she want to cower and hide; no longer did she want the protection of her mommy and daddy.

Something snapped inside her as she crossed an invisible line, a tipping point. She felt, for the first time in her life, that she didn't need anybody. All she needed was herself. Instead of fearing the moment, now, she relished it.

Scarlet felt herself infused with rage, rising from her toes, through her body, all the way to her scalp. It was an electric emotion that she didn't understand, one she had never experienced before. She no longer wanted to run away from these boys. She didn't want to let them get away, either.

Now, she wanted vengeance.

As the three boys stood there, staring in shock, Scarlet charged. It all happened so fast, she could barely process it. Her reflexes were so much faster than theirs, as if they were moving in slow motion.

Scarlet leapt into the air, higher than she ever had, and kicked the boy in the center, planting her two feet on his chest. She sent him flying back, like a bullet across the alley, until he smashed into the wall and collapsed.

Before the other two could react, she wheeled and elbowed one in the face, then spun and kicked the other in the solar plexus. They both collapsed, unconscious.

Scarlet stood there, with Ruth, breathing hard. She looked around, and saw all five boys sprawled out around them, not moving. And then, she realized: she was the victor.

She was no longer the Scarlet she once knew.

*

Scarlet roamed through the alleyways for hours, Ruth by her side, putting as much distance between herself and those boys as she could. She turned down alleyway after alleyway in the heat, getting lost in the maze of narrow side streets in the old city of Jerusalem. The midday sun beat down on her, and she was beginning to feel delirious from it; she was also feeling delirious from the lack of food and water. She could see Ruth panting hard beside her as they meandered through the crowds, and she could see that she was suffering, too.

A child passed by Ruth and grabbed her back, yanking on her playfully, but too hard. Ruth turned and snapped, snarling and bearing her fangs. The child screamed, cried, and ran away. It was unlike Ruth to behave this way; usually, she was so tolerant. But it seemed the heat and the hunger was getting to her, too. She was also channeling Scarlet's own rage and frustration.

As much as she tried, Scarlet didn't know how to turn off her residual feelings of rage. It was as if something inside her had been unleashed, and she couldn't reign it back in. She felt her veins pumping, the anger pulsing, and as she passed vendor after vendor, displaying all manner of food that she and Ruth could not afford, her anger grew. She was also beginning to realize that what she was experiencing, her intense hunger pains, weren't just typical hunger. It was something else, she realized. Something deeper, more primal. She didn't just want food. She wanted blood. She needed to feed.

Scarlet didn't know what was happening to her, and she didn't know how to handle it. She smelled a hunk of meat and squeezed her way through the crowd, right up to it, staring. Ruth squeezed in, beside her.

Scarlet elbowed her way right to the front, and as she did, a resentful man in the crowd shoved her back.

"Hey girl, watch where you're going!" he snapped.

Without even thinking, Scarlet turned and shoved the man. He was more than twice her size, but he went flying backwards, knocking over several fruit stands as he fell to the ground.

He scrambled to his feet, shocked, looking back at Scarlet, trying to figure out how such a small girl could overpower him like that. Then, with a look of fear, he wisely turned and hurried away.

The vendor scowled down at Scarlet, sensing trouble.

"You want meat?" he snapped. "You have money to pay for it?"

But Ruth couldn't contain herself. She lunged forward, sunk her fangs into the huge slab of meat, tore off a hunk, and swallowed it down. Before anyone could react, she lunged forward again, aiming for another hunk.

This time, the vendor brought down his hand, as hard as he could, aiming to smack Ruth hard on the nose.

But Scarlet sensed it coming. In fact, something new was happening to her sense of speed, her sense of timing. As the vendor's hand began to descend, Scarlet found her own hand shooting up, almost without her, grabbing the vendor's wrist right before he hit Ruth.

The vendor looked down at Scarlet, wide-eyed, shocked that such a small girl could have such a strong grip. Scarlet squeezed the man's wrist, and tightened her grip until his entire arm started shaking. She found herself scowling back up at him, unable to control her rage.

"Don't you dare touch my wolf," Scarlet snarled back at the man.

"I'm…sorry," the man said, arm shaking in pain, eyes wide with fear.

Finally, Scarlet released her grip, and hurried away from the stand, Ruth by her side. As she hurried to get as far away as she could, she heard a whistling behind her, then frantic shouts for guards to come.

"Let's go, Ruth!" Scarlet said, and the two of them hurried off down the alleyway, getting lost in the crowd. At least Ruth had eaten.

But Scarlet's own hunger was overwhelming, and she didn't know if she could contain it any longer. She didn't know what was happening to her, but as they walked down street after street, she found herself examining people's throats. She zoomed in on their veins, saw the blood pulsing. She found herself licking her lips, wanting—needing—to sink her teeth in. She craved the idea of drinking their blood, and found herself imagining what it would feel like when the blood poured down her throat. She didn't understand. Was she even human anymore? Was she becoming a wild animal?

Scarlet didn't want to hurt anyone. Rationally, she tried to stop herself.

But physically, something was taking over her. It was rising, from her toes, her legs, through her torso, to the crown of her head and to the tips of her fingers. It was a desire. An unstoppable, unquenchable desire. It was overwhelming her thoughts, telling her what to think, how to act.

Suddenly, Scarlet detected something: in the distance, somewhere behind her, a group of Roman soldiers were chasing after her. Her new, hyper-sensitive hearing alerted her to the sound of their sandals slapping on the stone. She already knew, even though they were blocks away.

The sound of their sandals slapping against the stone only irritated her further; the noise mingled in her head with the sound of the vendors' screaming, the children laughing, the dogs barking.... It was all becoming too much for her. Her hearing was becoming too intense, and she was too annoyed by the cacophony of noise. The sun, too, was feeling stronger, as if it were bearing down just on her. It was all too much. She felt as if she were under the microscope of the world, and about to explode.

Suddenly, Scarlet leaned back, overflowing with rage, and felt a new sensation in her teeth. She felt her two incisor teeth expand, felt long, sharp fangs growing, protruding from them. She hardly knew what the feeling was, but she knew she was changing, into something she could hardly recognize or control. She suddenly spotted a large, fat, drunk man, stumbling through the alley. Scarlet knew that she either had to feed, or to die herself. And something inside of her wanted to survive.

Scarlet heard herself snarling, and was shocked. The noise, so primal, stunned even her. She felt as if she were outside her body as she pounced, leapt through the air, right for the man. She watched in slow motion as he turned to her, eyes open wide in fear. She felt her two front teeth sinking into his flesh, into the veins on his throat. And a moment later, she felt his hot blood pouring into her throat, filling her veins.

She heard the man scream, just for a moment. Because a second later, he was collapsed, on the ground, she on top of him, sucking out all of his blood. Slowly, she began to feel a new life, a new energy, infusing her body.

She wanted to stop feeding, to let this man go. But she couldn't. She needed this. She needed to survive.

She needed to feed.

CHAPTER SIX

Sam sprinted through the alleys of Jerusalem, snarling, red with rage. He wanted to destroy, to tear apart everything in sight. As he ran past a row of vendors, he reached out and swiped their booths, knocking them over like dominoes. He bumped people deliberately, as hard as he could, sending them flying every which way. He was like a wrecking ball, out of control, hurling down the alley, knocking over everything in his way.

Chaos ensued; cries rose up. People began to take notice and started to flee, to jump out of his way. He was like a freight train of destruction.

The sun was driving him crazy. It beat down on his head like a living thing, filling him with more and more rage. He had never known what true rage was until now. Nothing seemed to satisfy him.

He saw a tall, thin man and he dove for him, sinking his fangs into his neck. He did this in a split second, sucking out the blood, then hurried on, sinking his fangs into another person's neck. He went from person to person, sinking his fangs and sucking the blood. He moved so fast, none of them had time to react. They all slumped to the floor, one after the other, and he left a trail in his wake. He was in a feeding frenzy, and he felt his body begin to swell with their blood. Still, it was not enough.

The sun was driving him to the brink of insanity. He needed shade, and he needed it fast. He spotted a large building in the distance, a formal, elaborate palace, built of limestone, with pillars and huge arched doors. Without thinking, he burst across the square and charged it, kicking open the doors.

It was cooler in here, and finally, Sam could breathe again. Just getting the sun off his head made a difference. He was able to open his eyes, and slowly, they adjusted.

Staring back at Sam were the startled faces of dozens of people. Most sat inside small pools, individual baths, while others walked around, barefoot on the stone floor. They were all naked. That was when Sam realized: he was inside a bathhouse. A Roman bathhouse.

The ceilings were high and arched, letting in the light, and there were large arched columns all throughout. The floors were a shining marble, and small pools filled the vast room. People lazed about, apparently relaxing.

That is, until they saw. They quickly sat up, and their expressions morphed to fear.

Sam hated the sight of these people—these lazy, rich people, lounging about as if they hadn't a care in the world. He would make them all pay. He threw his head back and roared.

Most of the crowd had the good sense to scurry out of there, to hurry to grab their towels and robes and to try to get out as soon as they could.

But they didn't stand a chance. Sam hurled forward, lunged for the closest one, and sunk his teeth into her neck. He sucked the blood out and she collapsed to the ground and rolled into a bath, staining it red.

He did this again and again, jumping from one victim to the next, men and women alike. Soon the bathhouse filled with corpses, bodies floating everywhere, all the pools stained red.

There was a sudden crash at the door, and Sam wheeled to see what it was.

There, filling the doorway, were dozens of Roman soldiers. They wore official uniforms—short tunics, roman sandals, feathered helmets—and held shields and short swords. Several more held bows and arrows. They pulled them back and took aim at Sam.

"Stay where you are!" the leader yelled.

Sam snarled as he turned, rose to his full height, and began walking towards them.

The fire came. Dozens of arrows went hurling through the air, right for him. Sam could see them in slow motion, glistening, their silver tips heading right for him.

But he was faster even than their arrows. Before they could reach him, he was already high up in the air, leaping, somersaulting over them all. He easily covered the span of the entire room—forty feet—before the archers even relaxed their hands.

Sam came down feet first, kicking the center one right in the chest with such force that he knocked back the whole crowd, like a row of dominoes. A dozen soldiers went down.

Before the others could react, Sam reached over and snatched two swords out of two soldier's hands. He spun and slashed in every direction.

His aim was perfect. He chopped off head after head, then turned and jabbed the survivors right through the heart. He cut through the crowd like butter. Within seconds, dozens of soldiers slumped to the ground, lifeless.

Sam dropped to his knees and sank his fangs into each one's heart, drinking and drinking. He knelt there, on all fours, hunched over like a beast, gorging himself with blood, still trying to fulfill his rage, which was limitless.

Sam finished, but was still not satisfied. He felt as if he needed to battle entire armies, to kill masses of humanity at once. He needed to gorge for weeks. And even then, it wouldn't be enough.

"SAMSON!" shrieked a strange female voice.

Sam stopped, frozen in his tracks. It was a voice he hadn't heard in centuries. It was a voice he had almost forgotten, one he had never expected to hear again.

Only one person in this world had ever called him *Samson.*

It was the voice of his maker.

There, standing over him, looking down, a smile on her gorgeous face, was Sam's first true love.

There, was Samantha.

CHAPTER SEVEN

Caitlin and Caleb flew together in the clear, blue desert sky, heading north over the land of Israel, towards the sea. Below them the land was spread out, and Caitlin watched the landscape change as they went. There were huge swaths of desert, vast stretches of sunbaked dirt, littered with rocks, boulders, mountains and caves. There were hardly any people, except for the occasional shepherd, dressed from head to toe in white, a hood covering his head to protect from the sun, his flock trailing not too far behind.

But as they flew further and further north, the terrain began to change. Desert gave way to rolling hills, and the color began to change, too, from a dry, dusty brown, to a vibrant green. Olive groves and vineyards dotted the landscape. But still, there were few people to be found.

Caitlin thought back to her discovery in Nazareth. Inside that well, she had been shocked to find a single, precious object, which she now clutched in her hand: a golden star of David, the size of her palm. Etched across it, in a small ancient script, was a single word: *Capernaum.*

It had been clear to them both that it was a message, telling them where to go next. *But why Capernaum?* Caitlin wondered.

She knew from Caleb that Jesus had spent time there. Did that mean he would be awaiting them there? And would her Dad be there, too? And, she dared to hope, Scarlet?

Caitlin scrutinized the landscape beneath her. She was amazed at how under-populated Israel was in this time. She was surprised to fly over an occasional house, since the dwellings were so far and few between. This was still a rural, empty land. The only cities she had seen were more like towns, and even these were primitive, with nearly all the buildings a simple one or two stories, and built of stone. She hadn't seen any paved roads to speak of.

As they flew, Caleb swooped beside her and reached out for her hand. It was good to feel his touch. She couldn't help but wonder, for the millionth time, why they'd landed in this time and place. So far back. So distant. So different from Scotland, from everything she knew.

She felt deep down that this would be the final stop in her journey. Here. Israel. It was such a powerful place and time, she could feel the energy radiating off of everything. Everything felt spiritually charged to her, as if she were walking and living and breathing inside a giant energy field. She knew that something momentous was awaiting her. But she didn't know what. Was her Dad really here? Would she ever find him? It was so frustrating to her. She had all four keys. He should be here, she thought, waiting for her. Why did she have to continue to search like this?

Even more pressing in her mind were thoughts of Scarlet. She peered down at every place they passed, looking for any sign of her, of Ruth. For a moment she wondered if she hadn't made it—but quickly put that out of her mind, refusing to allow herself to go to such a dark place. She couldn't bear the thought of a life without Scarlet. If she learned that Scarlet were truly gone, she didn't know if she'd have the strength to carry on.

Caitlin felt the Star of David burning in her hand, and thought again of where they were going. She wished she knew more about the life of Jesus; she wished she had read the Bible more carefully growing up. She tried to remember, but all she really knew were the basics: Jesus had lived in four places: Bethlehem, Nazareth, Capernaum, and Jerusalem. They had just left Nazareth, and were on the way to Capernaum now.

She couldn't help but wonder if they were on a treasure hunt, following in his footsteps, if maybe he held some clue, or if one of his followers held a clue as to where her Dad was, where the shield was. She wondered again how they could be connected. She thought of all the churches and monasteries she had visited throughout all the centuries, and felt there was a connection. But she wasn't sure what.

The only thing she knew about Capernaum was that it was supposed to be a small, humble fishing village in the Galilee, along the northwestern coast of Israel. But they hadn't passed any towns for hours—in fact there had hardly even been a soul in sight—and she had seen no sign of any water—much less a sea.

Then, just as she was thinking it, they flew over a mountaintop, and as they crossed its peak, the other side of the valley opened up before her. It took her breath away. There, stretching out forever, was a shining sea. It was a deeper blue than she had ever seen, and it positively sparkled in the sunlight, looking like a treasure chest. Bordering it was a magnificent shore of white sand, and the waves crashed against it, as far as the eye could see.

Caitlin felt a thrill of excitement. They were heading in the right direction; if they stayed along the shoreline, it must take them to Capernaum.

"There," came Caleb's voice.

She followed his finger, squinting into the horizon, and could just barely make it out: in the distance sat a small village. It was hardly a city, hardly even a town. There were maybe two dozen homes, and a large structure, nestled against the shoreline. As they got closer, Caitlin squinted, examining it, but could hardly see anyone: only a few villagers walked the streets. She wondered if it was because of the midday sun, or because it was uninhabited.

Caitlin looked down for any sign of Jesus himself, but saw none. More importantly, she did not sense it. If what Caleb said was true, she would sense his energy from far off. But she didn't sense any unusual energy. Once again, she started to wonder if they were in the right time and place. Maybe that man was wrong: maybe Jesus had died years before. Or maybe he wasn't even born yet.

Caleb suddenly dove down, towards the village, and Caitlin followed. They found an inconspicuous place to land, outside the village wall, in a grove of olive trees. Then they walked through the town gate

They walked through the small, dusty village, and it was hot, everything basking in the sun. The few villagers who ambled about barely seemed to notice them; they seemed only intent on seeking shade, on fanning themselves. One old lady walked to the town well, raised a large spoon to her hand and drank, then reached up and wiped sweat from her brow.

As they traversed the small streets, the place seemed utterly deserted. Caitlin scanned for any sign, anything, that might point to a clue, to any sign of Jesus, or her father, or the shield, or Scarlet—but found nothing.

She turned to Caleb.

"Now what?" she asked.

Caleb looked back blankly. He seemed as at a loss as she was.

Caitlin turned, surveying the village walls, the humble architecture, and as she looked through the town, she noticed a narrow, well-worn pathway, leading down to the ocean. As she followed its trail, through a town gate, in the distance, she saw the glimmer of the ocean.

She nudged Caleb, and he saw it, too, and followed her as she walked out the town, towards the shore.

As they neared the shoreline, Caitlin saw three small, brightly-colored fishing boats, weathered, half-beached on the sand, bobbing in the waves. In one sat a fisherman, and standing beside the other two, ankle deep in the ocean, were two more fishermen. They were older men, with gray hair and matching beards, faces as weathered as their boats, suntanned, deeply lined. They wore white robes and white hoods to block out the sun.

As Caitlin watched, two of them hoisted a fishing net and dragged it slowly through the waves. They pulled at it, fighting the waves, and a small boy jumped out of one of the boats and ran to the net, helping them pull it in. As it reached the shore, Caitlin saw they had caught dozens of fish, squirming and flopping. The boy squealed in delight, while the old men were somber.

Caitlin and Caleb had snuck up on them so quietly—especially with the sound of the crashing waves—that they still didn't know they were there. Caitlin cleared her throat so as not to startle them.

They all wheeled and looked her way, and could see the surprise in their eyes. She didn't blame them: they must have been a shocking sight, the two of them, dressed in all black from head to toe, in modern leather, battle gear. They must have looked as if they'd dropped straight down from the sky.

"We are sorry to bother you," Caitlin began, "but are we in Capernaum?" she asked the nearest fellow.

He looked from her to Caleb, then back to her. He slowly nodded back.

"We are looking for someone," Caitlin continued.

"And who might that be?" the other fisherman asked.

Caitlin was about to say "my Dad," but then stopped herself, realizing that wouldn't do any good. How would she describe him anyway? She didn't even know who he was, or what he looked like.

So, instead, she said the only person who came to mind, the only person they might recognize: "Jesus."

She half expected them to mock her, to laugh at her, to look at her as if she were crazy—or to have no idea who Jesus was.

But to her surprise, they didn't seem surprised by her question; they took her seriously.

"He left two weeks ago," one of them said.

Caitlin's heart skipped a beat. So. It was true. He was really alive. They were really in his time. And he had really been here, to this village.

"And all his followers with him," said the other. "Only the old folks like us and children stayed behind."

"So he's real?" Caitlin asked, in shock. She could still hardly believe it; it was almost too much to comprehend.

The boy stepped up, walking close to Caitlin.

"He fixed my grandpa's hand," the boy said. "Look at it. He was a leper. Now he's healed. Show her, grandpa," the boy said.

The old man slowly turned and pulled back his sleeve. His hand looked perfectly normal. In fact, as Caitlin looked closely, she saw one hand actually looked much younger than the other. It was uncanny. He had the hand of an 18-year-old boy. Pink, rosy and healthy—as if he'd been given a new hand.

Caitlin couldn't believe it. Jesus was real. He really healed people.

Seeing this man's hand, this man who was once a leper, perfectly healed, sent a chill up her spine. It brought it all home. For the first time, she had hope that she might really find him, and really find her Dad, and the Shield. And that they might lead her to Scarlet.

"Do you know where he went?" Caleb asked.

"Jerusalem, from what we hear," yelled out one of the other fishermen, over the sound of the crashing waves.

Jerusalem, Caitlin thought. It felt so far away. They had flown all the way up here, to Capernaum. And now, it was feeling like a wild goose chase. After all that, they would have to turn around and leave empty-handed.

But she could feel the Star of David burning in her hand, and she felt certain that there had to be a reason they were sent to Capernaum. She felt there was something more, something they needed to find.

"One of his disciples is still here," a fishermen said. "Paul. You can ask him. He might know exactly where they're going."

"Where is he?" Caitlin asked

"Where they all spent their time. The old synagogue," the man said. He turned and pointed back over his shoulder with his thumb.

Caitlin turned and looked over her shoulder, and there, sitting on a hill, overlooking the ocean, she saw a beautiful, small, limestone temple. Even in this time, it already looked ancient. Bedecked with intricate columns, it looked out over the sea, with a direct view of the crashing waves. Even from here, Caitlin could sense that this was a holy place.

"It was Jesus's synagogue," one of the men said. "It was where he spent all his time."

"Thank you," Caitlin said, beginning to walk towards it.

As she walked, the man reached out and grabbed her arm with his new, healthy hand. Caitlin stopped and looked at him. She could feel the energy pulsing through his hand, into her arm. It was unlike anything she'd ever felt. It was a healing, comforting energy.

"You're not from here, are you?" the man asked.

Caitlin felt him looking into her eyes, and could tell that he was sensing something. She realized there was no use in lying to him.

Slowly, she shook her head. "No, I'm not."

He stared back at her for a long time, then slowly nodded, satisfied.

"You will find him," he said to her. "I can feel it."

*

Caitlin and Caleb walked up the shore, waves crashing beside them, the smell of salt heavy in the air. The cool breezes were refreshing, especially after so much time in the desert heat. They turned and ascended a small hill, at the top of which sat nestled the ancient synagogue.

Caitlin looked up as they approached: built of a worn limestone, it seemed as if it had been here for thousands of years. She could feel the energy coming off the place; this was a holy place, she could tell already. Its large, arched door was ajar and creaked as it swayed in the wind, rocked by the ocean breezes.

As they hiked up the hill, they passed clumps of wild flowers, growing seemingly right out of the rock, in an array of bright desert colors. They were the most beautiful flowers Caitlin had ever seen, so unexpected, so unlikely in this desolate place.

They reached the top of the hill and walked right up to the door. Caitlin felt the Star of

David burning inside her pocket, and she knew this was it.

She looked up and saw over the doorway, embedded in the stone, a huge, golden star of David, surrounded by Hebrew letters. It was amazing to think that she was about to enter a place where Jesus had spent so much time. Somehow she had expected to enter a church—but, of course, as she thought about it, she realized that wouldn't make sense, since churches weren't built, of course, until after he died. It seemed strange to think of Jesus in a synagogue—but then again, after all, she knew he had been Jewish, and a Rabbi, and so it made perfect sense.

But what relevance did all of this have for her search for her Dad? For the shield? She was increasingly feeling that all this was connected, all the centuries and times and places, all of the searching in all the monasteries and churches, all of the keys, all of the crosses. She felt that a common thread was sitting there, right before her eyes. Yet she still didn't know what.

Clearly there was some holy, spiritual element to whatever it was she needed to find. Which also seemed strange to her, because after all, this was a world of vampires. But then again, as she thought about it, she realized this was also a spiritual war, between supernatural forces of good and evil, those who wanted to protect the human race, and those who wanted to harm it. And clearly, whatever it was she found would have huge ramifications not only for the vampire race, but for the human race as well.

She looked at the ajar door, and wondered if they should just walk in.

"Hello?" Caitlin called out.

She waited a few seconds, her voice echoing. No response.

She looked at Caleb. He nodded, and she could tell he also felt they were in the right place. She reached up, lay her palm on the ancient wooden door, and gently pushed it. It creaked as it opened, and they entered the darkened building.

It was cooler in here, protected from the sun, and it took Caitlin a moment for her eyes to adjust. Slowly, they did, and she took in the room before her.

It was magnificent, unlike anything she had ever seen. It wasn't grand, like so many churches she'd been in; it was actually a humble building, built of marble and limestone, adorned with columns, and with intricate carvings over the ceiling. There were no pews, no places to sit—just a large, open space. At the far end was a simple altar—but instead of a cross above it, there sat a large Star of David. Behind that was a small golden cabinet, with images of two large scrolls carved into it.

Only a few, small arched windows lined the walls, and while sunlight streamed in in places, it was still dim. This place was so silent, so still. Caitlin could hear only the distant crashing of the waves behind her.

Caitlin and Caleb exchanged a glance, then together walked slowly down the aisle, heading towards the altar. As they walked their footsteps reverberated off the marble, and Caitlin couldn't shake the feeling they were being watched.

They reached the end of aisle and stood before the golden cabinet. Caitlin studied the diagrams etched into the gold: they were so detailed, so intricate, they reminded her of that church in Florence, in the Duomo, of its golden doors. It looked as if someone had spent a lifetime carving this one, too. In addition to the images of scrolls, Hebrew letters were embedded all around it. Caitlin wondered what was inside.

"The Torah," came a voice.

Caitlin wheeled, shocked to hear another voice. She didn't understand how anyone could have kept so quiet, managed to avoid her detection—and how anyone could, on top of it, read her mind. Only a very special person could achieve this. Either a vampire, or a holy person, or both.

Walking towards them was a man wearing a white robe, hood pulled back, with long, disheveled light brown hair and a beard to match. He had beautiful blue eyes, and a compassionate face, lit up with a smile. He looked ageless, maybe in his 40s, and walked towards them with a slight limp, holding a cane.

"They are the scrolls of the Old Testament. The five books of Moses. That is what lays behind those golden doors."

He kept approaching until he was just a few feet away, then stopped before Caitlin and Caleb. He stared right at her, and Caitlin could feel the intensity coming off of him. Clearly this was no ordinary person.

"I am Paul," he said, not extending his hand, which he rested on his cane.

"I am Caitlin, and this is my husband, Caleb," she replied.

He smiled widely.

"I know," he answered.

Caitlin felt foolish. Clearly, this man, able to read her mind so easily, knew a lot more about her than she did about him. It was an eerie feeling, that all these people, in all these centuries and places, knew about her, had all been waiting for her. It made her feel a sense of purpose, a sense of mission, even more. But it also made her even more frustrated that she didn't know what it was, or where to go next.

"We are sorry to intrude," Caleb said. "But we were told that Jesus prayed here. That he was here recently. Is that true?"

The man nodded slowly, keeping his eyes fixed on Caitlin.

"They left for Jerusalem some time ago," he said. "If you were one of the masses coming to be healed, I would tell you it's too late. But then again, I know you have not come to be healed. No. You have a very different purpose, don't you?" he asked, still staring at Caitlin.

Caitlin nodded back, sensing that this man already knew everything. And for the first time in her life, she had another feeling: that this man was close to her Dad. That he knew where he was. The feeling sent a chill through her body. She had never felt so close to him before.

"I'm looking for my Dad," Caitlin said, and could hear her own voice trembling with anticipation.

The man smiled back.

"And he is looking for you."

Caitlin's eyes opened wide in surprise.

"Do you know him?" she asked.

The man nodded back.

"Where is he?" Caitlin asked, impatient.

But the man merely sighed, turned, and walked to a window pane. He stood there for a long while, looking out at the sea.

"It is not for me to say."

All of these riddles were driving Caitlin crazy. She couldn't take it anymore. She *had* to know where he was.

"Why can't you just tell me?" Caitlin asked, upset.

The man paused.

"I could tell you," he said, "but you wouldn't listen."

That only deepened Caitlin's confusion. She had no idea what he meant.

"You are in the final time and place," he continued. "You are closer to finding your father than you can imagine. But there are also powerful forces at work. Dark forces. There is much at stake, and they want the shield. And they will stop at nothing to have it.

"The time is coming when you are going to have to make a choice. To make a great sacrifice. Remember that your father and the shield must come before all else. Before all personal desire. Even before family. Do you understand? It won't be easy. There will be hard choices for you to make. But you must make them. For all of us. Do you understand?" he asked again.

Caitlin slowly nodded back, but she didn't quite understand. What choices would she have to make? Was this man seeing her future? She had an eerie feeling that he was.

"We are all counting on you," he added. "You must find your father. You must get the shield before they do. If they get it first, there will be unthinkable evil and cruelty for all time to come."

Caitlin felt more of an urgency than ever to find her Dad, and the shield, especially before the others. But she still had no idea where to begin.

"You cannot meet your father until the timing is right. Not one second before, not one second after. There is a cycle of fate in the universe. The stars must line up perfectly. And then, and only then, will you meet."

The man turned and faced her, and Caitlin sensed that he knew even more—not only about her father, but about Scarlet.

"And what of my daughter?" she asked. "Is she here? In this time and place?"

"Yes," the man replied simply.

His direct answer surprised Caitlin, and thrilled her at the same time. Scarlet was here. She was alive. She felt flooded with relief—and also anticipation. She *had* to find her.

"Where is she?" Caitlin demanded.

The man shook his head.

"Again, that is not for me to say. But I will tell you this: until you find your father, you will not find Scarlet. Search for Scarlet, and you will lose them both. Search for your father, and you will find them both."

"But I don't know how to find him," Caitlin snapped, frustrated.

"Oh, but you do," the man replied. "You have already found the first clue. You trusted your intuition, and it has worked. It sits there now, in your hand."

Caitlin suddenly remembered: the Star of David. She held it in her palm, examining it, wondering.

The man crossed the room slowly, reached out, and took the star. He held it up, examining it. He nodded in satisfaction.

"See?" he said. "I could not have found this. It was meant for you. And you alone. Only you can use it."

Caitlin looked over at Caleb, befuddled. He looked back at her blankly.

Use it? she wondered.

"How?" she asked.

He looked over at the golden pedestal before the cabinet, and Caitlin followed his gaze.

There, in the center of the pedestal, was a hollowed-out shape. As she looked closely, she was shocked to realize that the shape was the exact size of the Star of David. She looked at the man for confirmation, and he handed the star back to her and nodded.

She turned and walked over to it. She gently held out the star, and placed it inside the pedestal. It was a perfect fit, sinking down into the small the space.

Suddenly there was a noise, high above her head. Caitlin looked up and saw a small portion of the ceiling retract, to the sound of scraping stone. As it opened, a shaft of sunlight streamed in at a sharp angle, illuminating a small patch of wall, about a foot wide.

Caitlin was shocked. She hurried over to the wall with Caleb, and as she looked closely, she noticed this section was different from the rest of the wall. As the sun hit it, she could just barely make out letters, carved into the stone.

It was a message. Carved in ancient, Hebrew letters, running from right to left.

She had no idea what it meant. She looked over at Caleb, hoping he did.

"Can you read it?" she asked.

He nodded, wide-eyed in surprise. He looked as if he'd just seen a ghost.

"It is a message," he said, and turned and looked at her. "And it is from your father."

CHAPTER EIGHT

Scarlet roamed the narrow streets of Jerusalem with Ruth, feeling unlike she ever had. She felt as if something inside her had been unleashed, something she didn't understand, and couldn't contain. She felt more animal than human. She was roving, looking for her next kill, and she didn't even trust herself.

The taste and smell of blood filled Scarlet's every pore. Her first kill had been indescribable, something beyond what she could have ever imagined. The feel of that man's blood filling her veins did something to her, something she couldn't explain: she felt filled with power and strength at the same time. Reborn.

Yet it also whet her appetite. It turned on a switch inside, made her realize how good it could feel—and it demanded more. She now roamed the streets wildly, watching people's throats, zooming in on the pulsing of their heartbeat. She felt an itch inside her veins, a thirst for more victims.

She also felt a fresh sense of rage, of entitlement, that she never had before. And of fearlessness. She turned down another alleyway, this one crowded with people, and this time, she no longer cowered, hid from anyone. Instead, she walked boldly, strutting right down the center. And when people got too close to her, she merely put her shoulder into them and knocked them out of the way.

"Hey little girl, watch it!" a man yelled.

Scarlet turned and smiled at him, feeling her fangs protruding, her eyes glowing red, and heard the guttural sound she made. She saw horror and fear on the man's face, and watched him quickly turn and run away. She knew that, now, she was a thing to fear.

Scarlet heard Ruth snarling beside her, too, and she felt more of a kinship with Ruth than ever. She could feel Ruth picking up on her rage, sharing it. The two of them were like a ticking time bomb, waiting to explode.

Scarlet spotted the vendor she had seen before, with his huge rack of meat. This time, she was determined to get Ruth fed.

The vendor saw her coming, and stood out before his booth. He reached up his hands and started whistling like crazy. It was a loud, piercing whistle, cutting through the crowd.

"Guards! GUARDS!" he shrieked.

But Scarlet didn't pause. She walked right up to him.

"You're going to jail this time, misses," he scolded. "Think you can steal someone else's food? Now you're going to pay. Stop right there!"

The big, beefy man reached down to grab Scarlet, and she felt his paws on her arm. He was strong, stronger than she could have imagined, and the old Scarlet would have slunk away in fear.

But now, she was unafraid. On the contrary, she hoped for this, relished it.

With an ease unlike any he could have imagined, she twisted his big arm around, leaned up her elbow, and brought it down the back of his, cracking his arm in half. The man shrieked out in pain.

She then reached over, grabbed him by the back of his shirt and hurled him through the crowd. The huge man, well over 300 pounds, went flying through the air as if he were a child's toy, and went crashing into the booths, knocking over dozens of carts. People screamed in fear and confusion and the crowd recoiled, away from Scarlet. They kept a safe perimeter, looking back at her with complete bewilderment.

Scarlet turned back to the meat on the spit. She grabbed the entire hunk, snatched it off, and held it out to Ruth. Ruth snarled as she tore off every last scrap of meat, eating the entire thing, which was even bigger than her. Ruth ate and ate, until Scarlet could feel that she was sated.

Scarlet suddenly heard a sharp whistling noise and turned to see dozens of Roman soldiers marching towards her from one end. She heard another whistling, and turned in the other direction to see dozens more marching at her from the other.

But again, Scarlet was unafraid. On the contrary, she looked forward to the idea of battle, to having an outlet on which to vent her unquenchable need for violence. She didn't wait for them to approach, but instead, charged right for them. They trotted towards her, hands on their swords and on their shields, but she sprinted for them at lightning speed.

Scarlet jumped into the air, and planted her two feet on the chest of the lead soldier, kicking him with such force that he went flying backwards, knocking down a dozen soldiers like dominoes.

The other soldiers jumped on Scarlet from behind, knocking her to the ground. But with hardly any effort, she merely jumped up and threw back her arms, and as she did, she sent them flying in every direction. They smashed into the walls, and collapsed onto the ground.

The remaining soldiers faced her, pausing, and she could see the fear in their eyes. Three of the them drew their swords and charged.

But from Scarlet's perspective it was as if they were moving in slow motion. She ducked and dodged, and their swords swung by harmlessly. She snatched one of their shields, then spun around and smashed one in the head, then pulled it back and threw it like a Frisbee, knocking another one in the chest and sending him to the ground.

Ruth came charging beside her, leapt into the air, and pounced onto the chest of the third soldier, taking him down before he could swing.

Scarlet looked down and saw the dozens of soldiers sprawled out before her, and she felt more invincible than ever.

That was when she felt it. Suddenly, from behind, she felt a net being hurled over her, enveloping her, and Ruth. She tried to yank it off, but as she grabbed it, she felt herself inexplicably weaken. The material was so cold, had such a strange sensation to the touch. And it was so heavy.

That was when she realized: the net was made of silver. And as it touched her body, it drained her strength and power. It made her weak, helpless, just like any other human.

She felt the bodies of the remaining soldiers pouncing down on her, pinning her to the ground.

And the last thing she saw, as she turned her neck, was the furious face of a Roman soldier, bringing his fist down hard, right for cheek.

CHAPTER NINE

As the sun set, Sam walked with Samantha in a desolate part of the streets of Jerusalem, far from anyone. They had been walking for hours, Samantha silently leading him, and he had followed without a word. There was something about her—there had always been something about her—that made Sam want to be with her, want to follow her, without even asking why.

Sam thought back to the very first time he'd met her, in the Hudson Valley, when she was living alone in that house. It was the first time he'd ever been smitten, and the first time he'd fallen in love.

As they walked for hours, Samantha leading him through obscure parts of the city, memories of their relationship came flooding back. Sam recalled their drive together that day in the Hudson Valley, their going to that trailer park, discovering that man who pretended to be his father was just an impostor, a creep. Sam remembered when he saw Samantha kill him—the first time he'd ever seen a vampire kill anyone. He remembered being transfixed by her.

He remembered their going to Boston, to the King's church, their losing the sword to Kyle. He remembered being captured, imprisoned, in New York. And most of all, he remembered that fateful night when she turned him. When she became his maker. At that moment the relationship between them changed from mere love to something endless, timeless.

Sam had thought that he'd put her out of his mind long ago—but truthfully, deep down, he knew that he had never quite forgotten. Memories of her had always lurked somewhere, deep in his consciousness. He felt himself drawn to her at times, like a magnet, like a servant wanting to return to its master. And now, with her by his side, he felt in some ways like he had found his way back home.

But he also remembered their parting. He remembered how she had urged him to kill his own sister, when he had fallen so completely under her spell, and had almost done it. Then he remembered breaking free from her, and never wanting to see her again. There remained a part of him that could still never forgive her for what she had done.

But now, here, in this different time and place, he was surprised to find himself happy to be in her presence. After all, he had changed: he was not the same person he used to be. Everything in the past that she had done, all of her violence, and ambition, and rage, and trickery—everything that had once bothered him so much—now, he liked. He admired it. The very same qualities he once despised, now, he looked up to. Now, he found himself wanting to be with her.

Yet as they walked in silence, Sam couldn't help wondering if all these memories of Samantha had flooded back to him naturally—or if Samantha had played one of her mind tricks, and had implanted all those feelings into his brain. Was she still manipulating him, even now?

But the funny thing was, Sam didn't care. He wanted to be with her. She was so overflowing with vengeance and darkness that he saw himself in her, and no longer cared about whatever dark place she would lead him.

Samantha reached over and took his hand and squeezed it hard. She looked over at him, and as he looked into her pale blue eyes, he could feel their connection grow even stronger. Before, roaming the streets of Jerusalem alone, he'd felt no sense of purpose. Now, with her by his side, he felt he was being led in the direction he was meant to go.

They continued down a narrow side street, up a steep hill, and as they went, Sam looked up and saw a huge structure awaiting them: an ancient, pagan Temple. Shaped in an octagon, it was surrounded by Roman columns and covered by a shiny, circular dome. There were eight columns and each took the shape of a different pagan God. Gargoyles stuck out from all corners, and even from here, as they walked towards it, into the blood-red sun, Sam could feel the evil energy coming off this place.

Sam could hardly believe they were back in a time and place where people still actively worshipped pagan gods. The old Sam would have recoiled from this place; but the new Sam looked forward to it. He felt that, behind those walls, were those like him. He couldn't wait to meet them.

"You are about to meet our leader," Samantha said to him, in a cold, raspy voice. "I've been sent to bring you back home. With us. Where you belong. This will be a great place of welcome and honor for you. The place where you can fulfill your destiny. You're one of us now, Sam. Your time for searching is over."

"I know," he replied, and was surprised to realize how gravelly his own voice had become.

They reached the top of the hill, walked across the wide marble plaza and up a long flight of marble steps leading to the temple entrance. Standing guard under the portico were a dozen huge vampires, dressed in all black. They wore elaborate velvet cloaks, despite the heat, with a broad red sash crossing over them.

They hissed back in greeting, and Sam could see their long fangs protruding. He looked down and saw their hands were irregular: each had only two fingers and a thumb, long and pointy, with nails that stretched for inches and were sharpened to a point. Their skin was stark white, and covered in blisters. These were no normal vampires, he realized. He had reached their capitol: the capitol of darkness.

They reached over, grabbed the large knocker and yanked open the enormous arched brass doors for them. They opened with a creak, and Samantha walked right in, not even hesitating. Sam followed. As he did, he felt a wind behind them and heard the door slam, just inches behind, locking them in.

Sam found himself in an octagonal room, framed by columns, filled with statues of pagan gods. It was a vast and open space that reminded him of the Pantheon in Rome, except on a smaller scale. Milling about were hundreds of vampires, dressed in black, some of them flying about the room, hovering in the air, but most on the ground, squirming. Among them were female humans, naked, sprawled across the floor. The vampires, Sam could see, were busy feeding on them.

The room was filled with the screams and moans of humans, suffering, trying to get away. But there was nowhere for them to go. It was a bloodbath: hundreds of vampires feeding on hundreds of innocent humans. The entire floor was alive, squirming with victims and victimizers.

On the far side of the room, all along the walls, more humans were chained to the walls, some of them crucified on crosses, others bound to columns. More vampires stood over them, behind them, whipping them, beating them with straps, and torturing them in all kinds of ways. Their cries punctuated the air, rising even over the cries of the vampires on the ground. Sadistic smiles lit up the faces of all the vampires, busy torturing the humans for sport. While in the past Sam would have recoiled from such a sight, now he enjoyed it. He understood it. Even sympathized. These vampires needed an outlet for their boundless rage and lust.

In the center of the room, on a throne, atop a raised dais built of solid gold, sat a single vampire, watching over it all, his back to them. Around him stood a dozen minions, awaiting his smallest nod.

Sam and Samantha took several steps in, and as they did, the seated vampire spun in his chair and turned to them.

Sam recognized this vampire. He had seen him once before, centuries ago, in New York City. Beneath City Hall. It was their grand leader. The ancient one, who had lived for thousands of years. Rexius.

A shriveled-up old man, his face covered in endless age lines, nearly bald, with white hair and drooping eyes, Rexius sat hunched in his throne, looking down on all of it with satisfaction. Sam could see he was living vicariously through all of it.

Rexius fixed his ancient, pale-blue eyes on Sam, and Sam could feel the evil emanating off of them, aiming right for him. Rexius reached up with his huge, golden staff, banged it several times, and slowly, all the motion in the room stopped. The room quieted, as much as it could amidst the screams and moans.

Samantha took his hand, and they walked through the room, through the crowd of bodies that parted ways, and right up to the dais. They looked up at Rexius, who gazed down at them. He was ancient, inscrutable, and Sam couldn't tell if he was looking at them with rebuke or approval—or both.

The room quieted, as hundreds of eyes turned to watch the encounter.

"So…" Rexius began slowly, in his deep, gravelly voice, "…the chicken comes home to roost."

He breathed deeply.

"I've been waiting for this moment for centuries. I should kill you now, just for making me wait so long."

Sam was not intimidated; instead, he felt a fresh dose of rage rise up within him. He could tear this man apart. How dare he—or any man—talk to him that way.

"And I should kill *you* for speaking to me this way," Sam responded, snarling, beginning to walk forward.

But he felt Samantha's reassuring hand stop him, hold his shoulder, and he hesitated.

Rexius' eyes opened wide, as an astonished gasp spread throughout the room. It was apparent that no one spoke to Rexius this way.

During the tense silence, Sam braced himself for an attack.

But suddenly, Rexius threw back his head and roared with laughter.

"That's what I like to hear," Rexius said. "Good. *Very* good. I like your hatred. It rejuvenates me."

Rexius surveyed Sam, nodding.

"Yes, yes," he said slowly. "You are truly one of us now, aren't you? Yes, very good. You will serve us well. You will serve our cause very well indeed."

He sighed.

"You have arrived not a moment too late," Rexius continued, his voice booming, echoing off the walls. "Now is a time of great urgency. Other forces are close to the shield. We must stop them. You are the final key to attaining the shield."

Sam stared back, racking his brain, trying to remember. *The shield.* He vaguely remembered…something about this father…. But it all seemed so hazy now, so far away. And with Kyle's spirit overwhelming him, and with thoughts of Samantha racing through his head, it was hard for him to think clearly.

"We stand at the precipice of history," Rexius said. "Now is our moment. If we find the shield before they do, we can dominate all humankind, all vampire kind, forever. There will be nothing but wars and bloodshed and chaos and destruction for all time. It is the moment we have all been dreaming of. For thousands of lifetimes. We are as close as we have ever been. And with you here, there is nothing left to stop us."

He breathed.

"But, unfortunately, your sister is searching, too. And she is very close. So is her husband. Your sister is the one I most fear, though. She's aligned herself with powerful people. Even as we speak, she is searching. And she is close. Too close. We must find it before she does!" Rexius suddenly screeched out, slamming his staff against the floor, the veins popping out of his face.

The entire room went silent.

Sam tried to concentrate, to remember all the details. His sister. His father. The shield. Somewhere, deep inside, he thought he detected remnants of feelings. Brotherly love. A desire to protect her.

But these thoughts were confused, muddled by other, new, feelings. Rexius' words hung in his ears, Kyle's spirit coursed in his veins, and Samantha squeezed his hand—and he found himself unable to focus, unable to think of anything but destruction.

"There is one other, too," Rexius continued slowly. "Just as grave a threat to us is this rogue, this rebel named Jesus. He walks about as we speak, preaching his idiotic sermons. We must kill him before he inflicts any more harm. He is the one your sister seeks. And if we don't reach him in time, they will join forces and find the shield. We cannot let that happen."

Rexius turned and nodded, and suddenly there stepped forward a single vampire, the only one of them dressed in white. He had black hair, a long black beard, and large black eyes. They were wide, and glowing with intensity as he stared right at Sam.

"Judas here will infiltrate Jesus' circle, and will help us bring him down. And then, we will catch your sister."

Rexius turned to Sam.

"But without you, we can't find her. Without you, we can't finish her off."

Rexius stood from his throne, staring down at Sam.

"Samson of the Blacktide Coven, are you prepared to help us in our cause? Are you prepared to help us find the shield, to help us kill Jesus, and to help us kill your sister?"

Sam stood there, feeling his body shaking, rising with thoughts of violence and destruction. He tried to think clearly, but all he could see in front of him were flames, rising higher and higher. It was a vision he could not shake, as much as he wanted to.

"I will kill anything and anyone in my way," Sam replied. He stared at Rexius. "I might even kill you."

Rexius stared down at him, and slowly, his surprised look morphed into a smile.

"Exactly the words I longed to hear."

CHAPTER TEN

As Caitlin and Caleb flew over the Israeli countryside, the sun beginning to set and the temperature finally cooling, Caitlin ran over in her head the inscription on the wall.

It had read: *Where the graves rise, the olive tree has many branches.*

She'd had no idea what that meant. Caleb explained that he thought it was a reference, a clue that they needed to go to the ancient Mount of Olives, the legendary mountain that sat on the outskirts of Jerusalem. It was a mystical place, he said, part cemetery and part olive grove, and had been one of the most important places of vampire power for millennia. It was rumored, he said, to be home to the most powerful vampire coven of all.

They hadn't stopped flying since, racing towards the Mount, towards Jerusalem. The entire time, Caitlin couldn't stop wondering if she would find her Dad there. Or the Shield. Or, she dared to hope, Scarlet. She couldn't get there fast enough.

The Israeli countryside below her was breathtaking. As they headed south, getting ever closer to Jerusalem, the terrain constantly changed, from desert, to mountains, to hills, to rolling green valleys. They passed rivers, rural towns, farms, and groves of palm trees. The country was barely populated, looking like one huge rural stretch of farmland, with just the occasional small village here and there.

As they rounded a bend, the sky now alight with shades of pink, Caleb suddenly pointed.

"There!" he said. "See that peak in the distance? That's it."

Caitlin squinted, and in the distance, she could barely make it out. It looked like every other mountain peak, except that she could see, even from here, it was completely covered in small olive trees, their silver branches glistening in the last light of sun.

"The Mount of Olives is famous not only because it towers over Jerusalem," Caleb said, as they flew closer, "but also because it is the place where Jesus gave his sermons. In the future, centuries from now, it will be home to one of the most important churches in all Christianity, and it has also, for thousands of years, been home to the most famous cemetery in the world. Everyone wants to be buried there, because the Bible holds that in the End of Days, when the Messiah comes, this is the place he will appear first, and that those buried here will be the first to resurrect."

"But I still don't understand: why does our clue lead us here?" Caitlin asked. "How is this related to our search?"

Caleb shook his head.

"I have no idea," he answered.

They dove down, circling the Mount. Up close, it was even more beautiful. Caitlin could see thousands of small olives filling the branches, the beautiful slopes rising up and down, the small, twisted trees. And over the edge of the mountain, on the horizon, she could just begin to see the ancient city of Jerusalem, nestled in the valley like a jewel shining in the sunset. She could feel its energy even from here. It was breathtaking.

Caleb dove for the mountaintop, and Caitlin followed. They landed high up, on a plateau, in the midst of the trees.

They stood there, getting their bearings, taking in the incredible vista, the sweeping sunset in every direction. Caitlin felt as if she were atop the world.

But as beautiful as it was, Caitlin still had no idea what they were doing there. She didn't know what to look for, and she didn't see any sign of her Dad, or of Scarlet—or anyone.

She did, in the distance, see a graveyard on one of the slopes and a row of small, marble headstones, and felt drawn to it. She walked amidst the stones, examining them. They looked ancient.

She saw a few stones which seemed bigger than the others and she knelt beside one, reached down and brushed off the dirt, sensing it was special. As she did, a name appeared.

Caitlin stood as if she had been struck by a lightning bolt. She could not believe it. It was a name that she knew.

Caitlin Paine.

She stood there, shocked, wondering what it meant. Caleb seemed equally surprised, and he knelt down beside the other and brushed that one off, too.

Caitlin was even more surprised: it was engraved with Caleb's name.

"What does it mean?" Caitlin asked.

"I don't know," Caleb answered, grimly.

The two of them stood there, frozen, almost afraid to check the third stone. Finally, Caitlin knelt down and brushed it off.

She could not believe it.

Aiden.

She turned to Caleb.

"Can it be? *Our* Aiden?"

As Caitlin saw his name, memories came flooding back. She recalled the last time she saw him, in Scotland, standing before the castle, informing her of all the tragedy that had befell their coven. Telling her she was their last hope, that she had to fulfill the mission. She thought of all the times she had seen him, all the places, going back to Pollepel, and she was overwhelmed with emotion.

"Yes, it is I," came a voice.

Caitlin wheeled, and was shocked to see standing there, barely a few feet away, the man himself.

Aiden.

He wore a long white robe and hood, with his flowing gray hair and beard, and stared back at her with his large blue eyes, as if he had just seen her yesterday.

Slowly, he broke into a smile.

"I thought you would get here sooner."

CHAPTER ELEVEN

Scarlet felt herself being pushed and prodded down the dark stone corridor of the prison, as they descended lower and lower into the earth. Her hands were clasped tightly behind her back with silver shackles, while Ruth was led beside her, a muzzle over her mouth. Scarlet was terrified as they went, hearing the distant shouts of prisoners, getting ever closer. They sounded like vicious people, and she felt as if she were being led into the depths of hell, towards an insane asylum.

As she was shoved again, hard in the back, Scarlet caught a glimpse of her warder: he was a huge man, with a big fat belly, unshaven, with missing teeth. She could smell his awful breath even from here.

"Keep moving, you little brat!" he said.

He then wound up and kicked Ruth hard in her back, sending her flying forward, and banging her head into a stone wall. Ruth yelped. There was nothing she could do, though, with the muzzle securely over her face.

Their warder laughed. Scarlet felt her rage well up, but there was nothing she could do: she tried again to twist her arms, her wrists, her hands. But she couldn't break free. They were securely bound behind her, and the silver made her powerless.

Scarlet thought back to earlier—her rampage, her first feeding, her fighting all the soldiers.... She regretted hurting anyone. She really hadn't wanted to. But the need for feeding, for blood, had consumed her so completely, she hadn't been in her right mind. No one had ever taught her how to feed. What to do. She had to fend for herself, and she did the best she could.

But she did not regret hurting those mean soldiers, and she was still furious they'd caught her in a silver net. She didn't feel that she deserved to be thrown into this dungeon, and felt more alone than ever. She could only imagine what horrors awaited her down below, as she was led deeper into the darkness, the corridors lit by flickering torches.

"You're a feisty one, aren't you?" came the guttural voice behind her. "They told me to take you to the lowest chamber, to the silver room. Lock you up behind silver bars. But I don't see how you need it. You're just a flimsy little girl, aren't you? No harm to anyone, are you?"

Scarlet felt his fat, sweaty palm suddenly grab the back of her neck, and then run up the back of her head, under her hair. She could hear him licking his lips, swallowing.

"Before I bring you down, I think I might teach you a thing or two. Break you in. Have my way with you, if you know what I mean?" he said with a laugh.

Scarlet felt the hair rise on her arms; she despised the sound of his voice. Beside her, Ruth snarled.

But she was helpless. She yanked again and again, but couldn't break free.

Suddenly, the man grabbed her and threw her into a side chamber. Scarlet sensed that he was defying orders, and that he was going to take advantage of her, for his own means. She looked up and saw the lustful look on his face, as he stared down, licking his lips and knew this would be bad.

He suddenly grabbed her by the shirt and tore at her buttons.

Scarlet squirmed, turning her back on him. She could feel her body shaking, and was more afraid than ever.

"Don't you touch me!" she screamed back. But she knew it was useless.

The man smacked her hard in the back of her head, and she cowered from the pain.

She then felt him unlock the silver clasps binding her wrists.

"You don't need these after all, do you?" he asked. "No. Taking them off will make my time with you more fun."

Scarlet felt the clasps slip off her wrists, then slink down to the ground. They landed on the stone with a clink.

She could not believe her luck. As the silver fell off her, a new power rose within her: it was as if a huge chain had been lifted from her. Now, she felt completely rejuvenated, felt all her power rushing back, infusing her from head to toe.

The man reached around and grabbed her from behind. He was strong, and his beefy hands clamped down on her. He reached up and began to squeeze her throat.

That was his last mistake.

Now Scarlet had strength to fight back. She grabbed his huge wrist, spun it around, and easily held it there, in mid-air.

The man looked down, eyes wide in shock, uncomprehending.

Scarlet held his wrist for several seconds, enjoying the moment, feeling so much stronger than he. Now the tables had turned. His hand shook as he tried to break free. But he could not. His astonishment deepened.

Scarlet slowly turned back his wrist, turning it nearly upside down, until the man finally dropped to his knees before her, crying out in pain. She kept turning it back, more and more slowly, relishing the moment.

Soon, the huge man was shaking, trembling.

"You little witch!" he screamed. "I'm going to kill you!"

Snap.

The man screamed out in pain as Scarlet broke his wrist.

Now, she wanted vengeance. Not just for her, but for any girl this man may have victimized. And, of course, for Ruth. No one treats Ruth that way.

Scarlet wound up and kicked him hard in the face, snapping back his neck, and he collapsed in a heap on the floor, not moving.

Scarlet ran over to Ruth and tore off her muzzle. Ruth snarled, and without missing a beat, leapt onto the man, sinking her teeth into his throat.

The man squirmed on the ground, in agony, then scurried to his hands and knees and crawled into the corner, covering his head with his hands, trying to get away. But Ruth kept biting him, leaving bite marks all over him, as the man cowered in the corner.

Suddenly, Scarlet felt a silver net cover her. She collapsed to a heap on the ground, powerless, and as several guards rushed in and stood over her, just as they threw another net over Ruth.

Scarlet chided herself. She should have been more careful, and made an immediate escape.

Moments later, the warder was back on his feet, bloody, and scowling down at them. He stared down at Scarlet with a hatred she had rarely seen.

"Now you're going to suffer," he said. "Before, I was going to put you in isolation, in the silver chamber. Now, I'm putting you in with the murderers. You just dug your own grave. I hope you enjoy it."

The warder marched out, moaning in pain, and as he did, the guards picked up Scarlet and dragged her out, back down the hall.

Scarlet, in the net, twisted and turned to break free—but it was no use. She was carried deeper down the corridors, and after several turns, they reached another level below ground.

She looked out and saw an endless row of bars, behind which was a cacophony of noise. Hundreds of voices screamed in the darkness. They were lit only by the torchlight, and as they shoved their faces against the bars, it made them look even more creepy. She could see the ugly and dangerous faces of dozens of treacherous types, sticking their heads through the bars, screaming out at her.

She swallowed. With the silver clasps back on her, she was weak and defenseless again. Surely, these prisoners would kill her.

The bars opened and the guards hoisted the net and threw her into the room. She landed hard on the stone floor, Ruth thrown in beside her, as the bars were slammed shut.

She scrambled to her feet and shook off the net—but she was still chained with the silver clasps. There she stood, in the midst of the cell, looking out at the faces of dozens of murderers. They stared back at her and licked their lips, as if a lamb had just been thrown into a lion's den.

Ruth squirmed beside her, but with her muzzle back on, she was useless.

"Well well well!" one of them, a particularly large and nasty-looking convict, said. "Look at what we have here!"

"If the lamb hasn't come to slaughter!" said another.

"I didn't have my breakfast yet today!" another one added.

"This is going to mean years of enjoyment for me. Do you know what it's like to suffer slowly, little girl?" another asked.

Scarlet squirmed against her shackles, but no matter how much she tried, she could not get free. The group of convicts slowly approached. She backed up, until she was flush against the stone wall.

Soon, she hit it, and there was nowhere else to go. Outside, she could see the guards watching, the sadistic smiles on their faces.

Clearly, they would revel in this, watching her suffer.

The crowd closed in, now only feet away.

Scarlet only wished that she didn't have to die this way.

CHAPTER TWELVE

Caitlin and Caleb followed Aiden as he walked down the steep slope of the Mount of Olives, turning amidst hidden paths in the trees. They walked in silence, Aiden several feet ahead.

Caitlin was burning with so many questions for him, as always. How long had he been here? How had he known she was coming? And most of all, why did all the clues lead to him? Was he her father?

They continued in silence, trailing behind, until they reached a plateau at the base of the mountain, well-hidden by the trees. She watched as he walked right into what seemed like a grove of trees. He disappeared amidst the foliage. After exchanging a look, Caitlin and Caleb followed.

As they did, she was amazed at what lay just beyond: nestled amidst a thick grove of olive trees sat a large villa, long and wide. Surrounded by columns on all sides, with wide-open arches, it looked like an ancient monastery, with its clean, simple lines and empty space. Inside was a broad, limestone interior, with a simple courtyard and roman fountains. It reminded her of all the monasteries they had visited over the centuries.

Milling about silently were dozens of Aiden's people, dressed in long, white robes, hands tucked in and heads lowered as they walked, as if in meditation or prayer. Caitlin was surprised they weren't sparring, training, as Aiden's coven always had. Here, they seemed more quiet, peaceful. Yet, at the same time, she could feel the power emanating off of them. She wondered if this silence, this meditation, was a form of training.

Caitlin couldn't believe it. Just when she'd thought they were all alone, they had found Aiden and his coven, here in this time and place. Here, at the base of the Mount of Olives. Had this been the purpose of all the clues? To lead her to him? Was it time for her to use the four keys that lead to her father?

Caitlin looked all about, looking for any sign, any clue, as to where the four keys might fit. But there was none. She felt more confused than ever, and hoped that Aiden had answers.

Finally, he stopped and faced them.

"Yes, you are right," Aiden began. "They are training."

Caitlin flushed, embarrassed he'd read her mind.

"You just don't see it, as you did in other times and places. In other days, it was a training of the body, a training of swords, and shields, and spears, and arrows. Here, it is a training of the spirit. Of the mind. It is a much deeper and more profound training. The final training, the final level of becoming a warrior. Here, our very souls are at stake."

Caitlin surveyed the building with a fresh respect for the coven members, many of whom simply stood there, staring off into the horizon, hands folded, eyes closed. She wondered what the training entailed, and how it made them better warriors. She thought back to some of her earlier training sessions with Aiden, when he had pushed her to look inside. To stop fighting. It had been some of the most powerful training she could remember.

She turned back to Aiden. She was burning with so many questions, she hardly knew where to begin.

"Are you my father?" she began.

Her words shocked even her. She hadn't meant to be so blunt, so direct—but the words just came flying out. She couldn't help it—she *had* to know. Was it him, all this time? A part of her felt that it was. But another part wasn't sure.

His response surprised her even more.

"That is a distinction of which I would be very proud," he said, smiling slowly. "But alas, it is not the case. No. I am not he. But I know him very well."

Caitlin felt her heart pounding. At least that put that idea to rest. But she was equally excited by the idea that Aiden knew him. And it made her wonder: was he here? In this place? Was she about to meet him now?

"No, he's not here," Aiden replied. "Nor can I reach him myself. If it were that easy, we wouldn't need you, would we?" He smiled, then asked: "Do you have the four keys?"

She nodded.

"Good. You will need them."

"But I still don't understand," Caitlin said. "Where is he? When will I see him?" Her heart was pounding with anticipation.

"There is a final relic waiting for you," Aiden said. "One last, final clue, that will lead you to him. We have been holding it for you here, in safekeeping. Of course, I cannot open it. Only you have the key."

Caitlin looked back at him, puzzled. *The key?*

He looked down at her necklace, and Caitlin suddenly remembered. She reached down and felt it, her heart pounding.

"Where is it?" Caitlin asked, expecting him to present her with perhaps a locked chest of some sort.

Aiden shook his head.

"Before I lead you to it, you must first complete your training. Tonight, you and Caleb will spend the night with us, and rest up for your final night before you see him. In the morning, we will ascend to the Mount, and you will complete your training. And then, you will meet your father."

Caitlin swallowed at the thought of it.

"Great forces are aligned against us," he continued. "Even now they have put into motion plans to destroy us. We have no time to spare. At the first light of dawn, we shall ascend to the mountaintop. And then you must find your father, and get the shield—quickly."

"What about Scarlet?" Caitlin asked the question burning most inside of her.

Aiden slowly shook his head, and Caitlin's heart sank.

"Of course, you ache to find her. But you must find your father first. Only by finding him will you find her. But I must warn you: you must keep sight of what is important. The shield. Humankind. The greater good. Saving us all. One day, you might have to choose. Between family, and humankind. Between your legacy, and your destiny. It will not be easy; in fact, it will be the hardest choice of your life. I cannot explain: this must all remain hidden for now. It will be revealed when it is meant to be revealed."

Caitlin racked her brain, trying to understand what he meant. But she had no idea. It was all too mysterious.

"I don't understand," Caitlin said. "Is Scarlet in danger? Right now?"

"Yes," Aiden answered flatly. "She is in grave danger. And only you can save her."

Caitlin's mouth went dry and her heart started pounding; she was overcome with a desire to leave and find her that very moment.

"Then I have to go," Caitlin said, turning to leave. "I'm sorry."

"And where will you go?" Aiden called out.

Caitlin stopped in her tracks.

"You don't know where she is," Aiden continued. "And you can't. Not until you find your father."

Aiden stepped forward and placed a hand on her shoulder. Slowly, she turned.

"You must trust me. Once you find your father, all will become clear."

Caitlin looked out at the blood-red sky, the sunset lighting up the slopes of olive trees, and wondered.

"Is my brother here?" she asked, softly, almost afraid to know the answer.

She looked at Aiden and saw the concern in his eyes. That told her everything.

"Sam…" he began, and turned away, as his eyes welled up. "I'm afraid…we have lost him. He is alive. But no longer one of us."

"Don't say that," Caitlin snapped, hearing the anger in her own voice. "He is my brother!"

Aiden shook his head.

"He was *once* your brother. Now…he has a different fate. I'm afraid we have lost him to the dark side."

Caitlin fought back tears, not wanting to believe it.

"I am sorry," Aiden said. "You two are of the same lineage, but you have vastly different destinies. It is your destiny—and yours alone—to find your father."

Aiden placed a hand on her shoulder.

"I know this is hard to hear. But you are alone now. Caleb and I are here with you, but it is you, and you alone, who can find your father. The final leg of the journey must be yours and yours alone. Caitlin," he said, with added seriousness, "after all these centuries and all these places and all these relics, the time has come. This is your time now. Use it wisely, and you will save mankind. But if you use it only for your own means….then there is no hope for any of us. Do not let us down. Whatever you do, do not let us down."

*

Caitlin sat in an alcove in her room, looking out over the Mount of Olives. She watched the fading light of day, the twilight illuminating the silver branches as they shimmered in the burgeoning moon. Far off, in the distance, she could just barely see the flickering torchlights of Jerusalem, beginning to light up against the night. It was so beautiful, so still, it looked like something out of a painting.

Caleb sat at the opposite end of the room, reclining in the chaise lounge. She sensed he was asleep. It had been a long day and night for them both, and when Aiden had suggested they retire to their room, they had gladly accepted. Aiden had told her the final training could not begin until sunrise, but even if she'd been allowed to begin now, she couldn't. She had never been so tired. In other places and times, she had been physically tired; but here, it was a different kind of tired: it was a psychic and spiritual exhaustion.

Caitlin felt so close to finding her Dad, she could hardly stand it. She felt as if she could find him at any moment, and the feeling was tiring her out. She also felt consumed by a burning need to find Scarlet, to save her from whatever danger she might be in, and the thought kept her on edge.

At least she had found Aiden. Caitlin felt so grateful to have found him, to be back in time with him, one last time, with his people, in his place. It was the first time she'd actually felt grounded in this time and place, felt a true sense of sanctuary. She felt reassured by his presence, as always, but at the same time, she had never seen him like this before. She could sense his nervousness, as if he saw some impending doom. And he was not surrounded by all the people she knew and loved from previous years. Polly, Blake, all the others…. It seemed as if they were all gone, as if, one by one, they were all killed over the centuries. Caitlin felt a profound sense of loss. She felt in some ways like she was the lone survivor.

It was odd, she thought, how much things had changed. In the beginning, she had felt like such a newcomer, such an outsider. Such a novice. And now, here she was, the last one standing, the oldest veteran of the bunch. Life, she realized, was always changing, and was never what it seemed to be.

Caitlin sat there, watching twilight turn into night, and finally pulled the burning candle closer to her. She rested on the small stone jutting from the wall, on which she laid her journal. As she'd set it down, she'd been shocked to see how worn and weathered it had become. By now, it looked like a museum relic. She turned the pages slowly, and they crackled with age. Each entry brought back fresh memories, and she had to fight to hold back her emotions.

Caitlin turned the pages until she finally came to the very last blank page. It was the final page of the book. She couldn't believe it. When she finished this entry, the journal would be finished. Forever.

She swallowed in anticipation. Did that mean her journey was over? For good? In some ways, it felt like it was. What did that mean the next step would be? Would there even be a next step? When it was over, would they all just die? Or would they go on living somehow? And what would happen to all the people that she loved?

Caitlin took a deep breath and, resting her head in one hand, she grabbed the quill and slowly began to write. The sound of it scratching against the parchment slowly filled the room.

My final journal entry. My final time and place. I miss everyone so much. Sam, my brother. Polly, my best friend. Yes, I have to admit, even Blake a little bit. Actually, any familiar face. If Cain were here, I'd probably miss him, too.

I miss other times, other places. When everyone was together, and happy. In this place, everything is so serious, so urgent, so somber. There is so much at stake. There are no celebrations. No lavish courts, castles. No balls, no dances. Instead, we go from holy place to holy place. And next, it seems, will be Jerusalem. I never thought in a million years I'd ever visit it.

But this is also such an exciting time. I can feel Dad, so close now, and the feeling is keeping me going.

The four keys are burning a hole in my pocket, and tomorrow morning, I will complete my training with Aiden. It's so crazy to think about: my final training session. Then what?

I'm so happy that Caleb is back here with me. We are together, finally. But I also fear for our future. I have a sense that we'll be parting. That I'll have to meet my Dad alone. I hope not.

I desperately miss Scarlet, and it's killing me that she's not here with me. I'm told I have to find Dad first. So I'll do everything I can to do that.

But then what? Will that bring back everyone I love? Somehow, I don't think so. I can't help feeling that everyone, and everything, I've loved will be lost forever.

And after all these times, and all these places, and all these clues and keys, I still don't know who my Dad is. I was sure it was Aiden. But, I learned today that I was wrong. Now, I have no idea who it can be. More than anything, I just want to see him. To know for sure. Who I come from. Who he is. Why it was all such a secret. What the shield is.

I feel the weight of the world on my shoulders. I would give anything for this to be over. Tomorrow can't come soon enough.

As Caitlin wrote her final sentence, filling the final page, she slowly closed the journal. It was finished. She could not believe it.

She held it there, in her hands, feeling the weight of it. A tear ran down her cheek as she pondered all the times and places she had written in it, all the hard times she had gone through. Somehow, she had survived. And this was her testament. Her vampire journal.

Caitlin closed her eyes and rested her head on it, and she didn't know why, but she began to cry. Her cries softly filled the air, blended with the cry of a night bird's song, and slowly, she lulled herself to sleep.

CHAPTER THIRTEEN

As the convicts crowded in around Scarlet, one of them stepped forward, the largest of the bunch. He towered over the others, and he looked to Scarlet liked he was seven feet tall. He was bald, with a huge scar across his nose, and bulging with muscles. He was clearly the leader in here.

He turned and faced the others.

"She's mine," he announced. "My plaything. Mine to torture as I wish. Any of you have a problem with that?"

The dozens of faces stopped, and Scarlet could see their fear. No one was willing to challenge him. Clearly, this creep was king of the hill in here. The others slowly slinked away, disappointed but resigned.

The creep turned and reached down and grabbed Scarlet with one hand by the back of her shirt. He picked her up high in the air with a single hand, and inspected her as if she were an insect. He was so powerful, he held her as if he were carrying a fly.

Scarlet wiggled and squirmed, struggling to break free as she was hoisted in the air and as he walked with her, bringing her to a dark, dark corner. She heard Ruth snarl down below, then watched the creep lean over, and kick her hard. Ruth went flying across the room, yelping, and hit a wall.

Scarlet was enraged, and tried harder to squirm away. But the man's grip was too strong. She was powerless.

"It's going to be great fun to torture you," he said. His voice was so deep, it sounded as if it came from the bowels of the earth. As he carried her, deeper and deeper into the darkest corner of the cell, Scarlet thought: this is what hell must be like.

They finally reached the darkest corner, and the creep set her down. He reached down, ran one hand down her back, down her arms—and then stopped at the clasps on her wrists.

"These won't do, will they?" he said. "That takes away half the fun."

He reached out and, with his brute strength, snapped the silver clasps in half, then yanked them off her wrists.

"I want you free when I have my way with you," he said.

And that was his last mistake.

Scarlet was suddenly overcome by a new energy, sweeping over her. She felt overwhelmed by a strength and a rage so primal, beyond anything she'd ever known, that she hardly knew what to do. As the creep reached for her, this time, she reached up and kicked him hard in the solar plexus. It was a perfect hit.

The creep went flying back with such force that he flew through the air like a missile, all the way across the cell, thirty feet, smashing against the metal bars. It was such a loud noise, it shook the entire cell.

Every prisoner stopped and stared, with looks of disbelief.

Scarlet didn't hesitate: she sprinted across the room, pouncing. Just as the creep was beginning to rise, she kicked him hard in the face. It knocked him back down to the ground, flat on his back.

But this man was strong. The kick would have rendered any other man unconscious, but he began to get up again.

Now, Scarlet was pissed. She reached down, grabbed him by the shirt, and to the disbelieving stares of all the other prisoners, hoisted him over her head. She spun him around three times, and then hurled him right into the crowd.

As he hit the crowd, he took dozens of prisoners down with him, falling like dominoes. The remaining prisoners stood and stared, looking at Scarlet with fear, as if a demon from hell had just landed inside their cell.

Outside the bars, the guards realized their mistake. They rushed to open the bars.

"I told you to put her behind the silver!" one guard yelled to the other.

Scarlet was enraged—and this time, nothing would quench it.

She charged the remaining prisoners. One by one, she punched and elbowed and kicked each one, spreading a wave of destruction throughout the cell. Within seconds, dozens of bodies lay on the floor. They scrambled, on their hands and knees, to get away from her, running over each other. But she wasn't finished: she grabbed them by the back of their shirts and threw them into the walls, into the bars. She was a one-person wrecking machine.

She stripped Ruth's muzzle off, and Ruth lunged into the crowd without missing a beat. She sank her fangs into the throats of several of them, and Scarlet, overwhelmed with the need to feed, followed suit: she went from body to body, sinking her fangs into their throats and drinking with all she had. She felt their blood infusing her, and she felt alive again.

But suddenly, before she could react, Scarlet felt herself covered by a silver net, once again. Her power deflated completely.

She looked up and saw several more guards. She chided herself: it had been stupid of her. She looked over, and saw Ruth muzzled again, too.

This time, the guards kept their distance—and instead of just a few guards, there were dozens of them. They all held out silver lances before them, staying far away. One guard approached her warily and clasped silver shackles again to her wrists, twice as thick. Then they all lifted her and carried her out the cell.

Scarlet was carried roughly by the large group of guards, and this time, they descended down several flights of never-ending steps. They went deeper than she could have possibly imagined, deep into the bowels of the dungeon.

Finally, they reached the end. There was a small room, dimly lit, with only a single cell. She could feel its silver bars, the energy radiating off them even from here. Moments later, there was a clanking of keys, and the cell was opened. She felt herself hoisted, then thrown in.

She flew through the air and hit her head against the wall, and collapsed on the floor. This time she was alone, only with Ruth, who was thrown in after her, the silver cell door slammed behind them.

This time, behind the silver, clasped in silver chains, she was utterly helpless. She knew that there was nothing left to do but await her fate.

CHAPTER FOURTEEN

Sam marched beside Rexius, Samantha and Judas down the cobblestone entranceway to Pontius Pilate's palace. Followed by a dozen members of Rexius' coven, they marched like a small army, dressed in all black, right down the center of the stone plaza. It was dark out, late into the night, the walkway was lit by flaming torches on either side of them. They came to a big arched gate, in front of which stood a dozen Roman soldiers.

To Sam's surprise, several of these soldiers had the temerity to step forward and form a wall to block their approach.

But the vampires kept marching, never even pausing, and as they did, Rexius merely smiled and held up a single hand before his face. Sam watched as the soldiers suddenly collapsed, slumping to the ground.

Sam marched with the others right over their bodies, and he could feel their soft corpses beneath his feet. They continued marching, across the big circular stone plaza, past the Roman fountains, past the perfectly trimmed cypress trees. They passed huge columns, rows of open arches, and saw the worried faces of the Roman aristocracy looking down. Their footsteps echoed as they walked right through the main entrance, and into the palace.

As they entered, a dozen more Roman soldiers approached. Another confrontation was about to ensue—until suddenly, Pontius Pilate, the Roman Prefect, appeared. He stepped up, front and center, to meet Rexius.

"Relax your guard!" Pontius commanded his men.

It was a wise move. His soldiers gave way, hurrying to the side, leaving Pontius alone to face off with Rexius.

Pontius stood there, wearing a royal Roman toga with gold trim and a red sash, with a look of grave concern across his face. Rexius stopped a few feet away from him, as did Sam, Samantha, Judas and the others. The tension was so thick, one could cut it with a knife.

"What is the meaning of this?" Pontius demanded to Rexius. "I was never informed you were coming."

Rexius smiled back, more of a snarl. He took his time.

"I will only inform you if it serves me," he answered slowly, in his gravelly voice. "You are my servant. I will call upon you anytime I wish."

Pontius' face flushed, as his brow furrowed.

"You cannot talk to me this way! I am governor of this district. I tolerate you only with mutual respect. If you don't show me that respect, I will have my soldiers send you out. We have silver weapons, you know."

Rexius laughed.

"And I have weapons far greater than yours."

Pontius, fed up, gestured to his soldiers as he stepped out of the way. Suddenly, a dozen archers stepped forward, pulling back their bows and aiming them at Rexius and his men.

It was a big mistake.

Sam burst into action, along with the rest of Rexius' men, and within the flash of an eye, before the archers could release their arrows, they all pounced on them, sinking their fangs into their throats and pinning them to the floor. In moments the marble floors were running red, streaming blood, every soldier down.

Pontius stood there, staring down at his soldiers, looking terrified. His face was ashen, his eyes open in fear. His body began to tremble.

Rexius' men regained their feet, standing beside him again, and Rexius smiled back.

"Are there any others you would like me to kill?" Rexius asked. "Or are you ready now to do my bidding?"

"What would…what do…what would…you like?" Pontius stammered, his voice shaking with fear.

"*Master*," Rexius corrected. "What would you like, *my master*."

Pontius swallowed hard.

"What would…what would you like…*my master*," Pontius said.

Rexius stepped forward, lay his old, wrinkled hand on Pontius' shoulder, and squeezed.

Pontius face creased in pain as he dropped to one knee, groaning.

"You are going to do me a great favor," Rexius said. "There is one who I despise. That rabble-rouser, Jesus. He stands in the way of my final plan. My soldier Judas is going to infiltrate his men, and when the time is right, he will betray him. And then you will put him on trial for all to see, and have him crucified. Do you understand?"

"I can't do that!" Pontius said through clenched teeth, squirming in pain. "His following is too great!"

Rexius squeezed harder, and Pontius groaned.

"Do you understand?" Rexius asked again.

Finally, Pontius groaned, lowering his head.

"Yes," he said, finally. "As you wish."

"Good. After his last supper, you will have him arrested, in the garden of Gethsemane.

Then you will have him crucified. Do you understand?"

"Yes," Pontius groaned.

"Yes, what?" Rexius pressed, squeezing harder.

"Yes…*my master*."

Rexius released his grip, and Pontius sighed in relief.

"There is one other matter," Rexius continued.

Pontius looked up, sweating, fear in his eyes.

"There was a young girl. The daughter of the one we are searching for. My friend here," Rexius said, gesturing to Sam, "tells me that he can sense where she is. That she is with you. Underground. In one of your dungeons. Behind silver bars. Is that true?"

Pontius looked at Sam in fear, then slowly nodded.

"My men did capture a young girl, yes. She was causing trouble in the marketplace this morning. They took her to the royal dungeons. She is behind silver. They are still not certain of the origin of her powers. She has caused us great trouble. Is she one of yours?"

Rexius ignored him, turning to Sam and smiling in recognition.

"You have served us well," he said to Sam.

Rexius turned back to Pontius.

"You will bring us to her," Rexius said. "Now."

"She's a danger to the state," Pontius pleaded. "I can't release her."

Rexius raised one hand and merely held it before Pontius' face. This time, his face crumpled in pain. Pontius reached up and grabbed his ears, holding his head, as if from some unbearable pain. He began to shriek.

"MAKE IT STOP!" he screamed.

"You will bring us to her," Rexius repeated calmly.

"OKAY! OKAY!" Pontius screamed.

Slowly, Rexius lowered his hand.

Pontius relaxed his grip on his ears, and slowly, his face returned to normal, though still breathing hard.

Rexius nodded, and several of his men hurried forward, grabbed Pontius, and shoved him out front, to lead the way.

Pontius stumbled down the hall, out into the night, across the courtyard, and out the palace gates. Several Roman soldiers began to come to his aid, but Pontius gestured to them to stay away. Clearly, he did not want to see more of his men die.

Rexius and his men followed him across several adjoining palace courtyards, then finally to a large building, over which were etched the words: "Royal Dungeons."

The guards lowered their weapons at the sight of Pontius, and as he approached, they all scurried to open the doors for him, bowing low. They walked right through the gates.

They marched down corridor after corridor, down staircase after staircase, descending lower, deeper into the bowels of the dungeon. The stairway became so narrow that they had to walk single file, and finally, they reached the darkest and lowest level, lit only by a single, barely flaming torch.

The crowd stopped before the silver bars. Pontius nodded to a guard, and he ran up and unlocked the cell.

Slowly, a single face emerged from the blackness. A child's face.

Sam looked down and recognized it instantly. It was his sister's daughter.

It was Scarlet.

CHAPTER FIFTEEN

Caitlin ran. She cut through a path in a never-ending field of wheat, the stalks reaching up to her chest, and ran towards an enormous sun, sitting as a ball on the horizon. The sun was just beginning to rise, the pre-dawn light blanketing the sky, and in the distance, she could see the silhouette of her father. He stood there with his hands outstretched by his side, as if waiting to embrace her. In each of his fingers dangled the four keys, glistening in the sun.

Caitlin ran with all she had, trying to get closer, but the more she ran, the farther away he seemed to get.

The next thing she knew, she was in a desert. She was running up a rocky hill, dust and dirt in her face, the sun beating down on her head. She looked up and saw she was racing towards a huge crucifix, mounted at the top. On the cross was Jesus, crucified, looking down at her.

Caitlin ran towards him, wanting more than anything to help him, to bring him down off the cross. But no matter how hard she ran, she kept slipping on the rocks, sliding back down the hill.

She felt a strong wind, and looked over her shoulder, and suddenly saw a huge sandstorm heading her way. She turned her head and covered her eyes with her forearm, just in time. Moments later she was enveloped by the tornado of sand, the sand whipping her face and skin and arms, scraping her, the noise pounding in her ears. She could barely breathe. It was like a million hornets descending on her.

Suddenly, the world went quiet. Caitlin blinked, and found herself atop a lone, grassy hill. Opposite her stood Aiden. He stood there, so still, so calm, gazing out at the horizon, his long staff in his hand, his beard blowning in the wind. He turned and stared right at her, his blue eyes glistening.

"It is me, Caitlin," he said. "I am your father." He took three steps towards her, grabbed her shoulders, and looked her right in the eyes. "Don't you realize? *I* am your father."

Caitlin woke with a start.

She sat there, breathing hard, and looked all about the room, in the pre-dawn darkness.

Caleb lay in bed beside her, still sleeping. As she caught her breath, she turned and looked about the room, wondering if she was really awake.

Caitlin looked across the room, and through the window, she could just begin to see the first light of sky breaking. She sat there, breathing hard, trying to collect her thoughts. It had all seemed so real, so vivid. Was it a message? Was Aiden really her father? Had he been tricking her all this time? Was he waiting to reveal that he was her father? Would he reveal it today, this morning, during their final training?

In many ways, it felt right to Caitlin that Aiden was her father. Still, somehow, she wasn't quite sure. A part of her still felt he was more like a mentor. She didn't know what to think.

Caitlin could barely contain her excitement for the day ahead. This just might be the biggest day of her life, she realized.

She jumped up and quickly dressed. This was her day. This was the day she would complete her training. The day she would meet her Dad. The day she would complete her mission. She felt thrilled and nervous at the same time.

Fully dressed, Caitlin crept across the room, not wanting to wake Caleb; but just as she reached the door and turned the handle, he sat up.

"Caitlin?" he asked softly in the darkness.

She stopped and turned.

"I have to leave now," she said, not wanting to be late.

"I know," Caleb said. "I just want to tell you that I love you."

Caleb blew her a kiss, and she blew him one back and hurried out the door, closing it behind her. She wanted to stay, to talk to Caleb—about everything. But there wasn't time for that now. She felt bad that the two of them hadn't had more time together to just sit down and talk since they'd been back here. But everything had been such a blur, non-stop traveling, searching. She promised herself that when she returned, she'd devote more time to their relationship. And she hoped that as soon as she finished the mission, she and Caleb would have all the uninterrupted time in the world to be together.

Caitlin burst out of the villa and found herself running, then sprinting, to the top of the Mount of Olives. Dawn was breaking, she had to meet Aden at mountaintop, and she couldn't be late. She considered flying, but she thought it best if she warmed up her muscles first, on foot. She ran past ancient headstones, past rows of trees, their silver branches glistening in the early morning light. It looked as if the entire mountain was alive, shimmering. It felt surreal, as if she were ascending to the very peak of heaven.

Caitlin reached the top, and as she did, she saw two things that took her breath away: one was the dawn, breaking over the horizon, filling the entire universe, lighting the valleys below, the mountain peaks on the horizon, and even the sprawling city of Jerusalem in the distance. It was magical.

The other was Aiden. He stood there waiting on the small plateau, his back to her, wearing his long white robe and holding a long, golden staff. He stood there, gazing out at the horizon. He didn't turn, but she was sure he sensed her presence.

She stood there, waiting, for several minutes, listening only to the sound of the wind in the early morning light. She knew it was best to wait until he was ready.

"Are you ready to complete your training?" he finally asked, still gazing out at the horizon, his back to her.

Caitlin swallowed, nervous, unsure how to respond.

"Yes," she finally said.

"Are you sure?" came a voice from behind her.

Caitlin wheeled and was shocked to see, standing just a few feet behind her, was Aiden, staring at her with his intense blue eyes, lit up by the early morning sun.

How did he do that?

"In this time and place," he began, "there exist stronger spiritual energies available to us. We are in less of a material world now, and more of a spiritual one. In future generations, the fights will occur mostly in the external world, with physical people and weapons and objects. But in this time and place, the greatest battles are unseen and unknown to us. They happen in the spiritual dimension. The good angels versus the bad ones. The forces of light versus the forces of darkness. They are battling all around us: we just can't see them. This is what you have left to learn."

He breathed deeply.

"Close your eyes," he said, as he reached out his hand.

Caitlin closed her eyes, and moments later, felt his fingertips on her eyelids.

"What do you see?" he asked.

She tried to clear her mind, to see something. But nothing came to her. Was she supposed to see something special? She felt embarrassed.

"I'm sorry," she said finally. "I don't see anything."

"Your problem," he began, "is that you're still stuck in the physical world. You still see battle as between person and person, object and object. You're missing the unknown. The unseen."

He breathed deeply.

"Where do people come from? Where do our kind come from? How did it all begin? There is a deeper level. This is what you are missing. You are not at this level yet."

After several moments of silence, Caitlin finally opened her eyes. She saw nothing. And Aiden was gone.

Caitlin spun in every direction, looking for any sign of him. But there was no trace whatsoever. For a moment, she couldn't help but wonder if she'd imagined the whole thing, if he had never been there at all.

"You still can't find me, can you?" came the voice.

Caitlin spun in the other direction, but she still couldn't see him.

"Find me," came the voice again.

Caitlin broke off into a sprint, running amidst the trees, looking on every side of the plateau, looking down every slope of the mountain. She even looked up. But still, she saw no sign of him.

"That is your problem," came the voice.

Caitlin spun, but the voice was not behind her.

"You're still looking with your eyes."

Caitlin spun again, but there was no voice there, either.

"You must close your eyes," came the voice. "And look inside."

Finally, Caitlin closed her eyes. She tried, again, to focus.

"Don't concentrate with your mind," came the voice. "Concentrate with your spirit. Your soul. Your nature."

Caitlin closed her eyes tight, trying to understand.

"You're trying too hard," came the voice. "If you try, you will not find. Let go of trying. Let go of everything. Just let the universe be."

Caitlin stood there, eyes closed, for several minutes. She was finally beginning to understand. She slowed, calmed down, forced herself to take a deep breath. *Let go of trying.* She just let the universe be, exactly as it was. She decided that whatever it was she was searching for, she could not find it: it would have to find her.

Slowly, Caitlin began to see something. At first it was just a glimpse. She felt her entire body relax, and as she did, the image became more and more clear.

Soon, it became more vivid, as if she'd opened her eyes. All around her was the Mount of Olives. But now, in the air, she saw legions of angels and demons, wrestling with each other. It was incredible, as if the spiritual dimension had revealed itself to her. As if a window had been opened up to the universe.

"Yes…very good," came Aiden's voice, deep in her mind.

"Now you are seeing. *This* is the real world. *This* is the world that is happening all around us, all the time—the one that we never see. Our physical world is but a manifestation of this world. We are puppets, all of us, in the physical realm."

Caitlin tried to focus even more deeply. Hovering over her she saw several guardian angels. One of them had the face of Polly. Another had Aiden's face.

"Yes…very good," came Aiden's voice. "Now tell me: where am I?"

"You're here," Caitlin responded. "You're everywhere, and nowhere at once. If I look for you in the physical world, I will not find you. And if I don't look for you, then I will see you."

"Yes…excellent," came the voice. "Now open your eyes."

Slowly, Caitlin opened her eyes. She saw Aiden standing before her, just a few feet away, holding his staff.

In his other hand, he held another staff, a bronze one. He threw it at her.

Caitlin caught it just in time.

He suddenly charged, swinging his staff down for her head.

Their final sparring had begun.

Caitlin blocked the blow, just-in-time. It clanged under the sky, the gold against the bronze.

Aiden swung again and again, from every direction. Each time, she blocked it. She was beginning to feel a new power, a new sense overtake her. In the past, she viewed battle as a struggle. Now, she was focusing on becoming one with everything.

Aiden swung faster and faster, but each time she managed to dodge it, jumping, ducking, weaving.

He pushed her back until she was standing at the edge of the plateau, with no room left without falling off the mountain. At the last second, as she was about to take her final step back, she suddenly flipped up in the air, high over his head, and landed on his other side.

As she did, she brought down her staff, and to her shock, she managed to strike Aiden hard, right on the shoulder. He reached up to block it, but was a fraction of a second slower than her. Caitlin was amazed: that had never happened before, not in all the years, all the centuries, all the places, she had known him. She had never seen anyone get a blow in on Aiden.

Her blow hit him hard, and Aiden sank to his knees. As he did, he dropped his staff, and it bounced off the ground and fell off the mountainside. It hurled, end over end, plummeting, bouncing off the rock, clanging as it went. It was a loud, surreal clang, one which shook the entire valley.

Aiden slowly turned and looked up at Caitlin. She had never seen him look so amazed.

She herself was flabbergasted, not knowing what she had just done. And then, she felt overcome with remorse. She had beaten her teacher.

"I'm so sorry," she said, extending a hand to help him up.

He shook his head, and slowly rose to his feet. As he did, his eyes filled with tears. Caitlin could see these were not tears of pain: they were tears of pride.

"The day has come," he said. "Now, finally, you understand. Now, there is nothing more I can teach you."

Aiden took two steps closer, held out his palms, and gently reached up and placed them on her forehead. He closed his eyes, and as he did, she could feel the incredible energy coursing through them, into her. She felt a transmission of power, a whole new energy, something she had never felt before. She didn't know what was happening to her.

"Caitlin of the Pollepel Coven," he slowly announced. "I hereby endow you with every power you will ever know."

Caitlin closed her eyes, feeling the energy coursing through her like a tidal wave. As she did, she was suddenly overcome with a series of visions.

She had a vision of war. She saw the skies blackening, saw an army of evil vampires filling the air, racing towards the Mount of Olives. She saw Rexius at their head, and to her disbelief, Sam, her brother, by his side. She could hardly believe it.

She saw them inflicting wave after wave of damage and destruction. She saw Caleb fighting them, and Aiden, too.

But she saw them losing. And then, to her horror, she saw Caleb get stabbed through the heart. Dying.

Caitlin opened her eyes with a cry.

She stared at Aiden, who stared back at her, grimly.

"What do you see?" he asked, his voice somber.

"I see a coming war," she said. "Here. On this mount. I see my brother. Attacking. I see….death. Caleb's death."

Aiden nodded back gravely.

"You see much," he said.

"Is it true?" she asked, afraid to know the answer.

Aiden turned away and gazed out, wordlessly.

"I won't allow it to happen!" Caitlin insisted. "I will stay here. I will defend the mountain, with all of you!"

"This is not where you are needed. You, and Caleb, and I, each have our own destinies. You are needed to find your father. The shield. That is the only thing that can save us now. You are our last hope. If you stay here and fight with us, we will all surely die. That much is certain. If you go, then there is a chance, a small chance, that we can survive."

Caitlin felt so torn inside, swirling with conflicting emotions. She didn't know what to say. She felt more helpless than ever, like a puppet in the hands of fate. On the one hand, she knew she had the power to make choices, to determine her destiny; on the other hand, she clearly saw that certain things were fated. But how much, she wondered? How much was everything fated? How much of life was destiny? Could fate be changed? Or was she helpless, were they all helpless, to just sit back and watch destiny unfold? These thoughts tore her up inside.

"You receive two powerful new skills today," Aiden continued. "Your final skills. The first is the skill to change properties: you can now change silver into an ordinary metal. Which means you can never be contained by silver. No other vampire has this skill. Only you."

Caitlin felt a new energy tingling in her arms, and felt more invincible than ever.

"And your final skill is the most powerful of all."

Aiden paused.

"It is the ability to choose your future place and time."

Caitlin stared back, thinking.

"What do you mean?" she asked, perplexed.

"Up until now, you have only been able to travel back in time. Vampires can never travel forward. But today, with the completion of your training, one exception is made, for one time only. If you survive, if you find your father, then you shall have one chance to choose. A time and place. In all of history. You will be able to choose your destiny."

Caitlin furrowed her brow, trying to process it all.

"Are you saying I can move forward, to the future?" she asked.

He shook his head. "Not without the shield."

"But with the shield?"

He looked back at her, noncommittal.

"When you have the shield, you will understand."

Caitlin tried to understand, but it all seemed so mysterious to her. She wanted to ask more, but she sensed he'd already told her all that he would.

"But I still don't know where to go next," she pleaded, "to find my father."

"You don't know because you're not seeing," he said. "Now tell me: what else do you see?"

Caitlin closed her eyes again. This time, she was flooded with a vision of a magnificent temple, stretching hundreds of feet in every direction, in the center of Jerusalem. She saw a square within a square, and a chamber in its center courtyard. She sensed that this was the holiest place on earth, and her final destination. She saw herself entering it, carrying an ivory staff.

"I see a vast and holy temple," she said, her eyes closed, struggling to make out the details. "I see myself entering it. And carrying a staff. An ivory staff. And I hear a voice. It says: *A square within a square.*"

Slowly, Caitlin opened her eyes, and as she did, she saw Aiden holding out a staff. She could not believe it: it was the staff of her vision. It was a weapon that Caitlin recognized, but had not seen in years: a four-foot ivory staff, intricately carved, with a round circular head and mysterious etchings all over it. The last time she had seen it had been in the Cloisters, in New York City. The crozier that Caleb had once used, one of the greatest weapons of their coven. It glowed like a thing of magic as Aiden held it out to her.

Slowly, her hand trembling, she reached out and grasped it. She could feel its ancient energy coursing through her.

"This weapon has been in safekeeping for thousands of years, reserved for the time of greatest war," Aiden said. "But it is also a clue, the final relic on the road to your father."

Caitlin surveyed it, in awe.

"Am I meant to bring it to the temple?" she asked. "The one in my vision? The one in Jerusalem?"

Aiden nodded back.

"And now, you must go. There is no time to waste. A war comes. Find your father, for us all. Go. Say your goodbyes to Caleb. Make it meaningful. It may be the last time you see him again."

Caitlin's heart stopped at his words, as she felt her eyes well up with tears.

"How can you say such a thing?" she asked, horrified.

Aiden stared back gravely.

"I only say that which you know yourself to be true. Sometimes our future is revealed to us, and it is one we must accept. I am sorry, but your destiny with Caleb must come to an end."

CHAPTER SIXTEEN

Scarlet stood in her cell, Ruth beside her, and looked up at the group of people before her. There must have been a dozen of them, and she could sense right away that they were different, like her. Vampires. Except, they were not like her. They had a very different energy—a dark energy. She sensed they had very dark intentions.

The guard opened the silver bars to her cell, and now they stood just a few feet away, staring down at her. The guard stepped forward and unlocked her silver shackles, and she rubbed her wrists, happy to have them free. She was tempted to try to make a run for it, to dart past them, between their legs, and up the stone staircase. But she knew she wouldn't make it. Ruth certainly wouldn't, either. So she stared back at them warily, waiting to see who they were, and what they had come for.

As she looked them over, she suddenly thought she recognized one of them. She did a double-take: could it be him?

Scarlet couldn't believe it. It looked just like him, although his face, the expression, seemed different. As if he were under a spell of some sort. And his eyes—they looked older, meaner, lifeless. But otherwise, she was sure it was him.

Sam. Her uncle. Polly's husband. The man she'd met back in Scotland, and had grown to love. The man who had once looked out for her, protected her. What was he doing with these creeps?

Seeing him, Scarlet could even see some of her mommy in him. It made her heart race, pine for her mother more than ever. Seeing him, she knew that she should feel relief that someone in her family was here, had found her. Rationally, she knew she should.

But emotionally, when she looked up at Sam, she felt nothing like relief. Instead, she felt fear. She couldn't understand why, but the way he looked down at her, it was like he didn't recognize her, like he didn't even care about her. Like he hadn't come here to help her, but rather to help this evil group of people. She couldn't understand.

"Sam?" she asked, as she looked into his eyes.

The rest of the group turned and looked at him. For a moment, just a flicker of a moment, she thought she saw his face flush with something like surprise. Or maybe, even recognition.

"Sam, don't you recognize me?" Scarlet persisted. "It's me. Scarlet. Your sister's daughter."

Sam stared back for several seconds, unblinking. He looked as if he were trying to figure it out, to remember.

But finally, his eyes did not fill with recognition. On the contrary, they continued to stare coldly down.

"I don't know you," snarled his guttural voice.

Scarlet shivered at the sound of it. It was a voice she did not recognize. It was not the voice of a human, but of a creature—of a cold, soulless person from hell. The tone of his voice, even more than his words, told her everything: this was not the Sam she once knew.

Her heart fell. She knew at that moment that her mother had not sent him. That he was not here to help. And that she was still alone in the world.

To Sam's side stood a woman with long red hair and large breasts, dressed in a tight black leather outfit, scowling down. Scarlet could see the meanness in her eyes, and she could also see the hold that she had on Sam, as if she had him in a spell. She wondered who she was.

On Sam's other side was an evil-looking man who seemed to be thousands of years old. From the way he stood, in the center of the group, she could sense that he was the leader. His pale blue eyes gazed down at her as if he were seeing right through her, and she felt a cold shiver run up her spine. She sensed he had come here just for her.

Ruth began to growl.

Scarlet wondered why they had come. Clearly, it was not to free her. And yet, she sensed, they weren't about to hurt her either. Not yet, at least. She sensed they wanted something from her.

The old, ugly man smiled down at her, his face collapsing into a million wrinkles. It was the most awful smile she had ever seen. She could feel the evil oozing off of him; more than ever, she longed for her mother, for any familiar face.

"You are a precocious little girl," the old man said. "Just like your mother. Do you know that I tried to kill her once? Centuries ago? Or I should say, centuries to come. In New York City. I doused her in a bath of acid. But it didn't work. Because, at the time, she was a half breed."

The man stepped forward, and narrowed his eyes at Scarlet.

"But you are not a half breed, are you? No. You are the real thing. The union of two vampires. A very rare and special thing. Vampires cannot procreate, you see. You are the exception. The thread in the eye of the needle. The one exception in the universe."

He paused, examining her.

"But why are you so special?"

He paused again, and as he did, Scarlet began to wonder. Was everything he was saying true? Did he really tried to kill her mommy? Would he try to kill her? Why?

"Yes, I would kill your mother now, if I could," the old man said, reading her mind, with a smile. "But the problem is, I don't know where she is. Not yet, anyway. You will lead us to her. And then, I can kill you and her together, at once."

His smile broadened, and Scarlet felt her heart stop at the viciousness of his words. He was the meanest man she had ever met. And she could tell from his tone that he really meant everything he said.

"I'll never tell you where my mommy is," Scarlet responded defiantly.

The old man laughed.

"That is because you do not know yourself," he answered. "But you will lead us to her nonetheless. You see, there is a very important weapon in the vampire world. It is called the Vampire Shield. And there is only one person in the world who knows where it is. And that, my dear, is you."

Scarlet narrowed her eyes back at him, fuming.

"I don't know about any shield," she answered, truthfully.

"I know you don't. It wasn't something you were told about. It was something you were entrusted with."

He took a step closer.

"You see, the hiding place can only be revealed by your lineage. And they couldn't risk entrusting it all to your mommy. So they split the clues. Half to her…and half, to you."

Suddenly, his eyes dropped down to Scarlet's wrist.

"They didn't tell you, of course. Why would they? They couldn't trust you. No. They implanted it on you. Your bracelet. The final clue."

Scarlet looked down at her wrist, at the dangling bracelet which that man had placed on her wrist in Scotland, which she had nearly forgotten. At that moment, as she looked at it, she knew it to be true, everything this man had said. She could suddenly feel the energy radiating off of it, its intense power practically burning through her wrist. She could feel that he was right, that it was some sort of clue. She was upset with herself that she hadn't considered it before, had never looked at it in that way. But now, suddenly, she knew that it was the key to finding the Shield. And more importantly, the key to finding her mommy.

And then, at the same moment, she realized that this clue could not get into this man's hands.

Scarlet suddenly reached down, snatched the bracelet off her wrist, and brought it towards her mouth, preparing to swallow it, to keep it away from them for good.

But, to her surprise, the old man's reflexes were faster than hers. He moved at the speed of light, and while her wrist was still moving towards her mouth, he reached out and grabbed it in mid-air. His grip was so cold, it felt like a block of ice had wrapped its claws around her skin. He held it with such force, it was as if he were an 18 year old man. Scarlet was strong as a vampire, stronger than she could imagine—yet, still, she was no match for this man.

As he squeezed her wrist harder, she found herself crying out in pain, then involuntarily opening her hand. The bracelet fell out, and the man grabbed it in mid-air, in his open palm.

Ruth suddenly lunged forward and tried to bite the man through her muzzle.

But he turned and kicked Ruth with such force that he sent her flying across the room and into the stone wall, yelping.

Scarlet had had enough. She reached up and lunged at the old man, and somehow moved fast enough to get her hands around his throat. She squeezed and squeezed the wrinkled skin, and took satisfaction in seeing his eyes open wide in surprise. She was really choking him. He was strong, stronger than any man she'd ever encountered—but so, she was realizing, was she.

A moment later she felt bodies descending on her, kicking and elbowing and pummeling her in every direction. They landed on top of her, tackling her to the ground.

Then she felt the silver shackles once again bind her wrists behind her back, as they planted her cheek against the stone floor. They grabbed her and dragged her to her feet.

Scarlet stood there, her face covered in dirt, scowling back at the old man, who now scowled back at her. She could see that she had shaken him.

"You insolent little brat," he snapped.

He held up the bracelet before her, dangling it in the torchlight, mocking her.

"You have just given me the key to the kingdom, the key to everything I need in life. I will now find the Shield, and I will take you with us. I will make you watch as I summon a greater evil than the universe has ever known. And then," he smiled broadly, "I will kill both you and your mommy with great delight."

*

Scarlet was prodded from behind, and after a strong shove, she stumbled several feet. Ruth snarled, protective of her, and turned and tried to snap the guard; but she was still muzzled, and there was little she could do.

Scarlet felt her rage heightening as she was led by the group of vampires down the back alleys of Jerusalem. Everywhere they went, crowds parted, scrambling to get as far away from them as possible. They must have sensed the evil energy of this pack, marching on a mission.

Scarlet desperately wanted to break free, to fight back, to make a run for it—but she could not. She struggled against the silver shackles binding her wrists, and realized she was helpless. She was at their mercy.

Sam and his girlfriend and the leader were in front as they twisted and turned through the alleys, marching on the ancient stone streets, going Scarlet could only guess where. They had taken Scarlet along, and while she was grateful to be free from that dark jail, she hardly felt at ease with this crowd. She knew that when they found whatever it was they needed, they would kill her. Or worse, use her to lure her mommy, then kill them both.

Scarlet felt another pang of fear, but there was little she could do. For the millionth time, she regretted allowing them to snatch that bracelet off her wrist. She should have thought of it sooner, should have figured out the bracelet led to something important, maybe even to her mommy. If she had known that, she wouldn't have worn it like that. She would have taken it off, and hid it in her pocket.

But no one had told her. Before she had been sent back in time, in that castle on that mountain in Scotland, that old man had shoved it on her wrist, right after he had given her something to drink. But he hadn't said anything, hadn't explained. She hadn't really thought of it, and had no idea how special it was.

Now, she felt terrible. She felt responsible—as if it were all her fault, as if she were the one responsible for leading this group to whatever it was they wanted to find. That stupid shield they kept talking about. As they hurried through the streets of Jerusalem, marching like a small army, she could see the determination on their faces. She had a sinking feeling they were going to a place of great evil. And that she, unwittingly, was leading the way.

They finally broke out of the alleyways and marched across a great stone plaza. The group of vampires pushed their way through the crowds of humanity, and bodies went flying in every direction. No one dared try to push them back. It was like a swarm of hornets cutting through the city.

They crossed the plaza and passed under an ancient stone arch. They continued down another alleyway, and down several flights of stone steps, the alleyways narrowing. As they went, even rats scurried to get out of their way, and old ladies, high above, slammed closed their shutters, afraid.

The alleyway seemed to end in a stone wall. As Scarlet looked closer, she could see that there was actually a door there, concealed in the stone. Above the door, in ancient letters, was etched: "Hezekiah's Aqueduct."

The old man nodded, and Sam lunged forward and kicked in the door. Stone shattered, revealing an arched passageway, heading further down, down another flight of steps, into the blackness.

Scarlet felt herself prodded from behind, and nearly tripped down the stairs as the group continued down a narrow stairwell. As they went, it got darker, and one of them lit a torch and held it high, barely lighting the way. Streaks of sunlight streamed in through small windows, high up, and Scarlet heard the distant sound of running water. It sounded like small underground streams, and it echoed in the darkness. It felt like they were entering an underground tunnel of some sort.

Finally, the stairs stopped, and Scarlet was marched down a high, narrow passageway, barely wide enough to fit two people side-by-side. She felt claustrophobic as the group made its way further and further down the tunnels. As they went, there were occasional small openings in the wall, and Scarlet could see streams of water rushing through.

She wondered where this was all leading. This was the creepiest place she had ever been. She wondered if they were going to just kill her and leave her here.

They continued down yet another passageway, and finally, they stopped.

Scarlet looked up, and before her, she was amazed to see, was a shining, gold door.

The vampires parted ways, and she watched the old vampire step forward and climb the four steps to the door. He stopped before it and smiled as he reached out, raised Scarlet's bracelet, held out the small golden key on the end of it, and inserted it into the lock.

It entered with a reverberating click. A perfect fit.

The old man turned the key, and as he did, the ground beneath Scarlet shook. He stepped back, and the gold door opened on its own.

The site took Scarlet's breath away. Shining, golden rays of light radiated out of the chamber, filling the tunnels. It was so bright, the vampires had to turn and look away. Only the old man continued to stare, his large pale blue eyes transfixed, as he stepped forward. He reached out, and grabbed hold of something with his hands.

He turned and held it up, high above his head, as he faced the others.

As he did, they all bowed down low to the ground.

It was a shield. It was a large, golden shield, and it was glowing, light radiating off of it. It pulsed and vibrated and turned colors, as if it were coming to life.

The old man held it triumphantly over his head, and as he did, all the age lines in his face began to disappear. Scarlet couldn't believe it. As she watched, he became younger and younger, right before her eyes. In just moments, he looked like an 18-year-old boy.

He threw back his head, and with a victorious snarl, he screamed:

"My fellow vampires! After three thousand millennia, I present to you the vampire Shield!"

CHAPTER SEVENTEEN

Caitlin stood beside Caleb, at the base of the Mount of Olives, her heart breaking inside. She had just completed her training and she knew it was time to say goodbye to Caleb.

They had to part ways; there was no way around it. Aiden had made it clear that she was needed out there, on the search for her Dad, and that Caleb was needed here, to stay and defend the coven, with Aiden. There was nothing Caitlin wanted less than to have to part ways with him. She wanted him to join her, especially now, on the final leg of her search for her father, for their daughter. She hated her destiny. Why couldn't they just stay together, live their lives together in peace? Why were they always destined to be torn apart?

As she stood there, looking into Caleb's eyes, she could see that there was nothing that he wanted more, too. But they were both dutiful warriors. They were both loyal to a fault, and they both knew where they were needed. They would not let others down. And they both knew that if Caleb were to leave now, with Caitlin, it would leave their coven defenseless. Especially after the massacre in Scotland, neither of them liked the idea of leaving Aiden's people defenseless again.

But still, Caitlin's heart broke at the idea of parting ways with him. Especially this time, this final time, with so much at stake. And especially because of Aiden's words, his dire prophecy. She hated Aiden for saying that, for saying that she and Caleb had different destinies, and she wanted his words to disappear from her mind. But deep down she sensed they were true.

She refused to think of it. Caitlin told herself that she would hurry, find her father, find Scarlet, find the Shield, and race back in time to help Caleb, and them all, just in time.

But she had a sinking feeling. As she looked up and stared into Caleb's large, brown eyes, glowing in the morning light, she had a horrible feeling that she would never see him again. And she could sense that he did, too. It deepened her sense of dread.

Caitlin stood there, trying to find the words, but she couldn't. After several moments, despite herself, she suddenly burst into tears, and embraced him.

Caleb hugged her back tightly, and she felt his muscles rippling across her back. She held him for a long time, crying, not wanting to let him go. Not wanting to say what could be her final goodbye.

Finally, he pulled back. His eyes were tearing just a bit, but he clenched his jaw, and she could see he was trying to be strong for them both.

"It will all be fine," he said.

But she knew, even as he said it, that he didn't really believe it.

"You are needed out there," he said. "And I am needed here. Find your father. Find our daughter. And bring them back."

He reached up and brushed the hair from her face.

"Don't worry," he said. "I will be fine here. We have fought so many battles together, throughout the centuries. I have always been fine, haven't I?"

She looked back and nodded. That was true, he had always been fine. But she sensed that this time something was different. She sensed something, she did not know what—some disturbance in the universe, some awful storm on the horizon.

"I just wish we could be together," Caitlin said. "I wish that Scarlet was here, with us. I would give up everything just to have us all together. Some place safe, and quiet, away from the world. Away from all this."

"I know," he said softly.

Caitlin felt torn up inside. On the one hand, she wanted nothing more than to stay here. Yet she knew that she had to do her duty, for the safety of them all. She hated having to choose like this. She hated that the universe was always forcing her to choose, could never just let her be.

Caleb smiled down at her gently, and swept her hair from her eyes.

"Remember that day we spent together?" he asked, nostalgia in his voice. "On the beach? The horses?"

Caitlin smiled, thinking of it. Of course she remembered. She thought about it all the time.

"Yes," she said.

"We have been together in so many places, so many times, so many centuries. That is what matters. Our memories together. The times we shared. No matter what happens, we will always be together."

Caitlin wanted to respond, to say: *Yes. You're right. We will always be together.*

But instead, she was overwhelmed with emotion. She burst into tears again, and hugged him tightly. It was the worst feeling of her life. Deep down, she knew it was the last time she would hold him again. She sensed it in every pore of her body.

She didn't how to handle it, how to say goodbye, how to let him go. So, without saying another word, without even looking into his face again, she suddenly pulled away.

She turned her back, took two steps off the side of the cliff, and leapt into the air. Her wings expanded, and she soared, higher and higher into the air.

She could feel Caleb behind her, watching her the whole time.

And she dared not, even for a second, look back.

CHAPTER EIGHTEEN

Scarlet stood there in disbelief, watching as the old man held the vampire shield high above his head, the ground beneath her quaking. She watched as he transformed, became younger, stronger. Rays of light continued to shoot out from the shield, completely filling the room, and the other vampires continued to bow low to the ground, shielding their eyes from the intense light. She too, had to turn away, so much light filled the room. Beside her, Ruth whined.

She managed to peek a glance, and as she did, she was confused by what she saw: shadows, then shapes, seemed to pour out from the shield. At first she thought maybe her eyes were playing tricks on her, but as she looked closely, she realized they weren't. It looked like spirits were flying out of the shield, forming in the light. At first, they took the nebulous form of shadows; but then they hardened, turned into shapes. And within moments, these shapes transformed into people.

Vampires.

Scarlet was even more surprised to see that these were vampires she recognized from other times and places. One of them had a face she would never forget: he was huge and bald, with one eye and a big scar across his face. Kyle. She'd thought he was dead for good, and was terrified to see him emerge from the light.

Within moments, he was standing there, back, alive again. He looked as ferocious as ever, more filled with rage than Scarlet had ever seen him, as if he'd just been let loose from a cage.

Behind him, more shadows emerged. There was another vampire she recognized, forming out of the shadows: it was the man she had seen back in Scotland, the one they had called Rynd. The one who had killed Polly.

Dozens and dozens more evil vampires and creatures emerged, each more hideous than the next. It looked like the shield was a portal, unleashing an army of demons.

Soon, the narrow tunnels of the aqueduct were filling up with creatures, screaming, shrieking. The scene became chaotic, and Scarlet feared for her life. She knew that now that she'd led them there, they would have no more use for her, and would kill her. She knew that she had to do something quickly, or in a few moments, she would be dead. Now was her chance.

Scarlet searched the tunnels, frantic for any way of escape. She realized that, with all the chaos, the vampires were distracted. She was still cuffed, but at least her warders had stopped paying attention to her—for the moment.

Scarlet saw her chance. She turned and nudged Ruth with her foot; Ruth, still sitting loyally by her side, seemed to understand, to pick up on the signal.

Scarlet nodded, and at the same time, the two of them turned and took off, running away from the crowd, back up the steps, back up the narrow alleyway. They ran back up flight after flight, Scarlet running awkwardly with her wrists chained in front of her. She glanced back over her shoulder, but saw nobody coming her way. They were all still staring at the shield, still transfixed.

It wasn't until she neared the top flight of steps, until she could see the doorway up ahead, that Scarlet heard screaming. She turned and saw the vampires pointing at her, then saw them all suddenly take off, charging right for her.

Scarlet doubled her speed, as did Ruth, and they burst out of the aqueduct, outside. She was so grateful to be out in fresh air, to be out from underground, and she ran as fast as she possibly could, hoping she could outrun them. She knew she didn't have much of a lead, but still, she ran, twisting and turning down alleyway after alleyway, praying she would not hit a dead-end. Ruth ran beside her, following close.

Scarlet turned a corner, and as she did, her heart stopped.

A dead-end.

Scarlet could already hear the rumble, and knew that, not too far behind, the vampires were chasing her down. She knew that, in just moments, she would be dead. She didn't care for herself anymore, but she cared so desperately for her mommy. She just wanted to see her one last time. To warn her. To explain that it wasn't her fault. To ask her forgiveness.

As Scarlet saw a figure fly down from the sky, right towards her, she knew that the end had come. She braced herself, and only wished that she didn't have to die this way.

CHAPTER NINETEEN

Caitlin flew as fast as her wings would take her, racing towards Jerusalem. She held in her mind that it still was possible to find her Dad, to find Scarlet, find the Shield, and to get back in time to help Caleb, Aiden and the others. She wiped away her tears, and tried to brush the negative thoughts out of her mind. She insisted on holding in her mind that all would be well. She flew even faster, determined to defy fate, determined to make everything okay.

Caitlin flew so fast, she barely even noticed the land of Israel below her, the rolling hills, beautiful in the morning light, barely even noticed the topography changing from mountains to valley to city. In fact, it wasn't until she was flying directly over Jerusalem that she was shaken out of her reverie. She looked down, and was taken aback by the site.

The city of Jerusalem, sprawled out below, was the most magnificent sight Caitlin had ever seen. She had been to extraordinary cities and countries in her lifetime, all throughout the centuries, and had seen some amazing things—yet nothing she had seen rivaled Jerusalem. The architecture was stunning; it was still simple, being the first century, with a large stone wall demarcating the city line, in which were several arched gates. Inside the city, she could see a network of twisting and turning alleyways and side streets, opening up onto small squares and plazas.

But dominating the city was the massive holy Temple of Solomon. It looked exactly like it had looked in her vision: it was enormous, its stone walls soaring hundreds of feet into the air, stretching in every direction, filling the city. She could feel in every fiber of her body that that was where she was meant to be. She felt that somehow, her father lay beyond those walls.

But it wasn't just the architecture of Jerusalem that left such a deep impression on Caitlin: it was its energy. Even from up here, soaring above it, circling, she could feel an intense spiritual energy radiating off of it. She felt it was the holiest, most charged place she had ever been. It was like one huge energy field.

The closer she flew to it, the more she felt the energy. The hairs on her forearms and on the back of her neck stood on edge. This place was positively tingling with electricity, and she could feel it her from her toes to her head. She sensed that there were incredibly powerful, unseen forces swirling in the air here, for good and for evil. That it was the spiritual battleground of the world.

Caitlin circled the city again and again, trying to take it all in, and as she did, she had an ominous feeling: she sensed Scarlet down there somewhere, and sensed she was in danger. She circled again and again, looking for her, but she could not find her. She tried to shake off the feeling, wondering if it was just her mind playing tricks on her. But deep down, she felt an even greater sense of urgency.

Caitlin focused on the Temple, realizing she had to get their as soon as possible, and find her Dad. That was the only way she knew to get Scarlet.

As she dove down, flying closer, she began to sense something else: a great disturbance. It felt as if a dark energy had been unleashed on the city. She couldn't understand: looking down, she could see no evidence of anything wrong. But she didn't like her sense of foreboding.

Caitlin landed right before the immense, arched stone gate leading to the Temple. She figured that the best way to enter, to find whatever what it was she needed, was to enter the proper way, through the main gate, and to see where her senses led her.

Caitlin landed behind a wall so as not to attract attention, then walked out, blending into the crowd and walking right through the immense entrance to the holy Temple. She squeezed in with hundreds of people, all rushing to enter, and could tell this place was always crowded, people always rushing to enter and pray. Hundreds of people were also lined up along its outside walls, praying, while hundreds more were streaming out.

As Caitlin passed through the gates and entered the temple mount, she looked up, in awe: spread out before her was a huge stone plaza, stretching hundreds of feet. People milled across it, praying, hurrying to and fro. In the center sat the holy temple. It was huge, a perfectly square structure, made of the finest marble, stretching hundreds of feet in every direction. People streamed in and out, many of them leading sheep and oxen. It looked exactly like the temple in her vision, and Caitlin sensed immediately it was where she needed to go.

A square within a square.

It was all starting to make sense. Caitlin could feel the ivory staff in her hands throbbing, warming her palm. She knew it. This was where she was meant to go.

Caitlin walked across the wide, stone plaza of the Temple Mount, feeling the staff grow warmer, feeling her body tingling as she approached. As she made her way through the crowd and got a good view of the structure, she was awestruck. Carved golden cherubs stared down at her from the temple entrance, their wings stretching outward. The columns before it, and all its cornices, were made of gold. Dozens of Roman soldiers stood near the entrance, watching the crowd warily.

Caitlin passed through its doors, and entered the huge main room of the temple.

Inside, it was overwhelming, packed with people and animals and noises and smells, the sounds of bleating sheep mixing with the sounds of people crying out in prayer. It was organized chaos. Before her was a huge, copper washbasin, and near that was an altar, towards which people were leading their animals. There was a long line, stretching around the room.

Caitlin watched the person at the front of the line walk forward with his sheep. As he reached the altar, the high priest said a prayer, then slaughtered the sheep with a sharp blade. The sheep collapsed, and the blood dripped down into a wide bowl beneath the altar. Two attendants hurried forward and carried the dead animal to the far side of the room, where there burned a roaring fire. As another high priest said a prayer, the dead animal was thrown into the flames.

Caitlin was amazed to watch a huge cloud of smoke appear, and consume the animal whole. It was as if the hand of God were reaching down and accepting the sacrifice.

This was the most intense place Caitlin had ever been. She searched the room, looking for any sign of where her Dad could be. Was he one of the high priests?

A square within a square.

Caitlin looked, and on the far side of the room, she saw a section of the room closed off by long, white velvet curtains on golden rods. There was a narrow crack in the curtains, and she could see through, just enough, to catch a glimpse of what lay beyond: a small structure, perfectly square, maybe twenty feet high and wide, made of solid marble. It had elaborate columns before it, bedecked in gold. More golden cherubs were mounted above it.

Caitlin could feel the energy radiating off it. She knew that behind those walls sat hidden the Holy Ark of the covenant, containing the tablets of God. The holy of holies.

A square within a square.

Caitlin suddenly felt the ivory staff burning in her hand. That was it. The holiest of holy sites within Jerusalem. Could her Dad be there?

Standing before it were dozens of rabbis, dressed in long white robes and hoods, praying. Among them were dozens of Roman soldiers, standing guard in case anyone attempted to approach. The holy of holies was clearly off limits. Caitlin could already tell this would not be easy.

She stepped forward to approach, and as she did, suddenly a Roman soldier blocked her way, scowling down.

"No one is allowed past this point," he snapped.

Caitlin looked around, and could see dozens of soldiers staring at her, ready to jump into action. She knew she didn't have much time. It was now or never.

She broke into action: she leapt up high into the air, over the soldier's head, and ran for the entrance. Luckily, she was much faster than anyone else, and before they could even react, she was already at the entrance. A huge outcry rose up throughout the room as people saw her charging for the holy of holies. She ran through the curtain, yanked open the marble door and, just as the soldiers were charging her, slammed it shut behind her.

Caitlin immediately heard dozens of fists pounding at the door, trying to get in. She found a spear and barred it, hoping it would hold. She only needed a few minutes to get this done.

Caitlin could feel the intense spiritual energy in here. It was almost suffocating, the strongest thing she'd ever felt. She knew that she couldn't stay long. She had to get whatever she could, and get out. Otherwise, the energy of this place would consume her.

On the far side of the room were more curtains, and a surreal light glowing from behind them. She sensed that behind them lay the holy Ark of God. And she knew enough to know that she could never dare approach it—and that she would die on the spot if she tried.

But she sensed she didn't need to: whatever it was she needed was right here, in this room. She looked around, searching, trying to drown out the banging on the door. She took several steps forward, examining the marble floor and walls, looking for any clue.

And then she saw it.

It was there, right before her, in the center of the room: a small, golden pedestal, maybe a foot high. Perfectly square. In the center was a round hole. Just the size of the width of her staff.

A square within a square.

She approached it slowly, her heart pounding, the staff throbbing in her hand. She reached up and lowered it, already knowing it would be a perfect fit.

It was. The staff slid down into the hole, and she let go. It slid lower and lower on its own, sinking into the earth. And that was when Caitlin heard it.

She turned, and her eyes opened wide: she could not believe what she saw.

CHAPTER TWENTY

Scarlet stood with Ruth at the end of the dead end, bracing herself for instant death. She looked up at the dark figure flying down towards her, saw it raise a weapon, and hurl it down right at her. It looked like a long spear. She ducked, bracing herself, and figured this was what it felt like to die.

Scarlet heard a noise of shattering metal, and braced herself for pain.

But as she opened her eyes, she was unhurt. She realized the noise she heard was the sound of her silver chains breaking. She realized that the weapon had been thrown to free her. And as the vampire landed before her, she realized it was not an adversary. It was a friend. Someone she recognized. Someone she remembered from her time in Scotland. Someone who had saved her life once before.

It was the man that Mommy once loved.

It was Blake.

*

Blake reached down and undid Scarlet's chains without hesitating. He undid Ruth's muzzle, and she jumped on him, licking him, remembering him, too.

"There's no time," he said urgently, fear in his eyes. "They're coming. Grab on."

Scarlet grabbed onto his back with her little hands, clutching for life, while Blake reached down and scooped up Ruth. A moment later he leapt into the air, his wings extending, flapping, soaring.

They flew above the city, above ancient Jerusalem, and as they did Scarlet was able to look down and see it all, the labyrinthine maze of alleys and side streets beneath her. She was amazed that she had been running down there, in that maze, and had been able to navigate it at all.

She checked back over her shoulder, still fearful of the hordes chasing her, and in the distance, could see a great black mass gathering on the horizon. She saw shadow after shadow, vampire after vampire, streaming out of the Aqueduct, on the far side of Jerusalem. It looked like a flock of bats surfacing from the bowels of the earth, spreading everywhere. Scarlet's heart stopped in her throat, as she feared they were coming after her.

But then her stomach dropped as she looked down and realized they were plummeting down, in a dive, straight towards the earth. She held on with all she had, screaming.

"HOLD ON!" Blake screamed.

They dove straight down, landing behind a large wall in another quarter of Jerusalem. Soon, they were back on the ground, in a remote alley, unseen. Blake carried them into a far corner, hiding, so that they would not be seen from overhead.

The three of them squatted there, waiting, watching the sky. Scarlet heard a great humming and buzzing noise, then a great commotion, like a flapping of wings. She looked up and saw hundreds, then thousands, of black wings covering the sky. It looked like an enormous flock of birds. When she was younger, she had once watched a never-ending flock cover the sky, migrating from one end of the earth to the other. She remembered watching for hours, as the world seemed to turn black. She had thought it would never end. This reminded her of that.

They crouched there silently, waiting. Scarlet held her breath the entire time, and she could feel how tense Blake and Ruth were, too. She prayed they remained undetected.

Finally, the vampires passed by. All was still. They were undetected. Blake had saved her. Again.

Blake stood, and Scarlet did, too. She looked up at him, more grateful to him than she had ever been. She was also happy to see him. A friendly face. Someone who she actually recognized and who was actually on her side. Someone who was friends with her mommy and daddy. She wondered if he could help lead her to them.

"Have you seen my mommy?" Scarlet asked without hesitating.

Slowly, Blake shook his head.

"I was going to ask you the same question," he said.

"I've been looking for her everywhere," she said.

"Me too," he answered.

Scarlet's eyes opened wide as she realized. She hadn't really considered it, but she could see now how much this man loved her mommy. It made her feel uncomfortable, as she thought of her daddy, and suddenly felt protective of him.

"She's *married*, you know," Scarlet said, with a touch of defiance.

Blake seemed taken aback.

"I…I…know," he stammered.

"So why do you want to see her?" Scarlet pressed.

She knew it was none of her business, and that she should be thanking him, not interrogating him—but still, she had to know.

"I..." Blake trailed off. "I know she's married," he said. "But I..."

He turned away, and Scarlet thought she could see tears in his eyes.

"I just have to see her," he said finally. "I've searched for her everywhere. I've been circling Jerusalem for days. I sensed a great disturbance in this time and place. I sensed that she needed me. That the others did, too. And then, today, I sensed your presence."

"I don't even know where to look for her," Scarlet said. "And I think I've done something terrible."

Blake narrowed his eyes.

"What?" he asked.

"All of those mean vampires...I think I lead them to something. The old one, he took my bracelet. I think it helped them. I didn't mean to. You have to understand. I didn't mean it. Now they say they're going to hurt my mommy. Is it true?"

Blake narrowed his eyes further.

"Where did you lead them?" he asked.

"I don't know," she said. "They took me down this long alleyway, underground. And then they found this golden door. And when they opened it, they took out this thing...it looked like a shield."

Blake opened his eyes wide in shock.

"A *shield*?" he asked. He seemed afraid to even pronounce the word.

"It was awful," Scarlet said, shaking her head. "All of these mean vampires came back to life. That one they called Kyle."

"Kyle?" Blake asked, astounded.

"Is it true? Will they hurt my mommy?"

Blake looked away. He looked as if he'd seen a ghost.

"There is no time to lose," he said, gravely. "We have to find her. We have to find her immediately."

"But I don't know where she is," Scarlet pleaded, feeling worse than ever.

Suddenly, Ruth turned and took off down the alleyway. Scarlet couldn't understand why; she had never seen her act like this.

"Ruth!" she screamed. She and Blake turned and chased after her.

As they chased her, down alley after alley, Ruth finally ran out into the wide open plaza before the holy Temple. Ruth stood there, barking and barking, as Scarlet and Blake finally caught up to her. Scarlet stroked her, trying to figure out what had gotten into her.

"What is it, Ruth?"

Scarlet followed Ruth's stare and looked out across the plaza. As she watched, suddenly a huge crowd started to form, gathering before a golden gate in the temple wall. The commotion increased as the gate began to open.

A single person appeared, flocked by followers.

Scarlet and Blake stood there, amazed. She could not believe who it was.

CHAPTER TWENTY ONE

Caitlin stood there, inside the holy chamber of the holy Temple, staring down at the floor. She could not believe what had just happened. As she inserted the golden staff, a secret opening in the floor slowly slid back, revealing a staircase, descending down beneath the ground. A golden light radiated down below, shining up the steps, and it looked as if it were a stairway descending down into heaven itself.

The pounding continued at the door, dozens of soldiers trying to knock it down, and Caitlin knew she had no time to lose. She hurried over and descended through the narrow opening, down the steps, towards the light. As she did, she felt the four keys burning in her pocket, and felt certain that this would lead her to her Dad.

Caitlin hurried down the winding, golden steps, deep beneath the holy Temple, and found herself inside a tunnel system, shining with light. She could hardly believe it: the walls and the floors were completely lined with gold. It was the most opulent place she had ever seen; she felt as if she were walking inside a treasure chest. As she walked down the long corridor, light bounced off of everything, perfectly immaculate and shining.

The corridors twisted and turned forever, an endless maze of labyrinths, like an entire city underground. She turned and turned, and felt herself being led deeper and deeper, towards a very special object—or maybe towards her Dad himself.

She thought of all the churches and cloisters and abbeys and palaces she had been to throughout the centuries, and she could hardly believe that this was her last stop. Her heart pounded in her chest as she wondered if maybe her Dad was waiting for her at the end of one of these halls. Or maybe the Shield itself. She could not imagine what else could be here.

Whatever it was, she knew it had to be very, very special. To be hidden inside the most holy Temple in the world—and inside its most holy chamber—beneath a hidden door, one that only she could open…she could only imagine what awaited her.

Caitlin briefly wondered how she would get out of here—but she tried not to worry about that now. Now, she tried to just focus on her Dad. She could hardly believe she was about to actually meet him. What would she say to him? Would he be proud of for? Who was he? Did he look like her?

And why was her lineage so special?

Caitlin's heart pounded as the walls glowed brighter, and the turns came more quickly. Finally, she began to run, unable to bear the anticipation. She made a final turn, down a short corridor, and at the end of it, a bright light, almost like a flood light, lit up everything with an intense glow.

At the end of the dead-end sat a small altar, made of solid gold. On top of this, sat a red velvet pillow. On top of this, sat a single, small object. Caitlin walked slowly towards it, breathing hard with each step, wondering what it could be.

As she reached it, she looked down and saw it was a small, golden box. It had a key slot, just big enough to fit a tiny key.

Caitlin examined it, wondering how she would open it, and then remembered: her necklace. She felt it vibrating around her neck, and she reached down and removed it. She reached out and inserted it, praying it would fit.

To her relief, it did. She turned it with a small click, and the floor beneath her began to tremble, as the tiny box opened.

Inside was a small, rolled up scroll, barely the size of her finger. She reached in, her heart pounding, and extracted it. It was so delicate, so fragile, it felt like it had been sitting there for thousands of years, felt like it might crumble in her fingers.

She slowly unrolled it, and stared down at the handwriting. It was an ancient script, and at first she was barely able to make it out. But as she squinted, slowly, the message appeared:

Your guide will appear at the Eastern gate.

She held it, reading it over and over again, trying to figure out what it meant, when suddenly, a side chamber opened in the wall, revealing a set of stairs.

Caitlin was flooded with relief: now she had a way out of here, a way to escape without having to go back through the Temple, through the angry mob awaiting her.

At the same time, she suddenly heard a thunderous, crashing noise: she looked over her shoulder and was amazed to see the ceilings and walls collapsing. Huge chunks crashed to the floor. Now that she had found the clue, this entire underground chamber was collapsing, she realized, hiding all traces of it. The crashing was heading right for her, and she turned and bolted for the stairs, escaping just before the ceiling collapsed on her.

Caitlin hurried up the staircase, running up as it twisted and turned, spiraling up, again and again, her feet echoing on the gold. She ascended, higher and higher, until finally it led her to a small, arched door. She opened it, and to her amazement, she found herself outside, back in Jerusalem, outside the holy Temple, on the far side of its walls.

As she stepped outside she heard a noise behind her, and turned and saw the door closing, then disappearing, blending into the wall. Within moments, she was amazed to see, the door seamlessly blended into the stone wall, leaving no trace there had ever been a door there at all. It was as if the Temple had ejected her outside its walls and sealed itself up again.

Caitlin stood there, on the outskirts of the holy Temple, in the streets of Jerusalem, trying to process it all.

Your guide will appear at the Eastern Gate.

She looked all around, and surveyed the wide stone plaza before the holy Temple. Hundreds of people milled about in every direction, streaming into the Temple, and in the distance she saw the soldiers still trying to break into the holy chamber, where they thought she was. No one suspected that she was out here, far from their eyes.

But now what?

Your guide will appear at the Eastern Gate.

As exhilarated as she was at finding this final clue, she was also disappointed. She had hoped to find her Dad there—or had, at least, hoped to find some sort of magnificent relic. Maybe even the shield.

But it was just another clue. She felt that this was the final clue. But she still didn't know what it meant.

Your guide will appear at the Eastern Gate.

She decided that she had to get up in the air, to look down at the city, to get a bird's eye view. Maybe that would help her understand.

She leapt into the air and in moments was up high, circling, looking down at Jerusalem. She felt certain that the clue had something to do with her Dad—and with Jerusalem. *The Eastern Gate.*

As she circled, she saw that Jerusalem looked much like a walled, medieval city: there was a large, stone wall surrounding it, and all around it were large, arched gates through which people were entering and exiting the city.

The Eastern Gate.

Caitlin circled, and the more she dwelled on it, the more she felt certain the final clue was a reference to the eastern gate of Jerusalem. She circled again, got her bearings, and headed towards the eastern side of the city.

As she flew closer, down below she sensed a great commotion. Thousands of people were milling around the eastern side of Jerusalem, and they all seemed to be congregating around one entrance. The eastern gate.

As Caitlin looked down, she saw the eastern gate: it was huge—a hundred feet high, arched and solid gold, with intricate carvings all over it. Above it, up high, in the ramparts, were dozens of Roman soldiers, patrolling, keeping watch on the city.

Caitlin dove down, landed out of sight, then hurried into the thick crowd, blending with the masses. She pushed her way through, towards the gate, trying to see what all the commotion was about. She felt certain that whatever was taking place was somehow related to her.

Finally, she broke through the rows of people, and stood there, looking up at the gate. There were thousands of excited and anxious faces, the crowd stirred up, agitated. She was dying to know what they were looking at. As she reached the front, she finally saw for herself.

A single person was entering through the gate, towards the crowd.

Your guide will appear at the Eastern gate.

She could not believe who it was. She had found, she knew, the man that would lead her to her father.

CHAPTER TWENTY TWO

Caleb stood there, at the base of the Mount of Olives, watching the sky. He had been unable to look away ever since Caitlin had left. Secretly, he hoped she would come back. But he knew she couldn't.

He felt a tightness in his chest, a sadness, and found it hard to breathe. He didn't know why, but he couldn't stop thinking about her, couldn't stop feeling as if it might be the last time he ever saw her. He thought back to all the times they had been together, to all the centuries, to his proposal, to their wedding. She was his life. She meant more to him than anything on this earth. And to watch her go, to fly away like that, broke his heart. He knew, rationally, that she should return. But deep down inside, somehow he felt that she never would.

So Caleb stood there, watching, hoping—and as he did, he began to feel something else: he began to sense a great disturbance in the universe. He had felt disturbances before, throughout the centuries, in his battles with Kyle, against the Blacktide Coven, and against a multitude of evil creatures. But he had never felt a disturbance like this. It was a disturbance that shook the very fabric of the earth. He felt the air shaking, the skies tearing apart. He sensed that something very evil—and powerful—had been unleashed. Something so powerful that it could not be contained. Something that might even bring an end to the very world.

Caleb sensed a presence, and looked to see Aiden standing there. Somehow, he had appeared beside him.

"You watch the skies for her," Aiden observed softly.

Caleb saw Aiden watching the skies, too, and could hear in his voice that he, also, missed her. There was a look of grave concern on his face.

"Yes I do," Caitlin responded.

"You and Caitlin, you have a very deep destiny. A fate. The two of you were meant to be. Nothing can tear it apart."

Aiden watched in silence.

"Sometimes," he continued, after a long while, "the world intervenes, and one person dies before the other. That doesn't mean though, that they are not together."

He turned and stared meaningfully at Caleb.

Caleb felt his heart pounding at his words. His ominous feeling worsened. Aiden had confirmed his worse fears. Would he die before Caitlin?

Or even worse: would she die before him?

Before Caleb could ask, he suddenly heard a shuffling, the sound of dozens of feet, and he turned and saw, to his surprise, dozens of Aiden's coven members. Somehow, they had all managed to creep up, silently, behind him. They all stood there, in their white robes, watching the skies. Caleb saw their worried expressions, and realized they sensed it, too. The entire coven was out in force, waiting. As if they already knew. As if preparing for a war.

Caleb stood there, and felt proud to be among them, proud to be with Aiden. He knew some terrible danger was coming, and no matter what the outcome, he felt proud to be able to make this last stand with them. If this were to be his final place on earth, the last battle he fought, he would proudly do it here, fighting with these men. And he would fight to his very last breath.

He sensed a shadow, and looked back up at the sky: as he watched, slowly, imperceptibly, it darkened. At first, Caleb thought perhaps it was a passing thundercloud—or maybe even an eclipse of the sun.

But as he looked closely, as he began to hear a great fluttering noise, to sense a tremendous vibration, he knew this was no cloud. It was no flock of birds. It was a legion of vampires. Hundreds of them.

No. *Thousands* of them.

They swarmed the skies like locusts, moving in a huge flock, right for him, right for the Mount of Olives. Caleb sensed immediately that they were the object of the attack.

And that they had come to annihilate them.

CHAPTER TWENTY THREE

Caitlin stood in the midst of the thick crowd, staring up at the Eastern gate, the sun glaring behind it. She had to squint, and for a moment, she wondered if her eyes were playing tricks on her. There was also such light radiating off the man coming through that it was hard for Caitlin to see where the sun ended and the man began.

Caitlin watched as the man, seated on a donkey, rode in through the Eastern gate. The animal ambled through the thick masses, as all around him swarmed dozens of followers, dressed in long, flowing white robes. The man himself wore a long, white robe and hood, which was lowered, exposing his face to the crowd. He had light brown hair going down to his cheekbones, and a short brown beard. His eyes were large and hazel, and they radiated light, like two glowing marbles. In fact, there was such light radiating off of him that Caitlin had to squint. He had such an aura of peace, she could immediately sense he was different. This was no ordinary person.

Caitlin could hardly imagine this was real. She felt as if she were in a dream, as if she were watching herself from the outside. And yet, from the pushing and shoving of the crowd, the noisy street, the smell, the braying of donkeys and bleating of sheep, the heat, the chaos, she knew it was real. It was very, very real.

To her astonishment, Caitlin realized that the man before her, the man entering in a donkey through the Eastern gate of Jerusalem, was none other than Jesus.

Your guide will appear the Eastern gate.

She could not believe it. She was standing there, at the doorway to history. In history. Watching it unfold as it happened.

Her heart started pounding, as she realized that all the clues, in all the places, had led her to this spot. To this moment in time. This was it. Jesus was her guide. He would lead her to her Dad.

As Caitlin watched him enter, she sensed it to be true. It felt right. Every bone, every vibration in her body told her that it was him, that *he* was her guide. That he would be the one to take her on the final leg of her journey, to meet her father, to bring her to the Shield.

She watched as he got closer, slowly riding through the crowd. He held up a single hand, palm out, eyes half-closed. As he went, she watched in disbelief as several crowd members, hunched over and limping, suddenly stood up straight. Healed. It was incredible.

Being Jerusalem, it was also a chaotic and crowded scene. Flooding into the gate behind him were dozens of followers, and behind these there appeared dozens of Romans soldiers, marching, trying to clear the way, to regain order and control. They had scowls on their faces, and looked deeply displeased that Jesus had come, that he had drawn this crowd. People elbowed to get closer to him, pushing each other out of the way. People screamed Jesus' name in every direction, wanting his attention, wanting to be healed. Others screamed curses at him, throwing stones, calling him a false Messiah.

Yet as the stones flew through the air, they fell harmlessly to the ground as they neared him.

It seemed like everyone in this crowd had a different opinion, a different agenda, a different perspective of him. Caitlin could see from the angry faces of the guards that the Romans were threatened by him and wanted him under a tight watch. Amidst the Romans she saw standing a single man, clearly their governor. She recognized his face from the history books: Pontius Pilate. The Prefect of Rome. The one who had killed Jesus.

Caitlin thought of history, and she knew what would happen. Jesus, riding now so harmlessly on his donkey, would soon be captured. Imprisoned. Put on trial. And then, crucified.

The thought of it made Caitlin cringe. She looked at him now—so serene, so peaceful—and it seemed hard to believe that any ill would ever come to him. Just being there, on the outskirts of the crowd, she could already feel a sense of peace. It was actually the first time she had felt a real sense of peace since she had arrived back in this place and time. She didn't know why, but she felt a great sense of comfort around him.

She also felt excited. Every clue she had ever found pointed her to this moment in time. She felt that, in just moments, he would lead her to her Dad.

As Jesus made his way through the crowd on his donkey, slowly, the crowd parted ways. Caitlin pushed her way through a row of people, trying to get closer. She had to see him up close. She wondered if he would even acknowledge her—or if she were just imagining all of this. Had the clue meant something else entirely?

She felt the urgency of time now more than ever. She didn't have a moment to lose.

Caitlin managed to edge closer, her heart pounding. As she neared him, she felt a warmth spreading throughout her entire body, and an indescribable sense of peace. Jesus was sitting straight up, eyes half closed, looking at everything and nothing at the same time. Caitlin hoped, prayed, that somehow he might acknowledge her. That he could lead her to her Dad.

As she got closer, he suddenly turned and looked directly at her. Then, he lowered his hand and held it out to her.

Caitlin could hardly breathe, she was so nervous. He was holding out his fingertips, as if for her to touch them. She reached out, slowly, her hand shaking, and the tips of her fingers just barely grazed his.

As they did, her entire body was electrified. The shock ran through her fingertips, down her arm, and through her entire body. The amount of energy that poured through him was more than she could fathom: it was like a tsunami. The energy rejuvenated and healed her at the same time. It made her aware of her own power. For the first time in as long she could remember, she felt truly alive.

Jesus looked down at her, expressionless, his eyes aglow, gazing into hers.

"I have been waiting for you," he said, softly.

Caitlin felt her eyes fill with tears. Waiting for her? Jesus? She couldn't even imagine. She felt so important. As if her entire life had a greater meaning than she ever knew. She had no idea how to respond.

"Follow me," he said.

The crowd surged forward and his donkey moved on, absorbed by the masses. Still trembling, she watched his back as he continued on. The experience left her speechless. She felt a greater sense of purpose than ever. She felt absolutely certain that if she followed him, he would lead her directly to her Dad. To the shield. She was so excited, she could hardly breathe.

But just as Caitlin took her first step to follow him, she suddenly stopped.

Because there, standing in the crowd, staring back at her, was a man with intense, sad eyes, a man she was sure she would never see again. She did a double-take, unable to comprehend if it was true.

After several moments, she realized it was.

It was really him.

Blake.

As Caitlin, already overwhelmed, tried to process this new twist, she was suddenly overcome by another shock: standing there, beside him, looking up at her with love and joy, was her daughter.

Standing there, was Scarlet.

CHAPTER TWENTY FOUR

Caitlin stood there, staring at Blake and Scarlet, speechless. Her heart soared at the site of them. Her eyes locked on Scarlet's, and at the same moment, they ran for each other. Scarlet's face lit up with joy, and beside her, Ruth, elated, ran to her, too.

Caitlin picked Scarlet up in her arms and hugged her with all she had. She could feel Scarlet's little hands hugging her back, squeezing tightly.

Caitlin felt hot tears streaming down her cheeks, felt Scarlet's tears on her own neck. She felt whole again. As if a piece of her had been returned. Her daughter was alive. And she was *here*, with her, back in this time and place. Safe.

"Mommy mommy! I missed you so much," Scarlet said, through her tears. Caitlin hugged her, never wanting to let her go.

"I know, sweetheart. I missed you, too."

Ruth barked and whined, jumping on Caitlin; Caitlin knelt down, and she licked her frantically all over her face.

Scarlet watched and laughed hysterically. Caitlin was so happy to hear that laugh again. Her life felt whole again.

Then Caitlin stood, suddenly remembering.

Blake.

He stood there, staring back with his large blue eyes. They were watering over as he smiled. Clearly, he was overjoyed to see this reunion—and more than that, he had been a part of it.

"Mommy, Blake saved me! And Ruth," Scarlet screamed.

Once again, Blake had saved Scarlet. Her daughter. She owed him a far greater debt than she could ever repay.

Caitlin stepped forward and wordlessly embraced Blake, hugging him tightly. At first, he hesitated, and then he hugged her back. His embrace became tighter and tighter, and she felt his muscles rippling. She felt his love pouring through, and she could feel how sad he was they were not together anymore.

After a long time, too long for just a casual friend, Blake finally, slowly, pulled back. He stood there, his eyes watered over, and looked down at Caitlin. She could see the longing and sadness in them. She could see in them how much he wished that things had turned out differently.

Caitlin felt indebted to him. But she was loyal to Caleb. Caleb was her husband, and

Scarlet was her daughter. So Caitlin did the loyal thing, and forced herself to look away. She took a deep breath, and turned away, not wanting to look into his eyes anymore, not wanting to think of him. She owed that to Caleb.

She hoped she didn't offend him. But she had to be strong. For them both.

Caitlin could sense Scarlet looking up, back and forth between them, trying to figure it out.

"I can't thank you enough," Caitlin said. But she was not looking into his eyes as she said it. She was looking away, refusing to meet that stare.

"I was looking for you, and I stumbled upon her," Blake said. "I came back in this time searching for you. There is nothing to thank me for. It was a great privilege."

Caitlin kept her distance. She turned and looked through the streets, trying to distract herself, to look at anything else. In the distance, she watched Jesus, riding slowly through the mobs. Some bystanders were cheering at his presence. Others were heckling him. She watched as he got further and further away.

Follow me.

She felt that she needed to go after him, that she couldn't let him disappear. She had to follow him. Wherever it was she needed to go, wherever it was he would lead her, now was the time. She felt a pang of anxiety at the thought of losing him.

"You are right," Blake said, reading her mind. "You must not lose him."

Caitlin blushed at her mind being read.

"You must follow him. Now. Take Scarlet. Don't let him get away. He will lead you to the Shield."

Caitlin blushed, embarrassed her mind was such an open book.

"And what about you?" Caitlin asked. "Where will you go?"

"As much as I would like to stay here, with you," he said, "there is business calling me elsewhere. Urgent business. There is a great disturbance in the universe."

Caitlin looked at him, unnerved to hear someone else say it.

"I can feel it too," she said.

"It is Rexius. And his men. And, I'm sorry to say, your brother, Sam. He is with them now."

Caitlin nodded, sensing it, too. She felt heart well up with shame and remorse at the thought of Sam helping the other side. But she didn't know what to do.

"They are attacking Aiden," Blake said. "Every moment counts."

As Blake said it, she could sense the power of these forces. She sensed that they had unleashed something very powerful, and she did not know what. She sensed it was heading right for Caleb.

"Caleb is with him," Caitlin said, feeling a sudden terror. "I have to join you," Caitlin said. "I can help you. And I can help Caleb."

Blake shook his head.

"No. You must find your father. If you come with us, you'll be just another soldier. That won't help us at all."

As he said it, Caitlin sensed his words were true. But it still hurt to hear them. More than anything, she just wanted to be by Caleb's side.

"I must go," Blake said, sadly.

As he did, Caitlin had a sudden sense this was the last time she would ever see Blake alive again, too. The feeling caused a pain in her heart. She tried to pretend it wasn't there, but deep down, she knew it was.

She looked at him one last time. She saw him staring back at her, and it pained her more than she could say.

"I don't know what to say," Caitlin said.

Blake took a step forward, standing just a few inches away. He reached up and held her cheek in his hand, smiling.

"Don't say anything," he said. "I know that you love Caleb. I'm happy for you. I'm happy for you both. Just do me one favor," he said, looking at her. "Just tell me one thing.... In the past, once, long ago…tell me that, once, you loved me."

Caitlin felt her eyes well up with tears and pain. She wanted more than anything to push thoughts of Blake completely from her mind. But, she had to admit, there had been a time. Once. When she did, indeed, love him. She thought back to Venice, to their magical time together. The costume ball. His dying for her in the Roman Colosseum.

Slowly, her voice trembling, Caitlin began to speak. It was hard to breathe.

"I…there…was a time…once… Yes, once, I loved you."

Blake stared at her for several seconds, then finally nodded. Satisfied.

He lowered his hand from her cheek. He leaned over and kissed her forehead. Then, he reached down and placed something in her palm, and closed it.

Then, without another word, he leapt into the sky.

Caitlin stood there, in shock, her heart in a million pieces as she watched Blake fly away, over the streets of Jerusalem, up higher and higher, towards the Mount of Olives, his wide black wings flapping. She knew, she just *knew*, that she would never see him again. She watched him disappear for far too long, wondering why they'd ever had to meet in the first place.

She looked down and slowly opened her palm, afraid to see what he'd placed inside. Her heart stopped as she saw a small, well-worn piece of sea glass.

And, despite herself, she burst into tears.

CHAPTER TWENTY FIVE

Now Caleb understood. As he stood there, looking up at the blackening skies, now he understood why he and Caitlin were meant to part ways. She wasn't destined to be here. She wasn't destined to witness this slaughter, to die with all of them, here, on this mountain. She had a different destiny.

He, Caleb, was the one destined to die today. In her place.

Caleb felt the old warrior inside rouse itself. He raised his chin proudly, held out his chest, and breathed in, jutting out his jaw, holding his ground. It was the stance of a warrior prepared to meet his death—and to go down with honor.

Caleb reached down and instinctively extracted his sword from his scabbard. It slid out with a metallic noise that echoed in the hills.

All around him, Aiden's coven members did the same.

Except for Aiden. He merely stood there, looking as relaxed as ever as he closed his eyes and merely raised his staff before him. Caleb could sense the energy radiating off of it. He had never fought with Aiden before, not shoulder to shoulder like this, and he wondered what it would be like.

Caleb's heart started beating faster as the black cloud grew thicker. The sound grew louder, incredibly loud, a million vampire wings flapping up above. As they descended, Caleb could see them taking aim, right for him.

As he raised his sword, bracing himself for the attack, he could feel the approaching army, before it even hit, coming at him like a gale force wind. The sound grew louder and louder and the skies blackened, as the entire horde descended.

Caleb looked to his left and right, and saw Aiden's men holding firm, veteran warriors, all holding the line. None of them even flinched.

The army approached. 100 yards…50…20…and Caleb could begin to see their faces. As they got close enough, he was shocked to see who was in front, leading the charge.

There, right in the center, was Kyle.

Caleb could not believe it. He was sure that Kyle was dead, gone forever. He could not understand how he could be here.

And there, beside him, he saw Rynd, another creature he was sure was gone forever. Caleb could not understand how they could be back in existence.

Beside them he recognized vampires from his days in New York, when he was infiltrating the Blacktide coven. Vampires who he knew were gone forever. He could not understand how all of them could be here.

And then, suddenly, it hit him. And the realization struck him deeper than any sword.

At that moment, he realized that all these creatures had been brought back from the other side. Resurrected. And there was only one weapon in the universe that had the power to do that.

The Shield.

The Vampire Shield.

Caleb's heart sank, as his breath was taken from him. They had found the Shield first. They had beaten them to it, and had already used it. These creatures, these thousands of demons, had all been resurrected with the Shield, dragged up from the depths of hell. The shield had fallen into the wrong hands.

That meant they had no chance. No chance at all of survival.

As they got even closer, Caleb looked up and saw Sam—and beside him, Samantha, a face he had not seen in years. As Sam neared, he could see Caitlin's face in him. It was hard for him to see his brother-in-law like this, so transformed, fighting for the other side. But there was nothing he could do. He would have to face off with him.

A moment later, there was impact. There came the awful sound of a million clashing swords and wings, as Sam dove down, a horrible grimace on his face. He raised his sword and aimed right for Caleb.

Caleb stood there proudly and met his sword with his own, blocking it. There was a loud clash, and an instant later, dozens of vampires landed all around him.

Aiden's warriors fought back bravely, blocking and dodging and ducking and slashing back. There was the clang of metal on metal, weapon on weapon, as they all fought expertly. Caleb caught a glance of Aiden: amazingly, he hadn't moved. He stood very still, his staff up before him, eyes closed. It was as if there was an invisible bubble around him, a shield, and everyone who flew towards him bounced back as they got close. He was untouched, standing there in his bubble.

But Caleb didn't have that power. He could feel the strength rippling through Sam's sword slash as he blocked it, the vibration of the metal shaking his entire body. He slashed back—but Sam was too fast: he blocked Caleb's every blow, and immediately slashed back. It was the toughest battle of Caleb's life, and he was being pushed back, with nowhere to go.

Making matters worse, dozens more vampires were landing all around him at every moment, encircling him from all sides. He was soon completely outnumbered.

Caleb fought furiously, swinging in every direction. The chaos helped him a bit, as some vampires, in the confusion, fought against each other.

He rolled away from Sam, not wanting to hurt him, and instead focused on other vampires. Moving with speed and dexterity, he managed to kill several of them. He was gaining momentum, when suddenly he felt himself elbowed hard in the back, right in the kidneys.

He wheeled, and found himself face to face with a hideous, sneaky creature.

Standing there, scowling back, missing one eye, was Kyle.

Before Caleb could react, Kyle raised his battle ax high and brought it down right for Caleb's head.

Caleb dodged at the last second, then reached over swung back, for Kyle's arm. Kyle blocked the blow with a shield, then leaned back and kicked Caleb in the gut, knocking him back.

Kyle came in for another blow with his axe, but Caleb anticipated it; he leapt over it, high in the air, and kicked Kyle in the chest, knocking him back. Now, Caleb had the upper hand.

But dozens more vampires continued to land, swooping down from every side. Caleb was already getting tired, already beginning to see this was a losing battle. He wondered what Aiden was thinking, trying to even face an army with only a few dozen men.

Just when Caleb thought things couldn't get any worse, suddenly, the earth around him shook. As he looked over in astonishment, he saw thousands of graves on the Mount of Olives start to shift; the dirt rose up, and bodies began to emerge from each grave—dark, demon souls, hideous-looking black shadows, with long, sharp fangs. As if the army in the sky weren't bad enough—now, Caleb was surrounded by thousands more evil creatures, from every side.

And that was when he realized that, in the coming minutes, his life would be finished.

CHAPTER TWENTY SIX

Caitlin stood there, watching the sky, wiping her tears, and finally tore herself away. She was jostled in the crowd, and felt a small hand grip hers, and finally snapped out of it.

Scarlet looked up at her with her joyful, innocent eyes.

"Mommy?" she asked.

Caitlin beamed at the site of her, forgetting all her sadness. She bent down and embraced Scarlet, holding her tight, smiling, radiant. And then she remembered: Jesus.

Caitlin took Scarlet's hand, checked to see that Ruth was there, and hurried through the mob, heading after him. They were jostled as they went, and it was an effort just to keep them together. The masses flocked around Jesus, who was far away now, and the crowd was growing thicker and thicker. He was such a polarizing figure, Caitlin could feel the tension in the air, so thick it was palpable. Brawls broke out, as some people wept openly, while others argued with each other. It felt like Jerusalem was on the verge of a revolution.

The Roman soldiers stood back, watching carefully, Pontius Pilate overseeing them. Caitlin saw more and more soldiers filtering in, their ranks swelling as they followed Jesus.

Caitlin had to get closer; she pushed her way through the crowd and narrowed the gap. In the distance he turned down a side street, and she lost sight of him. She elbowed with more force, but the crowd was thick—and growing thicker by the second.

Suddenly, Pontius Pilot gave his soldiers a signal, and they rushed into the crowd, cordoning off the street where Jesus had went. The crowd booed and screamed, trying to follow him, but the soldiers wouldn't let them. The crowd got pushy, and the soldiers started to raise their clubs and beat them back.

A riot ensued. People started fighting, then stampeding toward Caitlin to get away from the soldiers' brutality. Caitlin could tell the situation was about to worsen, and realized that if she didn't do something fast, they'd all be trampled to death.

Caitlin hoisted Scarlet onto her back, grabbed Ruth with her free hand, and leapt up into the air. Her wings caught, and soon she was flying, up above the crowd. She made it just in time, right before the stampede. She didn't like to fly so conspicuously in front of humans who she knew would spot her. But she had no choice.

They spotted her indeed—and the effect was electrifying. Caitlin heard the shocked cries and looked down to see hundreds of crowd members stopping and turning, pointing up at her.

"Witch!"

"Heretic!"

"Demon!"

Several people grabbed rocks and hurled them up towards Caitlin.

But Caitlin flew higher just in time, and the rocks sailed by, missing. In moments, she was higher, and higher, far away from them, over Jerusalem. She kept flying, and soon she was over the barricade set by the Roman soldiers.

She gained speed, and within moments was able to spot Jesus and his apostles, down below, on a quiet side street. They had just finished ascending a small hill, and were entering a large, Roman house.

Caitlin dove down, landing out of sight, then hurried to catch up to the last of the apostles, just before he entered the house.

As she ran up to him, he turned and faced her. Caitlin braced herself, assuming he'd tell her to go away; but to her surprise, he smiled.

"We were hoping you would come," he said, looking at Caitlin, then down at Scarlet and Ruth. "Will you join us?"

Caitlin nodded, relieved.

"It is the Passover meal," he said. "It is our last supper before the holiday begins."

He stepped to the side, and motioned for Caitlin to enter.

The Last Supper. The words rang through Caitlin's head. She could hardly believe it. Here she was, with Jesus and his apostles, on Passover evening, during the Last Supper—the night before he was crucified. The night he was betrayed by Judas. She could hardly believe it. She was right in the middle of history. Could she somehow change it?

Caitlin entered the small house, holding Scarlet's hand, Ruth beside her, and followed the apostle down a corridor. They passed a small, open-air courtyard in the middle of the house, framed by columns and arches, with immaculate gardens and olive trees. They continued down another corridor and up a flight of stairs, and she saw the apostles clustering around a door.

The energy was palpable. There was excitement, preparation for the holiday and for the meal. They filed into the room one by one, and she followed on their heels.

As Caitlin entered the room, it took her breath away. There, spread out before her, was a long, wide table. The apostles were taking their seats, all alongside it. And there, sitting in the center, was Jesus. He sat with his eyes closed, palms out, as if meditating.

As she entered the room, he opened his eyes and gazed right at her. She could feel the intense energy radiating off of him; it was unlike anything she had ever experienced. It was like the sun, trapped in a room.

"I am glad you have come," he said to her.

Once again, Caitlin found herself unable to respond. She was overwhelmed in his presence.

The apostle gestured towards empty seats not too far from Jesus, and Caitlin and Scarlet took their seats. Caitlin could see the wonder on Scarlet's face, and wanted to explain it all to her. But she hardly knew what to say.

Caitlin saw a man sitting to Jesus' side, and recognized him from paintings. Judas. The one who would betray him.

Caitlin felt an urge to jump up, to warn Jesus, to tell him that his time was limited, that this was his last supper; that they were coming for him; that tomorrow they would crucify him; that he should beware of Judas.

But she didn't want to cross a line, and she didn't know if it was her place to do so. She felt she was caught up in the hands of history, and that it wasn't her role to try to change it. And she didn't know if she could change it if she tried. After all, could Jesus really *not* be crucified? How would that affect history?

So instead, Caitlin sat there, trying to be in the moment, to experience this. For whatever reason, she had been led to him, and she tried to understand why. She just wanted to see her Dad, and she tried to imagine how and when Jesus would lead her to him.

Small foods and delicacies were passed along the table, and some were placed before Caitlin and Scarlet. On her plate was placed a round, flat cracker. Unleavened bread.

Each person was then handed a large, bejeweled goblet. Caitlin took hers, as did Scarlet. It was heavy, made of solid gold.

As soon as she held it, Caitlin could sense what was inside. Every pore of her body screamed out for it.

It was blood. The finest, purest, white blood she had ever seen.

Each apostle raised a glass. They held their glasses in mid-air for several seconds, as if praying silently. Caitlin followed suit. And then, each of them drank.

Caitlin sipped it, and as she did, she immediately felt the blood rush through her veins, feeling instantly restored, rejuvenated. It was the finest blood she'd ever drank. She looked over and saw Scarlet drink, too, and was relieved to see the color returning to her cheeks.

One of the apostles handed Ruth a large slab of raw meat, and Caitlin was relieved to see

Ruth eat, too. Finally, she felt at ease. She wished that Caleb could be here to share this with them.

Everyone set down their goblets, as Jesus cleared his throat. It was clear that all the disciples were patiently awaiting his teachings.

But as he spoke, it was Caitlin who he turned to, who he looked at. She felt nervous.

"When you are brought before rulers and authorities," he said, "do not worry about how you will defend yourselves or what you will say."

Caitlin flushed, embarrassed; it was as if he had read her mind. Yet at the same time, she found peace in his words. He was talking to all of his disciples, but she felt as if he were talking directly to her. She looked around the room and saw his disciples taking in every word, eager to hear more.

He half-closed his eyes, and seemed to enter back into a meditative state. Caitlin felt so peaceful around him; yet, on the other hand, she couldn't stop worrying. She worried about finding her Dad in time; she worried about what would become of Caleb, and Blake, and Aiden; she worried about not returning fast enough. She tried to find peace, as all the other apostles seemed to, yet she couldn't stop her mind from racing.

Jesus spoke again:

"Who of you by worrying can add a single hour to her life?"

His eyes were closed when he said it, but still, Caitlin felt as if he were speaking right to her. His words brought her a sense of peace: he was right. Worrying would change nothing.

A thick silence pervaded the room, and Caitlin sat there, wondering what it all meant. When would he lead her to her Dad? She felt as if she were closer to her Dad now than ever—there were no more keys to find, no more clues to uncover. All she had to do was follow Jesus. It seemed easy enough. Yet, at the same time, it also felt so vague. She wished there was something more concrete she could do.

She looked around the room, wondering if maybe one of these apostles could be her Dad.

She was burning with a desire to speak up, to ask Jesus questions about him, about what she was doing here, about what she should do next. She felt so overwhelmed, she could barely contain herself. But she felt it would be disrespectful, somehow, to speak up at this table.

Suddenly, Judas leaned over and whispered something in Jesus' ear. Jesus slowly stood, and all the other apostles stood, too, out of respect. Caitlin did, too.

Jesus slowly exited the table, followed closely by Judas.

As Caitlin watched them go, she wondered what Judas had whispered into his ear. It sent a chill through her: she knew that Judas was betraying him somehow. And she wanted to stop it.

Caitlin knew it was not her place to get in the way of history—but still, she was burning up inside. She couldn't just sit there and watch this happen.

So, despite herself, she jumped up, ran around the table, and stood before Jesus and Judas, right before they exited the room. She blocked their path, and they both looked at her.

"I…uh…" Caitlin began, at a loss for words. "Please. Please don't go," she said.

She felt protective of him. She couldn't stand to let this happen.

Jesus reached out and placed a palm on her shoulder. As he did, she felt a tremendous heat rush through her shoulder and body. It was a healing power, electrifying.

"Forgive them," he said softly, "for they know not what they do."

Caitlin felt tears welling up. It was all too much for her to bear. Here she was, so close to finding her Dad; to fulfilling her mission; to finding whatever it was she needed to help her husband. And Aiden.

And yet, she was helpless. All she needed to do was follow Jesus—and yet, she knew that

Judas was leading him to be betrayed. And that she might not ever see him again.

She wanted to stop all this. To prevent them from leaving. To stay by Jesus' side. To protect him.

And yet she knew from his words that that was not what was meant to be. What was meant was for her to step aside and let them pass.

So she did.

Caitlin stepped to the side, and Jesus walked past her, followed by Judas, who scowled down at her.

And moments later, they were gone.

Caitlin turned back to the others and did as she was supposed to, taking her seat again at the table.

"Mommy?" Scarlet asked. "Is everything OK?"

Caitlin wiped away tears as she sat there, her heart pounding, waiting for them to return. She tried to put it out of her mind. She tried to be patient. She tried to have faith that everything would be okay.

But after several minutes of waiting, of knowing her destiny might be slipping out from under her, of knowing her husband was out there, in danger, she couldn't take it anymore. She no longer cared if she got in the way of destiny. She felt she had to take action.

Caitlin jumped up from the table, grabbed Scarlet's hand, and bolted from the room—determined to save him.

*

Caitlin ran from the room, leaving the last supper, ran down the corridor, clutching Scarlet's hand, Ruth following, and ran down the flight of stairs. She ran past the courtyard, down another corridor, then finally burst out the rear door. She knew from history that Jesus had been betrayed in the Garden of Gethsemane, and she knew that the garden adjoined the house of the last supper. As she burst out the back of the house, she prayed this was the right place.

It was. There Jesus stood, alone with Judas, in a small, ancient garden in the rear of the house, filled with olive trees. Behind them, the sky was filled with the most dramatic, blood-red sunset Caitlin had ever seen.

Caitlin stood there, gasping for air, and the two of them turned and looked at her.

Judas's face suddenly filled with apprehension at the sight of her, and he quickly turned and hurried out of the garden, slithering through a side entrance.

Now Jesus stood there, all alone. Caitlin could feel that his time was limited, and despite herself, she started to cry.

"Mommy, what's wrong?" Scarlet asked, also out of breath. Beside her, Ruth whined.

But Caitlin couldn't even respond. She didn't know what to say. She didn't know if she was too late.

Jesus turned to her.

She had so many questions she was burning to ask. But she found herself completely tongue-tied.

Jesus took a step closer to her, and spoke:

"Only be careful, and watch yourself closely so that you do not forget the things your eyes have seen or let them slip from your heart as long as you live. Teach them to your children and to their children after them."

Caitlin tried to understand what he meant. Was he referring to Scarlet? What did she need to teach her? And how did that relate to her father?

Jesus was about to speak again, and Caitlin sensed that he was on the verge of revealing to her something momentous. Something that would make her whole life make sense. Something about her father.

But before he could speak, the whole world changed.

Scarlet turned and pointed up at the sky.

"Mommy, look!"

Caitlin looked up and saw the sky blacken. Thousands of vampires suddenly descended, flying right towards them.

At the same moment, the doors to the garden burst open, and in rushed Judas, followed by dozens of Roman soldiers. They charged right for Jesus, just as the vampires dove down.

It all happened so fast, there was hardly time to react.

They grabbed Jesus, who did not resist, and Caitlin began to run to help him.

But before she could reach him, at that moment, a lone vampire she did not see suddenly dove down, right for her. She turned at the last second, and prepared to defend herself.

She raised her fists, ready to knock him down.

But then, at the last second, she saw his face. It was a face she knew. A face she loved.

And she lowered her defenses.

There, flying right at her, was her brother. Sam.

Caitlin stood there, shocked, horrified.

"Sam?" she asked.

She stood there, her guard lowered, expecting him to embrace her, to rescue her.

But to her amazement, the last thing she saw, before her world went black, was Sam raising his fist, and bringing it down, right for her face.

CHAPTER TWENTY SEVEN

Caleb could not believe what he was seeing: all around him, the graves were rising on the Mount of Olives. He remembered the prophecy for the end of days—that the first to resurrect would be those buried on the Mount of Olives—and knew the prophecy was coming true.

That meant that the end of days was at hand. Right here. Right now.

The thought struck him like a lightning bolt. The apocalypse. It was really happening. Something horrific had been unleashed, and the dark side had gotten to it first. His sense of dread deepened: now, his death seemed inevitable.

Caleb turned back to the battle at hand and fought furiously, blocking Kyle's battle axe just in time. He leaned back and kicked Kyle hard, right in the chest, sending him flying backwards.

Another sword came slashing down for his head, and Caleb blocked it with his sword, then spun around and kicked his assailant hard in the gut, knocking him down. It was Rynd. Kyle's old accomplice.

Caleb was at the peak of his strength, fighting well, faster than ever. But he also knew he was badly outnumbered, and could only hold them off for so long. He hoped that Caitlin would come back, and bring her Dad with her.

Suddenly, Caleb noticed a lone figure, diving down from the sky, right to him. At first, he braced himself for an attack—but then sensed a friendly energy. His heart leapt, as he thought it might be Caitlin.

The figure swooped down, right before Caleb, sword outstretched, and blocked the below that was about to strike him.

Caleb couldn't believe it. It was his old rival for Caitlin's love: Blake.

Blake had just saved Caleb from a life-threatening below, and Caleb was more grateful than he could say. Caleb felt re-energized at this presence, and he used this opportunity to leap over Blake's head and kick another vampire hard in the chest with both feet, just before the vampire struck Blake. Blake had his back, and now Caleb had his.

But the graves were still resurrecting, and the first of the shadow creatures charged right for Caleb. One of these shadows grabbed him from behind, and his touch sent a chill through Caleb, and deepened his sense of dread. The shadow was so cold and slimy, like a demon from hell.

Caleb threw his arms back and managed to throw it off, sending it flying and knocking into several others. But still more came.

Aiden swung his staff, and Caleb was shocked to see the staff stretch out before him, grow before his eyes. It grew to fifty feet, then a hundred. As it did, Aiden swung it around in a wide circle.

It had a tremendous effect. Aiden managed to knock down every creature that came within a hundred feet of him, establishing a wide perimeter. He killed a hundred creatures in a single blow.

With Blake here, and Aiden's staff, the momentum was beginning to turn. Caleb felt as if they might stand a chance, especially as he spotted Aiden's coven members: these soldiers, dressed in their white robes, each wielded a sword and a staff of his own, and each swung them in slow but deliberate ways. They were channeling some sort of energy Caleb was not aware of, and as they spun their staffs, they each managed to knock out twenty vampires in a single blow. Clearly, Aiden's men were infused with a special power, a high state of training that Caleb had never seen.

Caleb lunged forward, transformed in his fury and newfound confidence, and killed a dozen vampires in a few seconds. Blake did the same. Within moments, Caleb and Blake were fighting back to back, each guarding the other. And they were succeeding. The tide was turning.

"Caleb," came a voice.

Caleb immediately spun. It was a voice he would recognize anywhere, and it sent an electric shock through his system. But it couldn't be. How could she be here?

"Help me, please!"

As he turned, Caleb was astounded to see who was standing there. Just a few feet away, right before him, stood Caitlin. She stood there, fighting off hordes of vampires, and they were beating her. He couldn't understand how she could be here, how she could have appeared so quickly; maybe she had dove down, and in the chaos, he had missed her.

He didn't have time to think about that. His first impulse was to save her, and he leapt into action, striking back the vampires attacking her. In moments, he managed to kill a dozen of them, and the others kept a wary distance.

Caleb quickly turned and looked at her. She stood there, looking so helpless, so afraid—and so beautiful. It was the Caitlin he knew. And he felt overjoyed to see her.

Yet at the same time, something bristled inside him; something deep down told him that something wasn't right, though he wasn't quite sure what.

He was so overjoyed to see her, he brushed his premonitions aside as he stepped forward to embrace her. She had been good to her word. She had come back.

"I came back for you," Caitlin said. "I couldn't stay away. I had to come and help you."

She stepped forward, lowering her sword to her side.

"Won't you give your wife a hug?" she asked.

Caleb stepped forward, took three big steps, opened his arms wide, and came in to hug her.

But as he got closer and closer, his body became cold, as something inside him screamed that something wasn't right. He didn't understand it. And by the time he realized, it was too late.

Caleb took one more, fatal, step towards Caitlin.

At the last moment, Caitlin's face collapsed into a scowl, as she pulled back her short silver sword, and plunged it right through Caleb's heart. She embraced him with one arm, holding the sword with the other, hugging him, driving it all the way through.

Caleb felt the breath rush out of him. The pain was so intense, so startling, his eyes opened wide, and he could hardly breathe.

Even worse, was the pain of betrayal. He had been stabbed in the heart by the one he loved the most, by the person he loved more than anything in the world.

Caleb looked up, into Caitlin's eyes, wondering how she could do such a thing.

"I told you I would have vengeance," she said, looking down at him.

Caleb didn't understand what she was saying. His whole world was going light, blurry, as he felt all the sensation leaving his body. He felt himself growing lighter and lighter, outside of himself as he watched his own body slump to the floor.

In his final seconds, lying on the ground, Caleb looked over at the battleground before him. It came to him in flashes. He saw Blake standing there, looking over, amazed, and then saw Rynd grab Blake from behind, while Kyle stepped forward and brought down his axe, killing him.

He saw Kyle take a long, silver spear, one he had never seen before, and charge, right towards Aiden. Somehow, he penetrated the shield, and the spear struck Aiden, right through the heart. He watched as Aiden slumped to the ground, lifeless.

He saw more and more graves open up, and Aiden's remaining warriors swamped by vampires and shadow creatures in every direction, getting killed left and right.

And then, finally, he looked up, one last time, back at Caitlin.

At that moment, her face changed: it became the face of his ex-wife. Sera. Scowling down, triumphant.

"I learned the shape-shifting trick from Sam," she said with a sneer.

But Caleb was too delirious. He did not see her face transform, did not hear her last words. In his last moments, he left the earth still thinking that it was Caitlin, his wife, his one and only love, who had betrayed him.

CHAPTER TWENTY EIGHT

Caitlin slowly opened her eyes, in excruciating pain. As the light hit her eyes, it felt like knives entering her forehead. She had to squint—even though it was dim in here, lit only by torches.

She felt aches and pains all over her body and as she tried to move, she realized she was chained. She looked over and saw chains binding her hands and feet to a wall. She was standing upright, arms and legs outstretched, chained, her back against a cold stone wall, the cold metal digging into her wrists and ankles. She struggled against her shackles, and realized they were silver.

She felt a huge welt forming on her cheek, and realized that was the spot where Sam must have hit her. The thought of that hurt her more than the lump. Sam. Her own brother. She could hardly conceive it. Had he so thoroughly turned to the dark side that he would attack even her?

Apparently, he had. And that hurt her more than she could contemplate. Sam, she realized, was no longer her brother. Their relationship was over. He was a stranger to her now. Worse:

he was an adversary. That thought made her feel more alone in the universe than ever.

She flashed back, trying to remember the chain of events. She remembered the last supper. Judas, leaving for the garden…Jesus…the sky darkening….Sam. Immediately, she thought of Scarlet. She forced herself to open her eyes all the way, to look about the room.

It was a huge, cavernous room, all stone, dark, lit only by torches. It was airless in here, and the only sound was the soft moans of other prisoners. She scanned the walls and saw several others, vampires and humans, chained, too. They were crying out in pain, tugging at their shackles. Caitlin knew how they felt: the tug of her chains was unbearable, and she wondered how long she'd been chained here like this.

She continued scanning the room, her heart pounding, desperate for any glimpse of Scarlet. And then, to her great relief, she saw her. She was chained to the wall, across the room. Her heart flooded with both relief and panic. Seeing Scarlet like that, chained, hurt her even more than her own captivity. Caitlin tugged again at her shackles, trying to break free and help her, but to no avail. Beside her, on the ground, muzzled and chained to the floor, was Ruth.

At least Scarlet was here. With her. Alive.

"Scarlet," Caitlin whispered, urgently.

Scarlet did not open her eyes, and Caitlin's heart sank. *Was she dead?* Caitlin wondered with a sudden panic.

"Scarlet!" Caitlin said, more forcefully.

Slowly, Scarlet's eyes fluttered, then began to open. She looked drugged. Or exhausted. Or sick. Caitlin wondered how long they had been here.

Caitlin's first impulse as a mom was to rush to Scarlet and give her a hug, to help her, to unchain her. But she tugged again at her chains, and cursed the fact that they were silver, and that her strength was useless against them.

Caitlin could sense that something terrible happened in the universe to make events get this far. To allow Jesus to be captured. To allow Sam to track her down, to hurt her like this. She had a sinking feeling that such chaos could only mean one thing: Aiden and his men had been defeated. And the dark side now had free reign.

And the only way that could have happened was if they'd found some sort of secret weapon.

Caitlin's heart stopped at the next thought: had they beaten her to the Shield?

Caitlin knew they had to get out of there fast. She had to find Caleb, to see if he was alive. She had to assess how bad the situation was. And she had to find Jesus, before they killed him. After all, he was her guide, the only person left who could lead her to her father. And in hours, he would be dead. Crucified.

This was her last chance.

As Caitlin tugged at the chains again, to no avail, she suddenly heard a noise, high up in the ceiling. She looked up, and as she watched, a barrel was lowered over the head of one of the captive vampires on the far side of the room. She watched as it slowly turned, showering liquid.

Caitlin watched, horrified, as the liquid poured through the air and landed a directly on the chained vampire's head. As it did, the vampire shrieked, in awful agony. Her shrieks filled the room.

Smoke rose up from her body, as there was a horrific hissing noise. Caitlin sensed right away what was in that barrel: ioric acid. She hadn't seen that since her time in New York. This, she knew, was Rexius' work: his favorite device of torture.

"Don't watch!" Caitlin screamed to Scarlet.

But Scarlet was watching, horrified, eyes wide open, and there was nothing Caitlin could do about it.

Caitlin watched as the acid ate away at the vampire. The vampire shrieked and shrieked, and after a long and agonizing torture, half of her face and body eroded. Yet somehow, she was still alive, stuck in a vegetative state, in indescribable agony.

Suddenly there was another noise, and another barrel was slowly lowered from the ceiling. This one was heading for the vampire next to her.

Caitlin could see that, one by one, each prisoner in this room was going to be tortured by the acid. And as the next barrel overturned and the shrieks of another vampire rang out, Caitlin realized she would be next.

And then, Scarlet.

"Mommy! Help us! Please! Do something!" Scarlet screamed.

Caitlin was frantic. She didn't know what to do.

And then she remembered: her training, her final training, with Aiden. She closed her eyes, forcing herself to concentrate. She focused on her new skill, the final skill Aiden had taught her. The ability to change any element. To change silver to metal.

Caitlin forced herself to relax. To center herself. To summon her ancient power.

Slowly, she felt an energy rising through her, felt her body warming, from her toes up through her legs, through her torso, and through her hands. She focused on the shape of the silver shackles, focused on their composition. And slowly, she willed them to change.

Suddenly, Caitlin felt the shackles around her wrists start to change. They were still there, but before her eyes, she saw the color change from silver to a dark iron. And just as a new barrel was being lowered and aimed towards her head, Caitlin realized she had done it: she had changed silver to metal. Now, they were ordinary shackles. Now, she could break free.

Without a second to lose, Caitlin snapped off her iron shackles. She shattered them one at a time, first each wrist, then each ankle. Finally free, she lunged forward.

Just in time. A split second later, the acid poured down, landing on the spot she had just been.

Caitlin sprinted across the room for Scarlet. As she went, she focused on Scarlet's silver shackles and willed the shape to change. By the time she reached Scarlet, she sensed that they had, and she reached out and tore off the shackles without hesitating. She then reached down and tore off Ruth's chains and muzzle.

Caitlin took Scarlet's hand and pulled her out of the way—a second before the acid fell.

The three of them sprinted across the room, and Caitlin saw the silver door up ahead, and changed the shape without even slowing. As they reached it she kicked it down and the three of them charged out of the cell.

They burst out into daylight, in a remote countryside, at the top of a mountain.

"Grab on!" Caitlin yelled.

Scarlet jumped onto her back while Caitlin grabbed Ruth and leapt into the air.

A moment later they were flying, soaring, getting farther and farther away from the place.

Caitlin looked over her shoulder, and saw that they had just flown out of an ancient, pagan temple. It looked like the Parthenon in Rome, but smaller, carved with demonic figures and statues in every direction.

Caitlin could see that their escape had caused a stir: dozens of vampires, dressed in all black—Rexius' people—scrambled on the hillside. They were blowing trumpets, sounding alarms, and moments later, dozens of them were up in the air, chasing after Caitlin. She knew that Rexius would summon all of his people after her.

But she didn't care. They had escaped. They were free.

Caitlin knew she should search for Jesus now, should continue her search for her Dad. But she couldn't stand to be away from Caleb for one more second. She had to see him first. Nothing in the world would stop her from finding her husband—and from doing everything in her power to make sure they were never apart again.

CHAPTER TWENTY NINE

Caitlin raced through the air towards the Mount of Olives. She managed to put a good distance between herself and her pursuers, and wasn't worried about them.

What she was worried about was what she might find. She had a pit in her chest, a deepening sense of dread she could not shake, that something terrible had happened, that all the people she loved in the world were gone. She felt as if she were already an orphan in the universe.

She thought back to Jesus' words, and willed herself to be calm.

Who of you by worrying can add a single hour to her life?

Caitlin flew across the arid landscape of Israel, watching Jerusalem and the never-ending palm trees beneath her. She was drawn to this city, yet found herself hating it at the same time. This place was too intense for her, and she associated it with everything that had gone wrong in her life. She just wanted to get away—far, far away, with Caleb and Scarlet. Alone. Just the three of them. To a place where they could live out their lives in peace. Where battles and clues and relics were a thing of the past.

But she was afraid that wasn't meant to be. She had a mission, a destiny, and she still hadn't fulfilled it—and still didn't know what it was. She knew she had to find her Dad, and knew that somehow Jesus would lead her to him. She knew, in her heart, she should go down below, and search for Jesus now. Right away. That he was her last salvation, her last hope to save the others.

But she just could not bring herself to. Every bone in her body led her to Caleb. She *had* to see him first. She had to see if he was in danger, and do whatever she could to save him.

As she rounded a peak, the Mount of Olives spread out before her. She saw the endless rows of olive trees, up and down the mountain, and on the far slope, the rows of graves.

Except now, something was different: the graves were opened. She saw thousands of patches of freshly opened dirt, and she could sense, even from here, that something was terribly wrong. It looked as if the earth had opened up and spit out thousands of corpses.

Already, even from here, she sensed a profound shift in the universe. She felt a terrible sadness, and sensed that below her had been a battlefield, that an epic battle had been waged here, and that thousands had died. She could already feel the tragedy. And she could already feel her remorse for missing it. She had abandoned her loved ones while they had fought; she had spent all that time searching for her Dad while she could have been here, helping them.

Caitlin dove lower, almost afraid to look; she felt the small hands clutching her tightly, and felt Scarlet tensing up, too. She assumed that Scarlet, as sensitive as she was, could sense it, too. After all, her Dad was down there.

Caitlin dove down sharply, between the rows of olive trees, heading for Aiden's villa. As she got closer, she spotted hundreds of corpses spread out, lying lifeless on the hills below. Vampires. Rexius' men. Slaughtered.

But as she dove closer, she could also see something else: corpses with white hoods and robes. Aiden's people. Before she even landed, Caitlin already sensed that the worst possible outcome had occurred: Aiden's coven had been wiped out.

She landed, and as she did she turned, surveying the mountainside, and could hardly believe what she was seeing. The site of devastation took her breath away.

And then she saw something else, something that left her speechless.

There, lying flat on his back, staff by his side, was Aiden, covered in blood, scarlet staining his robe. His eyes were open, staring up at the sky.

Caitlin walked over slowly, not comprehending what she was seeing. How was it possible? Aiden? Her mentor? Her guide? The man she had thought was her father? The man she knew to be invincible? Dead?

But there he was. Still. Lifeless.

Caitlin was struck by a terrible thought: if Aiden was dead, what hope was there for the rest of them?

She was afraid to look anywhere else, not wanting to see who else might be laying there. So instead she walked over to Aiden's side. She knelt down, and could see he was not breathing. He was stiff, and clearly he had been this way for a while. Beside her Scarlet was crying, and Ruth whining.

"Don't look," she said softly to Scarlet.

Caitlin reached out and gently lay her fingers on Aiden's eyelids. She closed them and left her hand there, resting on his forehead. She was sending him whatever love she could, in whatever form he was.

She flashed back, remembered the first time she had met him, on Pollepel. Whether he was her true father or not, he had been a father to her. The closest thing to a father she'd ever had. She felt indescribable gratitude for that. And seeing him here, like this, tore her heart in two.

Caitlin quickly got up, and turned Scarlet away.

"Don't look, sweetheart," she said again.

Ruth ran over and licked his face several times, and Caitlin forced herself to turn away.

Caitlin surveyed all the corpses—thousands of them—and could not comprehend the scale of disaster that must have taken place. There must have, she realized, been a powerful weapon, something she didn't know about, to enable them to do this kind of damage. But what?

Caitlin slowly scanned the bodies, walking forward; she was looking for any sign of Caleb, but at the same time, prayed she would see none. Maybe he had escaped? She hoped. But deep down, a part of her sensed that was not the case. Already, she could feel her heart beginning to break.

Caitlin rounded a corner, and as she did, she stopped.

There, lying lifeless, his back to her, was a body she sensed she knew. He lay on its side, and she couldn't tell who it was. Slowly, she walked towards him.

"Look away, sweetheart," Caitlin said, and Scarlet turned.

Caitlin took the final few steps, knelt down, grabbed his shoulder, and pulled him to his back.

There, lying lifeless, eyes open wide to the sky, was Blake.

Caitlin felt as if a small dagger had been thrust into her heart. Blake. Dead. And, she could see, for good this time, struck by a silver axe. Already, Caitlin sensed whose work this was.

Kyle.

But how was that possible? Was Kyle resurrected? How?

Caitlin immediately rose, forcing herself to look away. She couldn't take it; it was too painful. Aiden dead. Blake dead….

That left only one person.

Caitlin hurried through the battlefield, tripping over bodies, scanning desperately, looking for any sign of her husband. Her beloved. Her one and only true love in life. She scanned each corpse, frantic.

"Caleb!" she screamed.

As she ran, she could already feel the tears pouring down her cheeks. Somehow, she knew. She just knew.

"CALEB!" she shrieked to the sky.

High up, a vulture echoed it.

She didn't even see him, yet already she knew she would. It was too much for her to bear.

Still, she had to know. She had to see. Maybe, some tiny part of her still hoped, maybe, just maybe, he was still alive. Maybe, somehow, he had survived. Or fled. Or maybe she would round the corner and find him alive, and she could take him, and they could leave, go far, far from here. Give up the search for her Dad. Start their lives over, somewhere far away from all this. Maybe they could close their eyes, and this would all just be one long, horrible dream.

But as Caitlin rounded the corner, she saw that it was just not meant to be.

There, lying among the field of corpses, flat on his back, eyes wide open and staring at the sky, was her husband.

Caleb.

Dead.

Caitlin felt all the wind knocked out of her. She dropped to her knees, in shock.

At that moment, everything she had ever wanted, everything she had ever hoped for in the world disappeared. She sank to her knees, in the dirt, far from him, already suffering, holding her head in her hands. She couldn't bear to get any closer.

She leaned out and let out a terrible wail.

Finally, Caitlin forced herself to her feet. She walked closer and closer to his corpse, each step feeling like the weight of the world, feeling as if she were walking through quicksand.

She reached his side and collapsed on top of him, holding him, hugging him. She sobbed and sobbed and sobbed and cries racked her body, as her wails reached up to the sky. It was so unfair. After all they had been through, all the centuries, all the times, all the places. After the deep love they had for each other. His proposal. Their wedding. Their child. After her going back in time, just for him. After everything, *everything* they'd been through. Now. Of all times. For this to happen. When they were so close. When she was just a hair's breadth away from finding her Dad. From finding the shield. From having all this be over, forever.

Caleb dead. And she and Scarlet completely alone in the world.

Caitlin knelt there, rocking him, holding him dearly, wishing her life would be over.

"Daddy?" came a hesitant voice.

At the sound of that voice, Caitlin's pain deepened.

Scarlet appeared, sobbing, and knelt down beside Caleb and hugged him, too. Hearing her cries was even more painful for Caitlin than anything else. She wished she could shield her from this.

"Daddy!" Scarlet screamed again and again, shaking him.

Caitlin wanted to comfort her. But she did not know how. She was too grief-stricken herself to know what to do.

"Do something mommy!" Scarlet screamed. "Do something! Bring him back. You have to! You HAVE to!"

But Caitlin merely shook her head. She did not know what to do. Caleb, her husband, was dead. Really dead. She sensed that his soul had left, that he was no longer on this earth. And there was no Aiden this time, hovering over her shoulder, telling her what to do. There was no one left.

"I'm so sorry, sweetheart," Caitlin said, feeling guilty, feeling like a failure, even as she said it, "there's nothing I can do."

Somehow, Caitlin felt as if it were all her fault. If only she had found her Dad sooner. If only she had found the shield. She felt as if she had let them all down.

"There is one thing you can do," suddenly came a deep, dark voice from behind her.

Caitlin did not need to turn to know whose voice that was. It was a voice that she had known, that had plagued her, for centuries.

Kyle.

Caitlin slowly rose and turned and faced him, feeling her grief quickly morph into rage.

"You can go to hell," Kyle continued, with a wide grin. "With your husband. And I can send you there."

Caitlin saw Kyle standing there, Rynd beside him, and behind them, Rexius' army. They were all facing her.

This time, Caitlin was ready. Her time for running was over. Now, she had nothing left to live for.

Now, she wanted vengeance.

CHAPTER THIRTY

Caitlin faced off against Kyle, Rynd, Rexius, and his legion of vampires. As she stood there, she could feel the rage slowly overcome her. She hadn't felt rage like this in she didn't know how long. It was a deep, primal rage, and it overcame her like a storm. It was the rage of a creature with nothing left to live for. It was the most powerful thing she'd ever felt.

Caitlin wanted vengeance. She *needed* vengeance. For Caleb. For Aiden. For Blake. For herself. Every ounce of her body geared up to fight this army. Her entire world turned red, and she knew that she needed to kill every last one of them.

Caitlin leaned back and roared, the roar of a thousand dragons. The ground beneath her trembled, as her battle cry reached up to the very heavens.

As the ground shook, she saw fear on the faces of Kyle and Rynd. They must have sensed that they were up against a changed person, against a person unlike any they had ever faced. This was the new Caitlin. The Caitlin who had completed her training. The Caitlin who had everything she cared for taken from her, and nothing left to lose.

Caitlin burst into action. With the speed of lightning, she leapt twenty feet in the air and kicked Kyle with both feet in the chest, so fast and so hard, he didn't even have time to react. He went flying, like a cannonball, right into the army of vampires behind him, knocking down dozens of them.

Before her feet had even touched the ground, Caitlin was already in motion, wheeling around and elbowing Rynd hard, right across the face. She heard the crack of his jaw breaking as he spun and dropped to the floor. Caitlin wound up and kicked him. The kick was so powerful, it sent him flying through the air, into the legion of vampires and knocked over dozens more, like a bowling ball striking pins.

Caitlin turned and leapt at Rexius. He was faster than the others, and as she brought her fist down for his face, he reached up and blocked it. But she immediately brought her other fist across, punching him, then leaned back and kicked him so hard in the gut, he went flying into the rows of vampires, knocking down dozens more.

Caitlin sensed an ominous presence behind her, and turned. There, staring back defiantly, was Samantha. She was shocked to see her, this girl who'd ruined her brother. And she was even more shocked to see Samantha holding Scarlet in a chokehold.

"Make one move, and I kill the girl," Samantha threatened.

Caitlin looked down, and watched as Scarlet's face transformed into one of rage. For the first time she saw the vampire instinct take over her daughter, watch her become a creature, like herself, a fearless warrior.

Before Samantha could react, Scarlet reached down, grabbed Samantha's wrist and snapped it back. To Caitlin's surprise, Scarlet exhibited the strength of a full-blown vampire. With just a quick move of her wrist, Scarlet twisted Samantha's arm all the way behind her, bringing her to her knees and breaking her arm. Samantha screamed out in pain—but Scarlet didn't hesitate. She picked her up and threw her, right into the army of vampires, knocking over several of them herself.

A vampire leapt out of the crowd from behind Scarlet, aiming right for her—but before he could reach her Ruth leapt into the air and sank her teeth into his throat, pinning him to the ground, dead.

Dozens of vampires charged Caitlin. She instinctively positioned herself between Scarlet and the army, and as the vampires charged, she fought them all. She kicked and punched and elbowed and leapt and spun—and was a one-person wrecking machine. She took down dozens at a time, smashing them into each other, incapacitating each one with deadly, accurate strikes. They dropped all around her like flies.

And still, they kept coming.

Caitlin grabbed a long staff off the ground—the one that had belonged to Aiden—and let out an unearthly shriek as she swung it. She swung in huge circles, and within moments knocked down dozens more. Soon the perimeter widened, as she knocked down row after row of vampires. Dozens dropped in a single blow, and she kept swinging, until hundreds were knocked out within minutes.

Caitlin managed to establish a wide perimeter around her of at least a hundred feet—and none of the vampires seemed to want to enter it. They were afraid. She could see them standing there, breathing hard, snarling, fangs extended—afraid to get any closer. Even Kyle, Rynd and Rexius stood at the perimeter, afraid to approach. She was a one-man army—and she was winning.

Suddenly, a lone vampire descended from the sky and swooped in, landing right before Caitlin. At first, Caitlin was surprised to see a single vampire brave enough to approach her in one-on-one combat.

And then, she saw who it was. And she was amazed.

It was her brother.

Sam.

He snarled at her as he landed, and this time, she snarled right back. She had no brotherly love left for him. Not after all he had done. They were adversaries now. Two children of the same father—pitted against each other. Caitlin had no love left for him, and clearly, he had none left for her. She could still feel the welt on her face, from where he had struck her. Finally, she was ready to fight him.

Sam suddenly attacked. He leapt into the air to kick her in the chest. At the last second, Caitlin sidestepped it, and at the same time, managed to elbow Sam hard in the face.

Sam landed flat on his back—hard. He looked stunned. Clearly he hadn't expected that.

He leapt to his feet, turned and charged again, going to tackle her.

But Caitlin was faster: she sidestepped again, grabbed him by his back and threw him, letting his momentum carry him. He went flying through the air and landed face-first in the dirt.

Sam jumped up and spun around, staring at her in surprise. He was humiliated, enraged.

In one quick move, he reached back, took a sword out of a scabbard mounted to his back, and threw it.

The sword hurled end-over-end through the air, right for Caitlin's chest.

At the last second, she dodged it. It flew by harmlessly, but came so close she could feel the wind of it grazing her face.

Sam stared at her with a look of shock. Clearly, he hadn't expected her to be this good.

Now it was Caitlin's turn.

She charged at him, wielding Aiden's staff. He drew his long sword, and they met in the middle.

They went blow for blow, brother and sister, in perfect harmony with each other. It was almost as if they were one person; neither could gain an advantage. His sword clanged against the golden staff as they used the entire battlefield, pushing each other backwards and forwards. The army stood to the side, watching, and it was clear that this solo combat would determine the victor of the war.

But neither seemed able to get an advantage. They were both locked in a deadly tug-of-war, moving at lightning speed, with breathtaking dexterity and power. Any of their blows would have rendered any other vampire dead on the spot.

Sam came down with an especially hard blow of his sword, and Caitlin blocked it high, over her head. His sword locked with her staff, and the two of them stood there in a pivotal moment, grunting from the exertion, locked in a deadly grip, just inches away from each other.

In that moment, Caitlin's entire world slowed down. She could feel the energy hanging in the balance, the good versus evil. She could feel that this would be a life-changing moment for either of them. His rage was overwhelming. But so was hers. They each carried a force beyond comprehension, and they each directed it at the other. Both of their lives hung in the balance.

Finally, Caitlin was thrown back. The scales had tipped, and not in her favor: Sam's power was just too much. His strength was greater than hers; it always had been. Not even her supreme rage could overcome that. She was the chosen one, but he was the stronger one. That had always been their destiny.

Sam looked down, seeing her on the ground, and realized this himself.

Without hesitating, he charged, coming in for the kill.

Caitlin regained her feet, and as he slashed, she parried, blow for blow. But now, he had the advantage: his blows were stronger than hers. With each slash, he came closer. She was getting weaker, and he was getting stronger.

As Sam spun around with another blow, this time, he was a fraction of a second faster and slashed her bicep, drawing blood. Caitlin screamed out in pain.

She slashed back, but he blocked it. He was too fast for her. Too strong. Caitlin realized he was going to win.

Sam charged again, and with a blow of supreme power, he managed to knock the staff right out of her hands. Caitlin was shocked to see Aiden's staff go flying through the air and land with a clang, several feet from her. And then, before she could react, in the same move he kicked her, knocking her to the ground.

Caitlin sat there on the ground, stunned, defenseless.

Sam raised his sword, grimacing, and aimed for her skull, for one final, deadly blow.

In that moment, Caitlin saw her life flash before her eyes, and felt certain that this was the moment she was going to die.

CHAPTER THIRTY ONE

"Sam!" screamed a voice.

Sam suddenly stopped, hypnotized by the voice, his sword frozen in mid-air.

"SAM!" screamed the voice again.

Sam turned and looked, and Caitlin saw who it was.

Scarlet stood there, hands on her hips, red-faced, screaming at Sam.

"Don't you hurt her! That's my mommy! What kind of brother are you?"

Scarlet stepped forward, fearless, and positioned herself between Sam and Caitlin.

Sam stared back, perplexed. He still held the sword, as if frozen.

"It's your job to protect her. Don't you remember? IT'S YOUR JOB!"

Sam blinked several times.

"You promised to protect her. And me. What kind of brother are you?" Scarlet screamed, chastising him.

There was something about the tone of Scarlet's voice—something so honest and real—that it seemed to break through an invisible barrier, to reach Sam. It seemed to reach to the core, to break him out of a trance, to reach all the way to Sam himself, to the man who was once a brother, who was once an uncle.

Slowly, Sam's face began to collapse; slowly, his scowl disappeared; slowly, his muscles went limp, and he lowered his sword.

Slowly, Caitlin began to see, once again, the face she once knew. The face of her brother. Her brother who loved her. Who had vowed to protect her.

"Caitlin?" Sam asked, sounding confused, as he looked down at her.

It was his voice—his *real* voice, back again. That voice she once knew.

Caitlin scrambled to her feet, holding Scarlet tight, looking back at Sam warily.

"Caitlin?" he asked again.

"It's me," Caitlin said.

Sam's face then slowly transformed into one of shame, of grief. Of self-hatred. He looked down at the sword in his hand with disgust, and confusion. He threw it down, then reached up and grabbed at his forehead, as if trying to tear the spirits out of his head.

"What have I done?" Sam pleaded. "WHAT HAVE I DONE!?"

"Kill her!" ordered a dark voice.

Caitlin looked over and saw Rexius standing there, his army behind him.

"Did you hear what I said?" Rexius said. "I gave you a command. I ordered you to kill her!"

As Caitlin watched, she saw Sam's face transform once again. Once again, it filled with rage. But this time, it was not directed at her. It was a rage, she could see, directed at Rexius. At his men. At everything they had done to him.

Sam's face glowered, as he reached for his sword. He pulled it out of the grass.

"Go," Sam said quietly to Caitlin. "Take your daughter. I will protect you. I vow. If I have to die here, I will protect you. And please," he added, "forgive me."

Caitlin felt her heart breaking. Sam was back, and she wanted to go to him, to hug him. She wanted him to come with her, wanted him to get out of here. Or, to fight by his side. Or, at the very least, to say goodbye. And to tell him that she forgave him.

But his face glowered, and she could see that he was set, that he would not leave this place, that he was determined to battle with Rexius. And there was no time left. She had to protect Scarlet. She had to find her Dad. It was now or never.

"GO!" Sam ordered.

And with that, Sam turned, let out a fierce battle cry, and charged Rexius and his men. He charged with all he had, just as Rexius' men charged him. Sam raised his sword and swung it wildly, and Caitlin could already see the bodies begin to fall.

There was no time left. Caitlin put Scarlet on her back, grabbed Ruth, and leapt into the air, flying high over the battlefield, while Sam held off Aiden's army below. She had to get far, far from this place.

And she knew exactly where she needed to go.

CHAPTER THIRTY TWO

As Caitlin flew away from the Mount of Olives, Scarlet on her back, holding Ruth, her heart was breaking in a million pieces. She was so overwhelmed, she hardly knew what to think. Down below, she was leaving Caleb, her husband, dead. Blake, dead. Aiden, dead. And her brother, Sam, alone to fight that army. He had finally come back to her, had become the brother she once knew. Her heart had soared to see him come back to himself. And abandoning him now, like this—after she had vowed to never abandon anyone again—was the most painful of all.

But at the same time, his remaining down there, fighting that army, was enabling her to flee, to search for their Dad—who, Aiden had said all along, was their last hope for salvation. Still, despite everything, she wished that Sam, the last familiar face in the world, could join her, could come with her to find their Dad together.

Caitlin recalled Aiden's words, centuries ago: she was the chosen one. Finding her Dad was her destiny, and her destiny alone. Sam had a different destiny. He was stronger, but he was not the special one. His destiny was to protect her.

It was hard for Caitlin to accept. He was her brother and she loved him, despite everything that had happened between them. It was hard for her to accept that she was more special than he. But she knew it was not meant to be. For the millionth time, she wondered how destiny worked, wondered why fate had to take the twists and turns that it did.

She also wondered why it had to take her husband away from her. Her heart was still breaking, and a part of her wanted to fly back there, to check Caleb's pulse one more time, to see if maybe, by some chance, he was alive.

But she knew he was not. She had held him, had looked into his eyes. She cried as she flew, knowing he was dead for good this time and that he would never come back to her. Behind her, clutching her back, she could feel Scarlet crying, too.

Since she had left the Mount of Olives, Caitlin knew there was only one place left to go. With Aiden gone, his coven gone, Caleb gone, Blake gone—even Sam gone—there was only one thing left she could do: find her Dad. Maybe, just maybe, if she found him, if she found the shield, it could somehow help the others. Maybe save Sam. Maybe, even bring Caleb back.

And the only person she knew who could lead to her Dad, the only lead she had, was Jesus.

Your guide will appear at the Eastern gate.

She flew away from the Mount of Olives determined to find Jesus, wherever he was. To free him from the Romans. To ask him where her Dad was. Where the shield was. And maybe, even, ask him to bring everyone back.

Suddenly, the sky above her blackened, became filled with dark, storm clouds, as if to match her mood. It was surreal: just moments before it was a clear day, not a cloud in the sky, and now the horizon loomed with the thickest, blackest clouds Caitlin had ever seen. They looked divine. It looked like the end of the world had come.

A single ray of light broke through a hole in the clouds, and it shined down, to a singular spot. The shaft of light landed on a small hill, overlooking Jerusalem, not far from the city. And it lit up one person—and one person only.

Caitlin didn't have to look. She sensed who it was. An electric jolt ran through her system, leading her like a magnet.

There, alone, atop a hill, was Jesus.

It was as if a flashlight from heaven were shining down on him. And to Caitlin's horror, she saw that he was crucified. He was alone atop the hill, crucified on a huge cross. Pegs were through his palms, through his ankles, and he hung on the cross, limp, in the ray of light.

Caitlin felt her heart breaking. She had been too late. Was he already dead?

She swooped down, flying for the hilltop. He was the only one on it, the crowds gone long ago. She landed right before him, setting down Scarlet and Ruth, right before his huge cross, and looked up at him.

There was such an intense energy coming off of him, as she looked up at him, it was like looking into the sunlight. It momentarily blinded her, and she shielded her eyes. Finally, her eyes adjusted and she looked at him closely, wondering, hoping, he was alive.

She saw the slightest flicker of his eyes, then saw him lift his head. He looked down at her, and despite the horrific agony he must be in, she saw a peaceful look on his face.

Caitlin suddenly felt herself fill with a warmth and peace unlike any she had ever known. It filled her entire body, and she felt a tingling. She didn't understand what was happening to her; it was like a switch had been turned on, one that could never be turned off. She felt a sense of belonging. Of being home.

And that was when it happened.

As she looked up at him, at the four corners of the cross, suddenly, she was awestruck by a revelation: as she looked closely, she noticed four large locks. One in each corner. Each holding Jesus's pegs in place. She examined each lock, and saw that each contained a keyhole.

At that same moment, the four keys in her pocket vibrated, practically burning a hole in them. An electric thrill ran through her, and suddenly, all became clear. All the riddles, all the clues, all the dreams, all the keys. All the churches, all the abbeys, all the monasteries.

The four keys. The four locks.

She was speechless. She barely had the strength to breathe.

And before Jesus even said the next words, she already knew what he was going to say:

"My daughter."

CHAPTER THIRTY THREE

Caitlin looked up at Jesus, unable to speak, unable to breathe. It was beyond what she could process. Yet at that moment, she knew it to be true.

Jesus was her father.

All this time, he had been the one she had been searching for.

Your guide will appear at the Eastern gate.

It was Jesus. He was her guide.

And he was also her father.

A feeling raced through Caitlin, a feeling unlike any she had ever had. It was a feeling of being special. A feeling of belonging. A feeling of pride. In her father, in herself. She was special. Her lineage was special. Beyond special.

Caitlin could hardly even conceive what it all meant.

She burst into action. After all, this was her father here, nailed to a cross, and she couldn't stand to see him suffer. She jumped up, and took out the four keys, already knowing they would each be a perfect fit. As she inserted each key, the earth shook and the skies thundered. It felt like an earthquake, as lightning bolts came down all across Jerusalem. It was surreal. It felt like the apocalypse had arrived.

Each key was a perfect fit, and as she inserted each one, each lock melted away.

She inserted the last one, and Jesus fell off the cross. He slumped down, limp, into her arms.

She caught him as he fell, and held his body. She knelt, holding him in her arms.

Her father, in her arms.

Her whole body lit up with an electric feeling. It was like holding the sun.

And yet she was also filled with a profound sadness. He was dying. Tears poured down her cheeks, and she didn't try to stop them.

He looked up at her, barely opening his eyes with what little strength he had left. She could sense these were his final moments on earth.

Jesus looked up, into her eyes, and as she looked down at his glowing green eyes, like two shining marbles, she could feel the love radiating off of him. She could feel that he was her father. That he had always been her father. She could feel how much he loved her. How proud of her he was.

As she looked at him, she realized: this was the man in her dreams. This was the elusive face, the silhouette against the sun. This was the man she had never been able to see. The man that was always just out of her reach, on the horizon.

And now here he was. Not just in her dreams. But real. He was really here. She held him in her arms, and it felt so good to know that he was real.

This moment, this one moment, made everything—all the centuries, all the battles, all the conflict—worth it. Finally, she had found him. Her father.

"I am with you," he said, his voice weak. "I have always been with you. And I am more proud of you than any father could be."

He smiled weakly, his eyes closing again, and Caitlin felt herself welling up with pride. These were the words she had always longed to hear from her father. For so long, she'd had so many things she'd wanted to ask her father when she found him, so many things she wanted to say.

But now that she was here, with him, she was speechless. She never expected it to be like this. She didn't even know where to begin. She struggled for the right words, but none came.

It wasn't fair. She had looked forward to this moment for as long she can remember, and now, finally, when she found him, he was dying. He was leaving her. She desperately wanted to savor each and every last moment.

He opened his eyes, and Caitlin could sense it was for the last time.

"I grant you the power and authority over every demon. The power and authority over every disease."

His eyes fluttered, then closed. Before he took his final breath, he said one last thing:

"I will always be with you, my daughter. Even in your dreams."

He then closed his eyes, and Caitlin could sense it was for the last time. Suddenly, there was a great rumbling of thunder, as his body went limp.

Ruth barked like crazy, as Scarlet wept behind her.

Caitlin let out a great wail, rising up, blending with the sound of the thunder. She felt she had lost the greatest thing she had ever found. She didn't even know what to say. How could she ever get over this?

Caitlin wanted to hold her father, to never let him go. But as she cradled him in her arms, suddenly, she felt his body lifting. To her amazement, right before her eyes, Jesus' body suddenly turned lighter, translucent. It lifted as she watched, ascended, higher and higher, up into the air. It became an orb of light, and went straight up, all the way to the heavens, right into the clouds themselves. There was another great clap of thunder, and of lightning, and then he disappeared.

"Caitlin," came a soft, female voice.

Caitlin wheeled, on edge, not knowing what was coming next.

Standing there, dressed in a white robe, with long brown hair and hazel eyes, looking down sweetly, was a woman she recognized. It was a woman she had seen photos of her entire life. She racked her brain, trying to remember.

Suddenly, it hit her. It was Mary. Mary Magdalene. Jesus' disciple.

Caitlin could hardly believe it.

Mary reached out a hand. Caitlin took it, and slowly rose.

"Caitlin," she said gently. "I am your mother."

Caitlin's heart stopped. It was too much for take in at once. Jesus, her father. Mary Magdalene, her mother. She hardly knew what to say, what to think.

Mary placed a hand on Caitlin's shoulder and looked down at her sweetly. In those eyes, Caitlin could feel all the love of a mother, all the love of the mother she never had. She felt overwhelmed by it, felt almost as much energy radiating off of her as from Jesus.

"We are so proud of you," Mary said. "You have unlocked the four keys. And now, the shield is yours."

Caitlin looked at her, perplexed.

"The shield?" she asked. "But I thought it was lost to us."

Slowly, Mary shook her head.

"There is a second shield. The first is merely a weapon. It is very powerful. But it is the lesser of the two. A decoy.

"The second, the more powerful, is the one that we guard. The one that only *you* could find. It is the divine one. The one meant only for the chosen one. For you."

Caitlin's heart pounded in her chest. A divine shield? She could hardly imagine what it was.

"Do you have the key?" Mary asked. "The final key?"

For a moment, Caitlin was puzzled. And then, she saw Mary looking down, at her throat. And she realized: her necklace.

Caitlin slowly removed her necklace and reached out to hand it to her mother.

Mary shook her head.

"No. It is for you to open."

Mary turned and looked up at the cross, at the huge crucifix on which Jesus had been crucified.

Caitlin followed her gaze, and examined it. In its center, where the four beams met, she saw a small keyhole. She was amazed. The final key?

Caitlin walked over, reached up and inserted her key. To her surprise, it was a perfect fit.

Suddenly, her necklace dissolved before her eyes, and as it did, a small compartment opened up inside the middle of the cross.

Mary walked over, reached in and extracted an object.

Caitlin watched in awe as Mary pulled out a bejeweled chalice, sparkling in the sunlight.

Inside it, was a white liquid.

"I present to you, the shield."

Caitlin stared, confused.

"The shield is the Holy Grail," Mary explained. "And the Holy Grail is the Antidote."

"Antidote?" Caitlin asked.

"Do you remember your father's final words? He has granted you power and authority over all disease. And that includes the disease of life."

Caitlin wracked her brain, trying to understand.

"The shield, the most powerful weapon on earth, is an antidote. An antidote to the disease of vampirism. When you drink this, if you choose to, you will unleash the antidote. You will cure the disease. From the moment it touches your lips, vampires will be no more. Including you."

Caitlin tried to process it all, flabbergasted.

"Using your final power, you will be able to make one last choice. You will choose where you want to live, as a human. You have to live in a world in which vampires do not exist. You will choose your loved ones, choose who you wish to surround you. Choose your place and time. Choose your age. And you shall live just as any other mere mortal. But it is a final choice, for all time. And by drinking from this Holy Grail, by opening this ancient shield, you will have saved mankind. Vampires will be no more. The world will be cured again."

Caitlin reached out and took the heavy goblet with two hands. She looked down at the white liquid and was overwhelmed, as thunder erupted all around her.

The ramifications of her choice were overwhelming. Where would she live? What time? What century? What place? Who would she want around her? Who would she be? How old would she be?

She would have to live a normal, mortal life. Just like any other human. Which meant that she would die. And which meant there would be no more vampires left in the world. Ever.

This was the shield. The ancient shield. She had found it. She could hardly believe she was holding it. And when she took a sip, it would change the course of history. Forever.

Caitlin slowly lifted it to her lips, feeling the tears run down her cheeks as she did. It would be the biggest decision of her life. She was scared. She could hardly imagine what would happen after she drank it. She knew that this would be her last moment as a vampire. She would come back somewhere, sometime, as a mere human. And all of this, her vampire life, would be a memory. Or maybe, not even a memory.

Caitlin closed her eyes and breathed deeply, her hands shaking. She slowly raised the chalice, and as she did, she felt the cool white liquid touch her lips. She felt it touch her tongue, then felt it slowly drip down her throat.

Mary gently took the chalice from her, smiling, and as she did, Caitlin began to feel her whole world spin. Caitlin reached out and held Scarlet's small hand, as she felt herself get lighter and lighter. Scarlet squeezed hers back.

Suddenly, Caitlin's mind filled with memories, as her whole life flashed before her eyes. She saw herself in New York, in Pollepel, in Edgartown, in Salem; she saw herself in Boston, Venice, Florence, Rome; in Paris, London and Scotland. She saw herself in castles, palaces, abbeys and churches. She saw herself with Caleb, saw herself meeting him for the first time, falling in love, getting married. She saw Caleb's child, Jade. She saw Scarlet. She saw Aiden, Polly, and anyone and everyone who ever meant anything to her.

It all came rushing back, so fast. She tried to grab onto the memories, to freeze them. But she could not. It was like trying to hold onto sand. Her life was already changing. And nothing would ever be the same.

As Caitlin felt herself grow even lighter, losing touch with her body, she knew the time had come. The time to say goodbye, to let it all go. She knew she had succeeded. She had found the keys, had found her father, had found the shield. She had found the antidote, the cure for vampirism for all time.

But this didn't feel like success. She just wanted to be here, alive, with everyone she loved. With her father.

She tried to hold onto something that might ground her, keep her here. Something tangible.

But she found that the only thing she could hold onto, the only thing that was real anymore, was love. Love for Caleb. Love for Blake. Love for Aiden. Love for Polly. Love for Scarlet. And love for her father.

She desperately tried to hold onto this; but even this slowly released from her grasp. Her world was turning white, too fast, and she knew, before it all ended, there was only time for one last thought. And as she closed her eyes, one last thought came to her:

I only wish that I see Caleb again.

resurrected

(book #1 of the vampire legacy)

morgan rice

"I grant you power and authority over every demon,
power and authority over every disease."
—Jesus, *Luke* 9:1

PROLOGUE

Rhinebeck, New York (Hudson Valley)
Present day

Caitlin Paine hurried through her house as night began to fall, trying to get everything ready in time. It was almost six o'clock, and in moments, everyone would be here. She rushed through her oversized, old Victorian house, feet creaking on the floorboards, as she hurried from room to room, tidying things. She wanted everything to be perfect for tonight.

Caitlin hurried into the large kitchen, grabbed the cake plate which she had been hiding, and hurried with it through the double doors. As she did, her large Husky, Ruth, followed at her heels, sniffing the cake and wagging her tail. As she set it down in the center of the dining table, she only hoped that Scarlet hadn't seen it yet. After all, tonight was Scarlet's big 16th birthday, and even though it was a weeknight, Caitlin had a special surprise in store for her.

Caitlin had been looking forward to this all week. Scarlet still thought they weren't going to celebrate until the weekend, since Caitlin had tricked her, had told her it would be more festive to wait until then. Scarlet had actually believed it, and Caitlin had secretly summoned the whole crew to be here, to surprise her when she got home from school. Not only did she make sure Caleb got home from work early to help her prepare, but she also made sure her brother, Sam, left work early, too—and that he brought his wife, and Caitlin's best friend, Polly. The four of them were as close as two couples could be—like one family—and Scarlet's birthday wouldn't be the same without them here.

The doorbell rang and Caitlin jumped. Ruth barked, and Caitlin ran through the house, praying Scarlet wasn't home early. Thankfully, she wasn't: Caitlin opened the door with huge relief to see her little brother, Sam, standing there, smiling, Polly on his arm, grinning and radiant as always.

"Did we make it on time?" Sam asked excitedly, as he stepped quickly into the house and gave Caitlin a hug.

"Barely," Caitlin answered.

"Sorry," Sam said. "Got stuck at work."

Caitlin was proud of her little brother. Only two years younger than she, it was hard for her to believe he was already 31. And even harder for Caitlin to believe that she, herself, was 33. That Polly was 32. And that Scarlet was turning 16. Where had the time gone? It had all flown by so fast. It felt like only yesterday that they were all teenagers.

Caitlin felt so fortunate to have so many people in her life who she loved. Life had been good to her, she had to admit. Or at least, lately it had. She and Sam's early years had been hard, raised only by their mother, in a dingy apartment in a bad neighborhood in New York City, with an absentee father they'd never met. Her mother died right after high school, and Caitlin and Sam had basically been left to raise each other on their own. Which was actually nearly an improvement from their unloving mom.

Sam, naturally, had gotten into a lot of trouble in his youth. How couldn't he? He'd even been thrown in jail once or twice, for misdemeanors, bar fights—once, for hitting a cop. He had a real issue with authority. But when he reached college age, after their mom died, Sam, with Caitlin's help, finally turned his life around. He got into college, graduated, and had been a model citizen since. Now he worked in a great job as a mentor, helping troubled youth at the local school. It was the perfect job for him, and Caitlin was so proud. In some ways, she felt like she raised him.

Polly stepped up and gave Caitlin a hug, and she hugged her back. Ruth barked and whined, and Polly and Sam knelt down and hugged her, too. Caitlin felt so lucky to have Polly in her life. In some ways, life had been a dream, working out so perfectly, her best friend marrying her brother. Their marriage was what had really grounded Sam, was what had given him the sense of stability and purpose he'd never had. The only thing missing from his and Polly's life was a child; they had been trying to get pregnant for years, but so far, with no luck. Still, Polly was beaming. Her whole life, as long as Caitlin had known her—since high school—she had been beaming.

"I'm so excited!" Polly screamed, bursting into the room, rushing right to the table, setting down an armful of presents and helping to prepare. "I found those candles she loves!" she added, as she emptied a paper bag and stuck thick, decorative candles all over the cake.

"Does she know yet?" Polly continued. "Does she have any idea? Oh my God, do you think she'll like this dress I got her? I was looking for it all day. You don't think it will be too small do you? Will she like the color?"

Caitlin smiled. That was Polly, always asking ten questions at the time, always in such an excited rush.

"I'm sure it will be perfect," Caitlin responded with a smile. "Thank you for everything."

Caleb hurried into the room, through the double doors, carrying a platter of carved turkey.

"Careful, it's hot," he warned, as he set it down. Caleb's muscles rippled through his tee-shirt, the product of years of training.

Every time Caitlin looked at Caleb, her heart soared. She had married the man of her dreams. Here he was, the model of a husband, tall, strong, with broad shoulders, a proud jaw, and beautiful brown eyes. And every time he looked at her, his eye were filled with love. She reciprocated. There was no one she loved more, even after all these years. He was the one and only true love of her life.

They had met the day Caitlin graduated high school, and she had fallen in love instantly. It was the strangest thing, but she'd felt, from the moment she'd met him, as if she'd known him her whole life. She'd gotten pregnant at 17, before they'd married, and back then, Caitlin had been terribly worried about it. Her mother of course didn't help, only having negative things to say.

But Caleb was never worried. He said he'd already decided he wanted to be with her, and was just grateful they had a child so soon. She took solace in his strength, and after all, she loved him as much as he did her. Nine months later, she gave birth—oddly, on the same day that her mother died of a heart attack. And shortly afterwards, Caitlin and Caleb married.

After they married, Caleb entered the Air Force. A fighter pilot for the Marine Corps, one of their best, Caitlin would watch him in awe as he would fly jets on a military base. It was incredible for her to watch him flying through the air at such speed, with such power. Sometimes she felt as if it stirred some memory, deep inside of her—but she was not sure what. It was an odd feeling that didn't make sense, as if somehow, she expected him to be soaring through the air. She knew it didn't make any sense, and she tried to push it out of her mind. But somehow, it lingered.

As they had gotten older, into their late 20s, Caleb had retired from the force, and had become a domestic pilot. He traveled a lot, though lately, he'd been home more often, which made Caitlin happy. Sometimes, on the weekends, he flew daredevil shows in small, local airplanes, to the delight of thousands of onlookers. He would soar in huge circles in the sky, dive down, then rise at the last second. Kids loved watching him, though Caitlin's heart sank every time he got in the cockpit. She just wanted him to be safe.

Sometimes, though, she would accompany him in the cockpit of a small, two-seater plane, and it would be just the two of them, flying locally, together. For their last anniversary, he took her up at night, during the summer, in a full moon. As the two of them glided through the night, it had felt as if they'd had the whole world to themselves. She loved it. It made her feel a sense of nostalgia, of belonging, though she didn't know why.

Caitlin was fine with the fact that Caleb traveled a lot, that he was busy. She liked having her space, and she was busy, too. After all, she had built an incredible career for herself. Her dysfunctional upbringing had resulted in her using her studies as a way of escape. The worse the neighborhood was that her mom dragged her to, the worse the school, the more she applied herself, the harder she studied. Through sheer force of will, she managed to get straight A's, and managed to get herself a scholarship to Columbia University. Ironically, it was only 15 blocks away from the bad neighborhood she was raised in—and yet, it was a universe apart.

In Columbia, Caitlin applied herself even harder, and after four years graduated with near-perfect grades, getting herself a scholarship to graduate school. She pushed herself even harder, until, at 26, she graduated with a dual Ph.D. in History and Antiquities. Caleb always joked with her, always would ask with a smile: *How many Ph.D.'s do you want?* But he was so proud of her. She could see it in his eyes.

What she should do with all of her knowledge was a question she'd asked herself many times, too. She still didn't know what she wanted to do, even after all the school, even after all these degrees. She knew that, for some reason, she was interested in history, antiquities, archaeology—and most of all, rare objects and books. With all her scholarship, she could have had a job anywhere she wanted. But instead, she chose to pursue her one great passion: rare books.

Caitlin didn't know why she felt so drawn to rare books; it didn't even make sense to her. But, for as long as she could remember, it was always what she loved. She still felt a thrill every time she picked up some ancient, dusty book, tried to decode it, figure out where it was from. How old it was. Who wrote it. What language it was in. How rare it was.

She'd held books that were worth tens of millions of dollars, one-of-a-kind, ancient books that had been seen and held by few people throughout history. She'd held original, first edition Shakespeare volumes, ancient Greek scrolls. She felt a connection to history as she did, and it made her feel alive.

She also couldn't help feeling, every time she picked up a book, that it held a riddle, a clue, some mystery to be solved. And that thrilled her. For some reason she always felt that there was some mystery lingering in her consciousness, something she needed to solve. She didn't know what. It didn't make sense to her, and that bothered her. When she worked on a rare book, at least she could solve clues that she couldn't put her fingers on in real life.

While she was raising Scarlet, Caitlin had worked part time in rare bookstores, and now that she was settled, she worked here, at the local university. They had a vast library, and an endless collection of rare books that had to be classified. They told her frequently how lucky they were to have someone of her caliber here, locally, to help them. It was true: with a mind like hers, Caitlin could have worked anywhere in the world. But Caitlin was happy to be here, locally, in this quiet town, to be able to raise Scarlet in a safe place, to give her the sheltered childhood that she'd never had.

Looking back, having Scarlet had been the best decision of Caitlin's life. She was the joy of her life—and of Caleb's, too. Caitlin firmly believed that even without a child, they would have married anyway. They had tried throughout the years to have more kids, but for some reason, they'd never been able to. So it ended up being just she and Caleb and Scarlet, just the three of them in this big house. Sometimes she wished they'd had more kids to fill the house. But she was grateful and happy for what she had.

They had both wanted to get away from New York City, wanted a wholesome life for Scarlet, so they'd headed two hours north and settled in a small, idyllic town in the Hudson Valley, a place where they could live in peace and tranquility. Caitlin had been thrilled when Sam followed them, and eventually, when Polly did, too. Life was finally coming together for her, all the pieces fitting. She felt so blessed to be able to live tranquilly in a small town, her family close by, with an adoring husband, a best friend, an amazing brother, and a child she loved more than anything.

Sometimes, she looked back at her childhood and felt pangs of anxiety and upset. Looking back, she wondered about her Dad. Who he was. Why he had abandoned them all. Why her mom had always been so mean to her. Why she couldn't have had a more normal upbringing, a less dysfunctional family.

But whenever these thoughts overcame her, Caitlin forced herself to just push it all to the back of her mind, to focus on what she had, on all the good in her life. She didn't want to linger in sorrow and guilt and upset. After all, it didn't do any good. She could just as easily choose to focus on all the blessings she had, all she had to be grateful for.

Growing up, everything had seemed so important. Her friends, her boyfriends, her parents, her school…. It had felt like everything had such importance, would last forever, and she'd been unable to see a life beyond that. But now, looking back, at 33, she realized how insignificant all of that stuff was. It all felt so distant, so far away. In retrospect, none of it even mattered anymore.

"Caitlin?" came a voice.

Caitlin blinked, snapping out of it. She looked over to see everyone staring at her.

"Hello, Earth to Caitlin?" Polly said, and they all broke into laughter.

Caitlin blushed. She must have zoned out again.

"Sorry," she said.

Caleb came over and kissed her forehead.

"You okay, baby?" he asked. "You've been spacing out a lot lately."

Before Caitlin could reply, suddenly Polly yelled:

"I see her! Scarlet! She's outside. Hurry!"

As everyone rushed to the front door, Caitlin quickly lit the 16 candles on the cake, then hurried towards the parlor to join them.

Caitlin positioned herself so that Scarlet wouldn't see the cake, standing right in front of the door, her heart racing. As she waited, she heard footsteps on the old porch, and was surprised to hear two sets of steps. She'd assumed Scarlet would be coming home alone, and didn't know who could be with her. Ruth whined like crazy, sensing Scarlet was coming.

Scarlet opened the door, and as she did, they all yelled: "SURPRISE!"

Scarlet lifted her head and stared back, wide-eyed, looking completely shocked. Caitlin could see real surprise in her face, and felt so happy, victorious, that she actually managed to surprise her. Scarlet, of all people. The smartest person she'd ever known. The hardest person to surprise with anything.

Scarlet was also the most beautiful. As she stood there, with her perfectly-chiseled pale face, her large, crystal-blue eyes, her flowing, red hair, she was breathtaking. In many ways, she reminded Caitlin of Caleb.

Ruth barked and barked and Scarlet hugged her. Scarlet's face lit with excitement, as she stood and broke into a huge smile, revealing perfect white teeth.

"That's why you didn't call today!" she said.

As she hugged her, Caitlin smiled over her shoulder.

"I wanted you to be totally surprised. Happy birthday, sweetheart. We love you so much!"

Scarlet then hugged Caleb, and he hugged her back firmly.

"Happy birthday, sweetheart," he said.

But as Caleb looked over Scarlet's shoulder, at the person standing the doorway, his expression hardened a bit.

Caitlin looked and saw that there, in the front door, stood a boy. He was maybe Scarlet's age, 16. Hands in his pockets, he wore a plaid shirt and jeans, with longish hair, and looked up warily at both of them.

Caitlin had never seen this boy, but she was suddenly overwhelmed by the strangest feeling that they'd met. He seemed so familiar that it bothered her, as if she'd known him forever. But she knew she did not.

Scarlet must have noticed the sudden tension in the air, because she turned.

"Um…guys," she said. "Like, sorry, I didn't realize that, like, everyone would be here. This is my boyfriend. Blake."

"*Boyfriend?*" Caleb asked warily, surprise rising in his voice.

Blake, Caitlin thought. How did she know that name? Somehow, she felt that she did.

Blake looked back and forth cautiously between Caitlin and Caleb.

"Um…hi," he finally said, shyly.

"Dad, be nice," Scarlet cautioned.

Caleb held out a large, firm hand, and Blake reached out tentatively. Caleb shook his hand hard—just a little bit too hard, Caitlin could see.

"Any friend of my daughter is welcome in our home," Caleb said, though Caitlin could see his jaw tighten. She also noticed he chose the word *friend*, not boyfriend.

"Hey Scarlet!" Sam yelled out, and came hurrying over and gave her a hug.

"Oh my god are you gorgeous or what!" Polly screamed, as she hurried over and wrapped Scarlet in a big hug, picking her up. "Oh my God, look at that hair. And those earrings. And those shoes? Where did you get those? Oh my god, you look stunning! Stunning!" Polly said.

Scarlet smiled wide as she embraced Polly, who was like a second mom to her.

"Thanks, Polly. You look great, too."

Caitlin gently prodded them towards the dinner table, and as they all were getting closer, she hurried around behind Scarlet and placed her palms over her eyes.

"Don't look!" Caitlin said, as she walked with Scarlet across the dining room.

As they approached the table, Caitlin pulled back her hands.

Scarlet's eyes opened in surprise, as her face broke into a huge smile.

"Oh my God, you got it for me!" she screamed, and turned and hugged Caitlin tightly.

Caitlin beamed with satisfaction. It was Scarlet's favorite cake, a red velvet cheesecake that she'd once had in Manhattan and never forgot. The bakery in the city was the only one that made it, and Caitlin had taken a special trip the day before just to get it for her.

Scarlet turned to Blake, lingering back behind the others, and grabbed his hand and pulled him forward, right next to her.

"Oh my god you don't understand," she gushed to him. "This is the world's best cake. You have to taste it."

As she spoke, Caitlin could see the love emanating on her face towards Blake. And it was reciprocal. That made her very happy—and nervous at the same time. She knew how easily Scarlet fell in love, and didn't want to see her get hurt.

Scarlet blew out all the candles, and as she did, everyone cheered.

"Thanks mom," she said, hugging Caitlin one more time, "you really surprised me. I love you."

"I love you too," Caitlin said.

*

They all had a lovely meal together. Blake joined them, and the six of them sat around, eating course after course, laughing, talking about the amazing year in store for Scarlet. Polly brought a bubbly, vivacious energy to the table, and having her and Sam there made the house feel so much bigger to Caitlin, so much warmer. It felt like a real home.

Having Blake there, Caitlin realized, was a welcome addition, too. The six of them all fit comfortably together, as if they'd all known each other forever. The conversation never stopped, and neither did the laughter.

They all ate way too much, then sliced the cake, and ate even more. Then came the coffee, and tea, and more desserts—boxes of cookies which Polly and Sam had brought. Ruth sat at their heels, and they had all thrown her scraps all night. Especially Scarlet, who Ruth adored more than anything. The love was reciprocal—most nights Ruth slept in Scarlet's room, and if anyone came anywhere near it, she growled.

Polly, so excited, couldn't wait any longer to give Scarlet her presents, so she, characteristically, gave her the gifts right there, at the table, and begged her to open them. Caitlin didn't know who was more excited, Scarlet or Polly. As always, Polly was way too generous. Scarlet opened gift after gift. Scarlet, so appreciative, got up and hugged her, and Sam.

After the conversation died down and they all began to get up from the table, Caitlin finally found her opportunity. She was dying to give Scarlet her gift, a very important gift, which she'd been waiting until her 16th birthday to give her. As the others began to filter out of the room, she went to pull Scarlet aside—but was surprised to see Scarlet reach for her coat.

"Scarlet?" Caitlin asked, surprised. "Are you going out?"

Scarlet paused in the doorway, with Blake, and looked back, hesitant, looking a bit guilty.

"Sorry mom," she said. "I didn't realized you expected me to stay. I was going to catch a movie with Blake. For my birthday, you know?"

Caitlin saw Caleb looking over, concerned.

"Um…if that's okay?" Scarlet added.

Caleb looked down at his watch, looking unhappy.

"Well, it is a school night," he said.

But Caitlin reached out and placed a hand on his wrist. She smiled.

"Of course it's okay, honey. It's your birthday. I'm glad that you guys are going," she said, meaning it. Caitlin felt a little sad for herself, because she wanted to hang out with Scarlet, to talk to her more on her birthday—

but she was genuinely happy for her that she had Blake.

Scarlet broke into a smile, looking relieved.

"But before you go, can I just have a minute?" Caitlin asked. "There's something I want to give you. It's your birthday, after all."

Scarlet's smile widened.

"Sure," she said. She turned to Blake. "Just wait for me out on the porch, I'll be out in a few minutes."

"I think porch time is a great idea," Caleb said, not missing a beat as he walked to Blake and draped his arm over his shoulder. "In fact, I think I'll join you. It will be a perfect opportunity for us to get to know each other."

Blake looked nervously back at Scarlet as Caleb led him outside.

"Dad, be nice," Scarlet cautioned.

Caleb turned and smiled as he opened the door, leading Blake to one of the overstuffed wicker chairs on their wide, Victorian porch.

"Don't worry honey," Caitlin said, as the door closed behind him. "I'm sure he'll be nice. And by the way, I really like Blake."

Scarlet's smile widened, and the two of them walked through the windy, quirky house to a small sitting room, lined with bookcases.

As they entered the room, Scarlet's eyes opened wide in surprise at the site of a small wrapped gift box sitting alone, on the coffee table.

Caitlin beamed. She had been preparing this for the longest time. Now, finally, it was the perfect moment.

"You really didn't have to get me anything, mom," Scarlet said. "That cake was more than enough."

That was Scarlet. Always so considerate. Always so selfless.

"This is an important one," Caitlin said. "Go ahead. Open it."

Scarlet lifted the small box and removed the delicate wrapping. As she did, it revealed an antique, mahogany jewelry box.

Scarlet looked over at Caitlin in surprise. Clearly, she was stumped.

She slowly opened it, and her eyes opened wide.

"Oh my God," she said, raising one hand to her mouth. "I can't accept this. It looks so valuable. It looks, like, ancient!"

Sitting there, against black velvet, was a small, antique silver necklace. An antique cross.

Scarlet held it up, examining it, struck by its beauty.

"Where did you get it?"

"My grandmother gave it to me," Caitlin said, "when I turned 16."

Caitlin came over, took the necklace, and got behind Scarlet and draped it around her neck, clasping it. She then came to her front and smiled wide.

"It fits beautifully," Caitlin said.

Caitlin had stumbled across the necklace just the other day, in the attic, and at that moment, she felt that Scarlet should have it. After all, she didn't wear it herself anymore. It was so beautiful, and mysterious, with that strange inscription in Latin on the back.

"I'll never take it off. I love you mommy," Scarlet said, hugging her.

Over her shoulder, Caitlin felt Scarlet's tears.

Caitlin had no idea what she'd done to deserve such a great daughter.

"I love you, too."

*

Caitlin lay there, in bed, late at night, the lights out, tossing and turning, thinking. Caleb had been fast asleep for at least an hour, and she could hear the steady, measured sound of his breathing. She was always amazed at how well he slept.

But not Caitlin. Most nights, she had a hard time falling asleep. She looked over at her bedside table, and turned the clock towards her:

12:30. She had laid down in bed over an hour ago, and still nothing.

She lay there, in the darkened room, lit only by the moonlight coming in through the drapes. She lay on her back, resting her head on the pillow, staring at the ceiling fan, thinking. Her mind raced and raced, and she could not get it to quiet down. Tonight was worse than usual.

She wondered if she was so stirred up because it was such a big day, with Scarlet's turning 16. She remembered when she, herself, turned 16, and she still felt in some ways like it was yesterday—to think of her daughter turning 16 was surreal. It was so weird to think of herself as a mom, as 33. In some ways, nothing had changed. Some part of her was still the same 16-year-old Caitlin.

But what bothered her most wasn't what she remembered—rather, it was what she could *not* remember. It was like there was some hazy corner of her consciousness that she couldn't quite get to come into focus, some deep part of her brain where things were murky. She willed herself to focus, to think back to the day when she herself turned 16, to remember everything that had happened that day, all the details—and she was frustrated to find that she could not.

Often, Caitlin tried to remember her upbringing, especially her early childhood, convinced that she must have some early childhood memories of her father. *Something.* But she often drew a blank, or drew some muted images, so vague and muddled that she didn't know if these were actually memories or just her imagination, just something she had concocted herself over the years. She wanted to remember. But she just couldn't summon it. It was like there was this huge black hole in her memory, this huge, hidden life that she once had that she just could not remember. And it bothered her to no end.

Maybe she was just imagining that there was something more, something else. Sometimes, Caitlin found herself feeling that she was destined for greater things. A bigger life. That she had some great fate and destiny, some huge purpose or meaning in the world. Sometimes she felt as if her life was meant to be so much bigger, that she had a secret mission waiting to be announced, at just the perfect moment. Then all the pieces would fall into place, then she would understand why it all had been kept so quiet, why her life had been so normal up until now.

But that day had never come. Caitlin felt special, but as she looked around—at her normal life, a life which seemed so much like everyone else's—she didn't actually see anything about her life that was that special. It seemed like a normal life, in a normal town. A part of her refused to accept that. And another part of her wondered if she was just going crazy.

After all, what was wrong with a "normal" life anyway? Wasn't having a normal life an achievement in its own right? Why did life have to be greater than normal? When Caitlin looked around and saw so many people she knew who were living such dysfunctional lives, with real problems, with broken marriages, with health problems—with *real* suffering—she realized that normal was OK. It was better than OK. She should be so grateful, she knew, just to have normalcy, just to have what she had. And she *was* grateful. She was not unhappy.

It was just that sometimes, she wondered, if maybe, she was meant to be something more.

Thinking of that necklace, the one her grandmother had given her, had also stirred her up. It brought flooding back memories of her grandmother—one of the few clear memories Caitlin still had. She remembered her grandmother, one of the few people she truly loved, on her eighth birthday, giving her a box of rare books. She remembered holding that box as if it were a treasure chest. She remembered all the times her mother insisted on getting rid of that box, every time they moved, and all the times Caitlin had refused, dug her heels in. She remembered one time, when she came home and discovered her mom had thrown it out—and Caitlin ran out and grabbed the box and brought it back and hid it. She kept it hidden, under her bed, for years, determined her mom should never find it again. And her mom never did.

Years later, when Caitlin moved to the Hudson Valley, to this big old house, she remembered one day getting a notice from an attorney about her grandmother's estate. Something about items that had never been properly dispersed. Caitlin had shown up, and they had given her several more boxes of rare books from her grandmother's estate. Caitlin had brought them home and had stored them in a far corner of her attic. A part of her had wanted to go through them all right away—but another part wasn't ready to. She couldn't explain why. There was something so personal about them, and she wanted to savor each book, every word. She felt she had to wait for exactly the right time to do that.

Caitlin tossed and turned, thinking about those books, and after hours, she didn't know how long, finally, she fell into a fitful sleep.

*

Caitlin was standing in a huge field of corn, at sunset, the only one left in a vast and empty universe. There was a narrow path, between the cornstalks, and she walked down it, under a sky alight with a million shades of reds and pinks. She walked towards the horizon, knowing for some reason that that was where she had to go.

As she did, she saw a lone figure standing there, on the horizon. It was a man, his back to the sun. A silhouette. Somehow, deep down, she felt she knew him. She felt as if, maybe, he were her father.

Caitlin ran, wanting to reach him, to see him, to talk to him. As she ran, the cornstalks changed to olive trees, their silver branches lit up beautifully in the last light of day. The terrain changed, too, to a mountain, and now she was running up. Church bells suddenly tolled. She felt herself getting closer, and as she did, he grew larger. As she nearly reached him, she looked up and saw him mounted on a crucifix. She could still only see his silhouette, and the image terrified her.

Caitlin ran even faster, wanting to free him, to help bring him down off the cross. She felt that if she could only reach him, everything would be okay.

"Caitlin," he said. "I am with you."

She got closer, and was just beginning to see some of the details on his face, and knew that in another moment, she would see who he was.

But then, suddenly, a flock of bats swooped down from the sky, descended on her like a swarm. Soon, they were all in her face and hair and eyes, and she was swatting them away like crazy. But there were too many of them, and they forced her down, down to her knees, to the ground, covering her like ants. She screamed and screamed, but no one heard her.

Caitlin sat bolt upright in bed, breathing hard, sweating. She looked all around in the silence, momentarily forgetting where she was. Finally, she realized: it had been a dream.

It had been such a terrifying dream, and Caitlin's heart was still pounding in her chest. She didn't understand it—none of it seemed to make any sense. It left her sad and scared and terrified all at the same time.

She jumped up out of bed and paced, too wound-up to go back to sleep. She looked over at the clock: 4:01. It was nowhere near daybreak, and she was wide awake.

As Caitlin paced the room, trying to figure out what to do, she felt more stirred up, more restless, than she could ever remember feeling. She felt as her dream were more than a dream: she felt it was a message. As if it demanded action of some sort. But what?

She felt she had to do something. But it was 4 AM, and where could she go?

Her mind was restless and she had to tackle something, to throw her mind into something. Like an old book. An intense puzzle. Something to engage her.

And then, suddenly, it struck her: the books she had been thinking about before bed. Her grandmother's boxes. Those rare books. The greatest puzzle of all.

Yes, that was what she needed. It would be perfect. It was a place where she could go and get lost, and not bother anyone.

Caitlin hurried out the room and down the hall. She grabbed a flashlight from a drawer and climbed the steep steps to the attic.

As she reached the top, she pulled the cord on a single bare bulb, and it lit a portion of the room in stark shadows. She turned on her flashlight and surveyed the dark corners: the attic was absolutely jammed with stuff. They had been living here so many years and had never bothered to clean it. They'd never had any reason to. It was airless up here and it wasn't insulated, and Caitlin hugged her shoulders in her pajamas, feeling a chill.

She could barely remember where she'd stored her grandmother's boxes. She swung the flashlight and searched through all the stuff, from one corner of the attic to the other. She began to walk through it all slowly, going from box to box.

Just as she was starting to wonder if this was a futile endeavor, suddenly, she saw it: a small stack of boxes in the corner which she recognized. Yes, these were her grandmother's books.

Caitlin move some things out of the way—an old high-chair, an old crib, an oversized toy horse—and managed to make her way to the stack. She opened the first box, and slowly, methodically, as she'd been trained to do, she extracted the books one at a time. Organized them. Catalogued them. Indexed them in her head. The professional Caitlin took over.

There were dozens of books, and this was exactly the kind of project Caitlin needed. Already, she could feel her racing mind and heart start to slow.

Caitlin sat there, cross-legged, taking her time as she picked through one book at a time. She sneezed more than once, the dust getting to her. But she was happy. She felt an instant connection to her grandmother as she went through each book, feeling each one, running her hands along the spine, feeling the binding, the old paper. She began to relax. Her nightmares were becoming more distant.

An hour passed in the blink of an eye, and by then, Caitlin had already finished going through most of the boxes. As she reached the final box, she went to open it, and was surprised to find it was sealed more securely than the others. She pulled at the layers of duct tape, but they would just not give. Caitlin wondered why this box would be sealed so much more carefully than the others. It looked older, too.

She was annoyed. She got up from her comfortable position and began combing the attic, looking for a razor, or scissors—or anything to help open it.

In the far corner she stumbled upon an old sewing kit, and extracted a small pair of sewing scissors. They were tiny, but looked like they would do the trick.

Caitlin went back to the box and set to work on cutting the tape. It took her several minutes to cut through it with the dull scissors, but finally, she did. She tore the box open.

Inside this box, Caitlin could see, were about 20 books. Most of them looked the same, typical binding, mostly classics.

But one book stood out immediately. It didn't look anything like the others. It was thick, overstuffed, weathered, with leather binding. It looked as if it had been through a war. Multiple wars. And it looked ancient. Positively ancient.

Caitlin was intrigued. As a rare book scholar, there was almost no book she could not decipher, categorize, in an instant. Yet this was different. She had never seen anything like it. And that both thrilled her, and terrified her. How could it be? This was unlike any book she had ever seen. And she had seen it all.

Caitlin's heart pounded as she reached in and delicately removed the book. She was shaking, and felt her heart pounding in her throat. She didn't know why. It was strange, but somehow, she couldn't help feeling as if she was led to it. To this box. To this book.

Caitlin pulled back the cover, and ran her hand along the first page and began to study the handwriting.

As she did, suddenly, her heart stopped. She couldn't understand it. It was a handwriting she recognized.

It was her own.

As she began to read, Caitlin could not process what was happening. She felt as if she were outside of herself, looking down. And she became more and more confused.

She read. And read and read.

Finally, it hit her like a lightning bolt: this book, it was *hers*. Her journal. The journal of a teenage girl. A journal of coming of age. Of going back in time. Of falling in love with a man named Caleb. Of having a daughter named Scarlet. Of becoming a vampire.

She wondered if she were losing her mind. What was this? Was it some sort of practical joke? Some sort of fantasy she'd had as a young girl? What was it doing here? How did her grandmother have it? And why did she only open it now, at this time?

As she turned page after page, transfixed, read story after story, entry after entry, as she sat there, frozen until long after the sun rose, finally, she realized: this was no joke.

It was real.

It was all real.

CHAPTER ONE

Caitlin's hands trembled as she drove. Her hands hadn't stopped shaking since this morning, since she'd put down her journal. She'd read every page, then started over, and read it all over again. It was like watching her life flash before her eyes. It was like reading about a life that had been kept secret even from her, a life she'd always suspected she'd had, but was afraid to believe was possible. It was like holding a piece of herself she never knew existed.

It excited and terrified her at the same time. She no longer knew what was real and what was imagined, what was her life, and what was a fantasy. The line was blurring so much, she started to wonder if she was losing her mind.

Being a scholar, a rare book expert, she also analyzed and scrutinized the book itself, with an expert's eye. She could tell, scientifically, objectively, that it was real. An ancient book. Thousands of years old. Older than any book she'd ever held. That in itself would have been enough to stump her. It didn't make any sense. How was it possible?

As Caitlin thought about it, she realized that her necklace, the one she'd given to Scarlet, was also ancient. And it had also come from her grandmother. She wondered who her grandmother really was, and what else she had in hiding. Her grandmother had said at the time that it had come from *her* grandmother. Caitlin couldn't help feeling some intense connection to the generations. But she didn't know what.

As she turned it all over in her head, it only raised more and more questions. And that, more than anything, surprised her. She was a world-renowned scholar. She could dissect and analyze any book within a matter of minutes. But now, with her own book, in her own attic—in her own handwriting of all things—she was completely stumped.

And that freaked her out more than anything. After all, Caitlin didn't remember writing any of it. And yet, as she read it, pieces of it seemed to come back to her, in some vague part of her consciousness.

The book had thrown her for a loop. Caitlin had come down from the attic late in the morning, to an empty house, Scarlet already gone to school, and Caleb already long gone to work. She was supposed to be at work herself hours ago, and hadn't even called in. She'd been in a daze, and had lost all sense of time and place. The only one still home to greet her had been Ruth, and Caitlin, in a daze, had merely walked past her, out the door, to her car, and had taken off, the book in hand.

Caitlin knew there was only one person in the world she could turn to for answers. And she needed answers now, more than ever. She couldn't stand to have something unsolved, and she would stop at nothing until she had all the answers she needed.

She floored it on the highway, racing down the Taconic Parkway, heading towards New York City, hands still shaking. There was only one man in the world who would know what to make of this—only one mind that was more brilliant than hers when it came to rare books and antiquities. Only one man who could explain the deepest truths of history, of religion, of the esoteric.

And that was Aiden. Her old college professor, her mentor all throughout her undergraduate and graduate degrees at Columbia. He was the one man she trusted and respected more than any man in the world. The one man who she considered to be a true father.

Aiden was the most venerated professor of antiquities and esoteric studies at Columbia, the shining star of the archaeological faculty, and the greatest scholar they'd ever had. If ever Caitlin encountered any rare book, or piece of history, or antiquity that left her stumped, Aiden was the one she could call. He always had an answer, for everything.

She knew that he would have an answer for this book, a scholarly way to explain it away that would both make her feel better and make her wonder why she hadn't thought of it. And he would do it with grace and charm, in a way that didn't make her feel stupid. In fact, knowing that he would have the answer was the only thing keeping her from losing her mind right now.

Caitlin was shaking with anticipation as she reached Manhattan. She sped down the West Side Highway, over to Broadway, and parked right before the entrance to Columbia. She parked right there, on Broadway, in a no parking zone, but she didn't care. She was hardly aware of her surroundings, hardly aware that she had left the house still wearing pajama pants, flip-flops and an old sweater, her hair undone. Life had been a blur since reading that book.

Caitlin jumped out of the car, snatched the journal, and ran through the gates of Columbia, stumbling on the uneven, brick-lined walkway. She hurried through the campus, and turned and ran up the wide, stone steps, taking them three at a time. She hurried across a wide stone plaza, found the building she knew Aiden would be in, hurried up more steps, through double doors, down a tiled corridor, up another flight of steps, turned down another corridor, and went right to his classroom. She didn't even think to knock, didn't even stop to consider whether he might be teaching. She wasn't in her right state of mind.

Caitlin opened his door and walked right in, as if she were still an undergrad.

She took a few steps in, then stopped, mortified. Aiden was standing there, at his blackboard, holding a piece of chalk—and the classroom was filled with about 30 graduate students.

"And the reason why the archetypical differences between the Roman and Greek values weren't considered—"

Aiden suddenly stopped speaking, stopped writing on the chalkboard. He turned and looked.

The graduate students all stopped typing on their laptops and stared at Caitlin, too, looking her up and down. Suddenly, she realized where she was, what she was wearing.

She stood there, mortified, like a deer in headlights. She finally snapped out of her daze, and realized what she had done. She must have seemed like a crazy person.

Scattered laughter broke out from the stunned classroom.

"Caitlin?" Aiden asked, looking back at her in astonishment.

Aiden looked just as she'd remembered, with his short, gray hair and beard, and intelligent light blue eyes. He stared back at her with kindness, but she also sensed surprise, and maybe even annoyance. Of course: she had interrupted his class.

"I'm so sorry," she said. "I didn't mean to interrupt."

Aiden stood there, perhaps waiting for her to explain, or perhaps waiting for her to leave.

But Caitlin couldn't bring herself to leave. She couldn't go anywhere, do anything, think about anything, until she had answers.

"Is there…something I can help you with?" Aiden asked, sounding unsure.

Caitlin looked down at the floor. She didn't know what to say. She hated to interrupt him. But at the same time she didn't feel like she could go.

"I'm sorry," she finally said, looking up at him. "I need to talk to you. Now."

He stared back at her for several seconds, and she could see his eyes narrowing. He slowly looked down at her hand, saw the book she was holding, and for the slightest moment, she saw something in his eyes like recognition. Astonishment. It was a look she had never seen before: Aiden had never been astonished by anything. He seemed to know about everything in the universe.

Now Aiden was the one who seemed caught off guard. He turned to the class.

"I'm sorry, class," he said. "But that will be all for today."

And with that, he suddenly turned towards Caitlin, walked to her, gently took her shoulder, and led her out the room, to the surprised gasps and muffled whispers of the students.

"To my office," he said.

She followed him down the hall, wordlessly, up the stairs, to the top floor, down another hall, and then finally, into his office. She walked in, and he closed the door behind her.

It was the office she remembered, and it felt like a second home to her. It was the office she had spent so many years analyzing and discussing and debating ideas with Aiden, as he advised her on her essays, on her thesis. It was a small office, but comfortable, every inch of it jam-packed with books, all the way up to the 14 foot ceilings. Books were stacked on the desk, on the windowsill, on the chairs. And not just any books—all sorts of rare and unusual books, esoteric volumes on the most obscure academic subjects. It was the quintessential scholar's office.

He hastily removed a pile of books from one of the seats across his desk, making room for Caitlin as she sat in the chair beside him.

Without hesitating, she reached out and held out her journal.

Aiden slowly took it with both hands. Gently, he pulled back the cover. His eyes opened wide as he read the first page.

But to Caitlin's surprise, he didn't go through the book, inspect it, turn it every which way, as he always did with an unusual volume.

Instead, he gently closed it. He reached out with two hands to give it back to her. Caitlin could not believe it. He didn't even try to read more. She was even more confused by his reaction.

Confusing her even more, he wouldn't look at her. Instead, he slowly got up, a grim look on his face, walked to his windowsill, and stood there, hands clasped, looking out. He was staring, looking down on the campus, on the hundreds of bodies scurrying below.

Caitlin could feel him thinking. And she knew, she just *knew*, that there was something here. Something that he knew about. Something he had never told her. And that frightened her all the more. She had so desperately hoped he would just dismiss it all as nonsense.

After moments of thick silence, Caitlin couldn't take it anymore. She had to know.

"Is it real?" she asked, cutting right to the chase.

After a long silence, Aiden finally turned.

Slowly, he nodded.

Caitlin couldn't comprehend what was happening. He was confirming her reality. This book. It was real. Everything was real.

"But how is that possible?" Caitlin asked, her voice rising. "It talks about the most fantastical things. Vampires. Mythical swords. Shields. Antidotes. It's thousands of years old—and it's all in my handwriting. None of it makes any sense."

Aiden sighed.

"I was afraid this day would come," he said. "It just came sooner than I thought."

Caitlin stared back, trying to understand. She felt as if some great secret had been withheld from her, and it frustrated her to no end.

"What day would come?" she demanded. "What are you telling me? And why didn't you tell me this sooner?"

Slowly, Aiden shook his head.

"It wasn't for me to tell you. It was for you to discover. When the time was right."

"To discover what?"

Aiden hesitated.

"That you are not who you think you are. That you are special. That you have a special past."

Caitlin stared back, dumbfounded.

"I still don't understand," she said, frustrated.

Aiden paced.

"As you know, history is part fact, part myth. It is our job to determine what is truth and what is fiction. Yet it is not as much of a science as we'd like to pretend. There are no absolute facts in history. History is written by the victors, by the biographers, by those with a cause and purpose and agenda to document it. History will always be biased. And it will always be selective."

"Where does that leave me?" Caitlin asked, impatient. She was in no mood for one of Aiden's monologues. Not now.

Aiden cleared his throat.

"There is a fourth dimension to history. A dimension discounted by scholars. But one that is very, very real. It is the unexplained. The esoteric. Some might even like to dub it a spiritual dimension. Some might call it the occult, but that term has been grossly misused."

"I still don't understand," Caitlin pleaded. "None of this makes any sense. I thought you would be the one person who would explain it away, who would tell me to forget it. But it sounds as if you're saying that it's all true, that everything in this book is true. Is that what you're saying!?"

"I know what you came here wanting me to say. But I'm afraid I cannot."

Aiden sighed.

"Some history had been obscured. By design. What if there was, indeed, a time when a race known as 'vampires' existed? What if you were one of them? What if you had traveled back in time? Had found the antidote, had wiped out vampirism for all time?"

Aiden paused.

"And what if there was one exception to the rule?" he asked, reflectively.

Caitlin stared at him, hardly believing what she was hearing. Had he lost his mind?

"What do you mean?" she asked.

"The antidote. The end to vampirism. What if there was one exception? One vampire who was immune to the antidote? One vampire yet to come? Immune because she had not yet been born, was not yet born at the moment you chose to come back?"

Not yet born? Caitlin wondered, racking her brain. Then, it struck her.

"Scarlet?" Caitlin asked, dumbfounded.

"You were warned you would have a very great choice to make, between your lineage, your legacy, and the future of mankind. I'm afraid that time has come."

"Stop talking in riddles," Caitlin demanded, standing, her fists bunched, red in the face. She couldn't listen anymore; she felt as if she were losing her mind. Aiden was the one man in the world from whom she expected rational answers. And he was only making things much, much worse.

"Tell me what you're saying about Scarlet?"

Aiden shook his head slowly, distressed.

"I understand you're upset," he said. "And I am sorry to have to be the one to tell you all this. But you must know. Your daughter, Scarlet, is the last of her kind. The last remaining vampire."

Caitlin looked at Aiden as if he'd lost his mind. She didn't even know how to respond.

"She is coming of age," he continued. "She will soon change. And when she does, she will unleash it on the world. Once again, our world will be under darkness, besieged by the plague of vampirism."

Aiden took two steps towards Caitlin. He placed a hand on her shoulder, looking into her eyes, as serious as she had ever seen him.

"That is why this journal came to you now. As a warning. You must stop her. For the sake of mankind. Before it's too late."

"Have you lost your mind?" Caitlin snapped back, but feeling unsure. "Do you even realize what are you saying? My daughter is a vampire? Are you for real? And what do you mean, stop her? What is that even supposed to mean?"

Aiden looked down at the floor, grim, looking much older in that moment than Caitlin had ever seen him.

And then, suddenly, Caitlin realized what he'd meant: kill her. He was telling her to kill her own daughter.

The realization struck Caitlin like a knife in the gut. She was so horrified, so physically sick from it, that she couldn't bear to be near Aiden for another second.

Without a word, she turned and bolted out of his office, running away, far away, like a madwoman down the halls—and determined to never come back again.

CHAPTER TWO

The entire drive home, Caitlin was sick with worry. She felt not only as if she were losing her mind, but also as if there were no rational person left in the universe. She had thought that driving into the city, speaking to Aiden, would calm her, would make her return home feeling better, everything explained and back in rational order.

But seeing him had made things a million times worse. Caitlin wished she'd never visited him—and she wished she'd never gone to the attic. She wished she'd never had that dream. She wished she never saw the journal. She wished she could just make it all go away.

Just yesterday, everything was perfect in her life; now, she felt that everything was upside down. She almost felt that, by going to the attic, and opening that box, and opening that book, she unleashed something horrible into the universe. Something that was meant to be kept locked away.

A part of Caitlin told her that all of this was ridiculous. Maybe Aiden had lost touch with reality after all these years of teaching. Maybe that book was just some weird relic of her childhood, some collection of fantasies she had scrawled as a young girl. Maybe she would drive home, put that book back in the attic, put today out of her mind, and everything would be fine, go back to normal, just as it always was.

But another part of Caitlin, a deeper part, felt an increasing sense of foreboding, one she just could not shake. She felt that nothing would be fine again.

Caitlin's hands were still trembling as she finished her two hour drive back from the city and pulled into her idyllic village, pulled down her quiet side street and into her driveway. She hoped the sight of her house would calm her, as it always did.

But as she pulled into her driveway, she knew immediately something was wrong. Caleb's car was in the driveway. He was home from work, in the middle of the afternoon. He never came home from work early.

Caitlin immediately checked her cell, to see if she had any missed calls from him, and that was when she realized: her phone had been off all day. She looked down now and saw it flashing: 9 missed calls in the last two hours. All from Caleb.

Caitlin's heart stopped. Caleb never used his phone. This could only mean an emergency.

Caitlin jumped out of the car, ran up the steps, across the porch, and burst through the front door—which was open and ajar, compounding her sense of dread.

"Caleb!?" Caitlin yelled, as she burst into the house.

"Up here!" he yelled back. "Come up here! Now!"

The tone of his voice set her into a panic. In all the years she'd known him, she'd never heard him scream with that sort of urgency, never heard his voice filled with fear.

Caitlin's heart pounded as she ran up the old staircase, yanking on the bannister, taking the steps three at a time. She raced down the hall, following the sounds, sounds like muffled cries.

"In here!" Caleb yelled.

Caitlin hurried right for Scarlet's room. The door was ajar, and she burst in.

She stopped cold, shocked at the sight.

Lying there on her bed in the middle of the day was Scarlet, fully clothed, and looking very sick. Standing over her, face grave with worry, was Caleb, holding a hand on her forehead.

Ruth sat by her bedside, whining.

"Where have you been?" he asked, panicked. "The nurse sent her home from school early. They said she has the flu. I gave her three Advil, but her fever's getting worse."

"Mom?" Scarlet moaned, weakly.

Scarlet lay there, twisting and turning, looking worse than Caitlin had ever seen her. Her forehead was damp with sweat and she groaned in pain, squinting with closed eyes as if fighting off some awful pain.

Caitlin's heart broke at the sight and she ran over to Scarlet's side, sitting on her bed, placing one hand on her arm and the other on her forehead.

"You don't feel warm," she said. "You feel ice cold. When did this start?"

"That's what's weird," Caleb said. "Her fever's getting worse—but in the wrong direction. She's abnormally low: 71 degrees, and dropping. It doesn't make sense."

"I'm freezing," Scarlet said.

Scarlet was ice-cold and clammy to Caitlin's touch. It was uncanny. Caitlin's heart pounded, unsure what to do: she had never seen anything like this.

"Mommy, please. It hurts so much. Please make it stop!" Scarlet groaned.

Caitlin's heart sank, wishing she could take the pain away. She sensed this was no ordinary sickness.

Scarlet began to cry.

"What hurts, sweetheart?" Caitlin asked. "You have to tell me. Please, calm down, and tell me," Caitlin asked firmly, feeling desperate.

"Exactly what happened to you? When did this begin?"

"This morning, when I went to school. I was sitting in class, and my eyes started to hurt. They hurt so bad. The light—it was so bright. And then my head hurt. I went to the nurse, and she shined a light in my eyes, and it made it much worse. Everything is killing. They had to put me in a dark room."

"I had to close all these blinds," Caleb said. "She said the light was killing her."

Caitlin surveyed the room, and noticed the closed blinds for the first time. Her heart dropped. Here was Scarlet, ice cold to the touch, unable to stand sunlight. Was there truth, she wondered, to anything Aiden had said?

"And now, my stomach, it hurts so bad," Scarlet said. "I can't explain it. It's like I'm hungry and thirsty at the same time. But not for food. For something else."

"For what?" Caitlin asked, sweating.

Suddenly, Scarlet shrieked and curled up into a ball, clutching her stomach. Caitlin was terrified. She had never seen her like this.

"We have to get her to a hospital," Caitlin yelled to Caleb, hysterical. "Call 911. NOW!"

"Mommy, please, make it stop. Please!"

Caleb turned to get his phone—but suddenly, he stopped in his tracks. And so did Caitlin.

Because at that moment, suddenly, there was a sound that shook the entire room, a sound that raised the hair on the back of both of their necks.

It was a snarl.

They both stopped, frozen, and slowly turned and looked over at Scarlet.

Caitlin could barely process what was happening: Scarlet was now sitting bolt upright in bed, and right before her eyes, she was transforming. She let out a snarl so vicious and hair-raising that even Ruth yelped and ran from the room, tail between her legs.

Caleb, a man who Caitlin had never seen scared of anything, looked absolutely petrified, as if he were caged in the room with a wild lion.

But Scarlet ignored them both: instead, she looked towards the open door.

In that moment, Caitlin suddenly understood. Suddenly, she had a flashback to some place—she could not remember where—when she herself was feeling the same thing as Scarlet. A hunger pang. A need to feed. Not on food. But on blood.

As she saw that look in Scarlet's eyes, that desperate look, the look of a wild animal, somehow she knew what she was thinking: she had to get out. To escape. Through that door. To sink her teeth into something.

It was at that moment that she knew, without a doubt, that Scarlet was indeed a vampire.

And that she, Caitlin, had once been one, too.

And that everything that Aiden had said was true.

Scarlet was the last remaining vampire.

And no matter what, Caitlin had to stop her from spreading it to the world.

As Scarlet began to get up, to go for the door, Caitlin suddenly screamed: "Caleb, stop her! Don't let her out. Trust me! Just listen to me! Don't let her out of this room!"

Caitlin didn't want to think of the consequences if Scarlet got past that door, out of the house, roamed the streets. It could change the entire world.

Scarlet, with lightning speed, was on her feet in a single leap, bounding towards the door.

Caleb, to his credit, acted fast. He listened dutifully to Caitlin and jumped in Scarlet's way, blocking her path. He managed to grab her from behind and held her tight, in a bear hug.

Normally, it would be no competition. Caleb, at six feet four, with broad shoulders, was twice the size of Scarlet, and it wouldn't even be a contest.

But to Caitlin's shock—and clearly, to Caleb's too—it was a struggle for him to hold onto her. It was as if Scarlet were overcome with a super-human strength. As she swayed, Caleb was thrown left and right.

Scarlet suddenly leaned over and threw back her shoulders, and as she did, to Caitlin's surprise, Caleb went flying across the room like a ragdoll, propelled through the air and smashing into the wall with such force, his whole body left an imprint on the sheetrock. He slumped down to the floor, unconscious.

As Scarlet turned back to the door, Caitlin leapt on her from behind, grabbing her in a bear hug the same way Caleb had. It was like trying to hold onto a wild bull: Caitlin was thrown all over the place, and she knew she was no match for her. After all, Caitlin was human. And clearly, she was in the presence of someone that was not.

Scarlet leaned back and Caitlin went flying through the air, propelled, until she smacked into a wall herself, slamming the back of her head.

Scarlet turned and raced to the door, and in another moment, she was gone.

Caitlin somehow managed to get to her feet. Dizzy, she ran out the room, down the hall, breathing hard, determined. She raced down the steps, four at a time, slipping, and then tore through the house.

In the distance, she saw Scarlet running towards the thick, oak front doors; without even pausing, Scarlet put her shoulder into them and smashed them to bits.

Caitlin ran after her, through the open front doors, and saw Scarlet bound across the lawn and without pausing, leap over the high bushes, a good ten feet.

She landed deftly in the middle of the quiet, suburban street. She stood there, and leaned back her head. As she did, Caitlin saw fangs begin to protrude from her teeth, saw her eyes begin to change from a blue to a glowing red.

Scarlet leaned back and roared, and it was a roar that shook the entire block, that reached up to the heavens themselves.

It was the roar of an animal that wanted to kill.

COMING SOON…

RESURRECTED:
Book #1 of the Vampire Legacy

Please visit Morgan's site, where you can join the mailing list, hear the latest news, see additional images, and find links to stay in touch with Morgan on Facebook, Twitter, Goodreads and elsewhere:

www.morganricebooks.com

Also by Morgan Rice

THE VAMPIRE JOURNALS SERIES

TURNED (Book #1 in the Vampire Journals)
LOVED (Book #2 in the Vampire Journals)
BETRAYED (Book #3 in the Vampire Journals)
DESTINED (Book #4 in the Vampire Journals)
DESIRED (Book #5 in the Vampire Journals)
BETROTHED (Book #6 in the Vampire Journals)
VOWED (Book #7 in the Vampire Journals)

THE SURVIVAL TRILOGY

ARENA ONE: SLAVERUNNERS
(Book #1 of the Survival Trilogy)

ALSO BY MORGAN RICE

ARENA ONE: SLAVERUNNERS (Book #1 of the Survival Trilogy)

"If you liked THE HUNGER GAMES, you will Love ARENA ONE."
--Allegra Skye, Bestselling author of *Saved*

From Morgan Rice, #1 Bestselling author of THE VAMPIRE JOURNALS, comes a new trilogy of dystopian fiction.

New York. 2120. American has been decimated, wiped out from the second Civil War. In this post-apocalyptic world, survivors are far and few between. And most of those who do survive are members of the violent gangs, predators who live in the big cities. They patrol the countryside looking for slaves, for fresh victims to bring back into the city for their favorite death sport: Arena One. The death stadium where opponents are made to fight to the death, in the most barbaric of ways. There is only one rule to the arena: no one survives. Ever.

Deep in the wilderness, high up in the Catskill Mountains, 17 year old Brooke Moore manages to survive, hiding out with her younger sister, Bree. They are careful to avoid the gangs of slaverunners who patrol the countryside. But one day, Brooke is not as careful as she can be, and Bree is captured. The slaverunners take her away, heading to the city, and to what will be a certain death.

Brooke, a Marine's daughter, was raised to be tough, to never back down from a fight. When her sister is taken, Brooke mobilizes, uses everything at her disposal to chase down the slaverunners and get her sister back. Along the way she runs into Ben, 17, another survivor like her, whose brother was taken. Together, they team up on their rescue mission.

What follows is a post-apocalyptic, action-packed thriller, as the two of them pursue the slaverunners on the most dangerous ride of their lives, following them deep into the heart of New York. Along the way, if they are to survive, they will have to make some of the hardest choices and sacrifices of their lives, encountering obstacles neither of them had expected—including their unexpected feelings for each other. Will they rescue their siblings? Will they make it back? And will they, themselves, have to fight in the arena?

ARENA ONE is Book #1 in the Survival Trilogy, and is 85,000 words.

"Grabbed my attention from the beginning and did not let go….This story is an amazing adventure that is fast paced and action packed from the very beginning. There is not a dull moment to be found."
--Paranormal Romance Guild {regarding *Turned*}

"A great plot, and this especially was the kind of book you will have trouble putting down at night. The ending was a cliffhanger that was so spectacular that you will immediately want to buy the next book, just to see what happens."
--The Dallas Examiner{regarding *Loved*}

"Jam packed with action, romance, adventure, and suspense. This book is a wonderful addition to this series and will have you wanting more from Morgan Rice."
--vampirebooksite.com {regarding *Loved*}

"Morgan Rice proves herself again to be an extremely talented storyteller….This would appeal to a wide range of audiences, including younger fans of the vampire/fantasy genre. It ended with an unexpected cliffhanger that leaves you shocked."
--The Romance Reviews{regarding *Loved*}

CPSIA information can be obtained at www.ICGtesting.com
Printed in the USA
LVOW091111120812

293983LV00001B/9/P